RETURN TO ASHES

CASSIE QUINN
BOOK 8

L.T. RYAN

with
K.M. ROUGHT

Copyright © 2024 by L.T. Ryan, K.M. Rought, and Liquid Mind Media, LLC. All rights reserved. No part of this publication may be copied, reproduced in any format, by any means, electronic or otherwise, without prior consent from the copyright owner and publisher of this book. This is a work of fiction. All characters, names, places and events are the product of the author's imagination or used fictitiously.

THE CASSIE QUINN SERIES

Path of Bones

Whisper of Bones

Symphony of Bones

Etched in Shadow

Concealed in Shadow

Betrayed in Shadow

Born from Ashes

Return from Ashes (2024)

Love Cassie? Hatch? Noble? Maddie? Get your very own Cassie Quinn merchandise today! Click the link below to find coffee mugs, t-shirts, and even signed copies of your favorite L.T. Ryan thrillers! https://ltryan.ink/EvG_

1

Dread followed the feeling of a looming presence at Cassie's back. An angry gaze bored into her skull until it felt like a physical pressure against her scalp, threatening to become a migraine. The silence in the air dripped with apprehension, but she couldn't tell if it was hers or his. In lieu of overanalyzing the atmosphere sweeping through her bedroom, she focused on the task at hand.

Packing.

Tennessee in April was cooler than Savannah, but still warm. Temperatures in the low seventies meant she could wear high-necked shirts to cover the scars along her chest without overheating, but she packed a few summer dresses in case she decided not to care about the stares people tossed in her direction upon seeing the map of destruction laid out over her skin. It had been years since she had been assaulted and left to die, and while her emotional wounds had coalesced into thin, neat lines scattered across her psyche, the physical manifestations of the worst night of her life were still jagged and angry. She might have grown used to them, but strangers often did a double-take. Some days she could handle it, and some days she just wanted to blend into the crowd. Be like everyone else. Even if that was a reality she would never experience.

A low, strained voice came from behind her. "Cassie."

She ignored it, her gaze skimming over the animals on her bed before landing on her luggage. It was bursting at the seams, but she didn't know how long she'd be gone or what kind of situations she'd find herself in. She had shoved everything from a cocktail dress to sweatpants into the purple rolling suitcase that had started falling apart about a decade ago. She could afford new bags, but having every scratch and tear memorized on this one meant it was easier to spot when it rolled off the carousel.

"Cassie," the voice repeated.

High heels and combat boots snuggled together at the bottom of her suitcase, and she walked over to her dresser to grab an extra couple pairs of socks. She was a firm believer that you could never pack too many socks. There was nothing worse than having to traipse all over a new city with soggy feet. And if she couldn't get to a laundromat right away, she'd at least have a few extra days before she had to worry about her shoes stinking up—

"Cassie."

Spinning around, she didn't let her gaze wander to the figure standing in the doorway of her bedroom as she returned to her suitcase and shoved the socks into one of its corners. If she tried to fit anything else, it was liable to burst open when they tossed it into the bottom of the plane, and then she'd have to watch from her seat as the wind carried her underwear down the tarmac.

A laugh crawled its way up her throat, but she clamped her mouth shut to keep it from escaping. Now was not the time. Not with what waited for her in Tennessee, and not with who glared at her from across the room.

A small whine left Bear's mouth from where he lay on the bed, his puppy-dog eyes peering up at her as his head rested on the lid of her suitcase. It only delayed the inevitable, but she allowed him a few more minutes of believing he could stop her from going if he held her suitcase down by sheer force of will.

Apollo was not so lucky. The chubby calico cat lay curled up inside her duffel bag, tail draped over his nose like he did when he was trying to stay warm while he napped, but his eyes were half-open, following her every movement. He wasn't fooling anyone.

Scooping him up into her arms, she snuggled him close and kissed the top of his head before setting him down on the bed. He stretched, emitting a little groan, then picked his way over to Bear and snuggled into the German Shepherd's stomach. Bear's tail wagged twice before falling still, torn between disappointment and comfort as Cassie filled her carryon and Apollo laid his head on Bear's shoulder and purred.

"Cassie," the voice insisted, closer now, almost in her ear. "Please."

Cassie closed her eyes and took a deep breath, inhaling for four seconds, holding it, and then exhaling for another four. She repeated this until her heartbeat slowed. It didn't ease her anxiety or frustration, but it calmed her enough to know that when she spoke, her voice would be even.

Turning, Cassie peered up at Jason, looking everywhere but his eyes. His olive-green shirt was rumpled, and his favorite pair of black jeans hung low on his hips. His hair was a little longer than he liked to keep it, and so was the stubble across his jaw. Most people wouldn't have said he looked ragged, but Cassie knew firsthand he hadn't slept well these last few weeks. She didn't need to look at the hollow of his cheekbones or the circles under his eyes to realize that. Even his dark, rich skin looked pale and drawn.

Now that he had her attention, he repeated what he'd been saying for the last few days. Only this time, he didn't hide that he wasn't asking. He was begging. "Don't go."

Tilting her chin up, Cassie met Jason's gaze, and the desperation in his eyes made her chest so tight, she had difficulty dragging in a breath. Counting again, she drew in air, held it, and then exhaled until she found her voice.

"I don't have a choice."

"Yes, you do," he said. "Don't do this. Please."

Weariness flooded Cassie's system, and she swayed a little on her feet. They'd had this same conversation countless times over the last month, but it hadn't become real until a few days ago. Not until Anastasia Bolton from Apex Publicity had called her up with a request to fly out to Nashville by the end of the week. Only, she wasn't asking. Not really.

Jason knew that, yet he insisted on having this argument.

Twisting away again, Cassie grabbed a spare outfit and shoved it into her carryon before throwing various chargers and electronics into the opening, going through the motions while her mind was hundreds of miles away. "We've been over this," she said. "There is no alternative."

When Anastasia had approached them a month ago with doctored footage showing Jason murdering Douglas Hughes in cold blood, Cassie had agreed to join Apex's team to keep him out of prison. It didn't matter that he hadn't committed the crime or that Hughes was the notorious Ash Wednesday Killer. If Apex wanted to put Jason behind bars for the rest of his life, they'd do it, one way or another.

"We'll figure something else out." Jason placed his hands on her hips and drew her into him. "We just need a little more time."

Cassie closed her eyes, reveling in the solid feeling of his chest against her back, his fingertips against her waist. Jason was warm and strong and comforting. But he was also wrong.

"We haven't been able to come up with anything in the last month. What makes you think a few more days will make a difference?"

Jason stiffened behind her, and he dropped his hands from her hips. "You're just giving up?"

Cassie didn't recognize the harsh laugh that escaped her mouth, like she was channeling someone much colder and crueler. When she turned back to Jason, she couldn't stop the clench of her jaw. She barely kept herself from poking a finger into his chest. "This is not me giving up. This is me fixing a problem. It's *one* job. And then I'm back home and you're safe and we can forget this ever happened."

"Did they actually say it was only one job? Or that they'd delete the video when you were done working for them?"

Cassie didn't bother responding. They both knew the answer.

The call with Anastasia had been short, just long enough to give Cassie the date and time of a meeting at their headquarters in Nashville, along with a promise to reimburse her for the plane ticket.

Someone would pick her up from the airport, and the hotel was already taken care of. The money for the ticket had hit her bank account last night, minutes after she'd emailed Anastasia the receipt. Cassie hadn't brought up the video in any of their exchanges, like she could pretend it wasn't real if she refused to speak it into existence. But despite the graininess of the footage, Jason's face was unmistakable as he peered up into Douglas Hughes' security camera. It didn't matter that it had been altered. People liked to believe what they saw with their own two eyes, and given Jason's military background, no one would question whether he was capable of ending a life.

The memory haunted her at night as she tried to fall asleep, and it was never far from her mind during waking hours.

"I wasn't about to discuss that over the phone." She had no idea if Anastasia recorded their phone calls, but that wasn't the only reason she hadn't brought it up. Clarifying the terms of their agreement was pointless. Cassie would do as many jobs as Apex required if it meant keeping her loved ones safe.

Jason was silent for so long, Cassie glanced over her shoulder to see if he was still standing there. The anguish on his face brought tears to her eyes, and before she knew what she was doing, she had wrapped her arms around him and buried her face in his chest. There was no hesitation in his movements as he engulfed her, resting his chin on top of her head.

"I hate this," he croaked.

Cassie sniffled, failing to hold back her own emotions. "Me too."

"If you won't let me go with you," Jason said, relinquishing his stance on yet another argument they'd been having for days, "then at least take Harris with you."

"I can't." Cassie leaned back to look up at him but didn't let go. She wanted him to see that this wasn't easy for her either, that she wasn't trying to be difficult or brave or arrogant. They needed to be smart and not let Apex know they hadn't given in to their demands or given up on the idea of taking them down once and for all. "She's the assistant chief of police now. She can't just pack up and go to Nashville for an extended period. And I'll be less suspicious if I'm there by myself."

"Anastasia knows what you're capable of. She won't underestimate you."

"She already has if she thinks blackmailing you will get her what she wants."

The corners of Jason's mouth tipped up, though his eyes remained clouded. "If I wasn't so terrified, I'd find that alluring."

"It'll be okay," Cassie said, infusing more confidence into her voice than she felt in her body. "We'll figure this out. Stay here and talk to whichever contacts you can trust. Help Lorraine gather more information on Apex and the people running the company." Her lips twitched into a smile of her own. "Keep Bear and Apollo from getting too lonely."

Jason nodded, his gaze sliding over to the animals on the bed, not returning to hers when he spoke again. "And you'll be in Tennessee."

"That's right. I'll be at Apex, and I'll find out exactly what skeletons they have hidden away in their closets."

2

The flight from Savannah to Nashville took less than ninety minutes, but a rush of relief flooded Cassie's body when she exited the plane. After purchasing the last-minute ticket, the only seats available were in the middle row, and she'd arrived to find herself sandwiched between two men who didn't know how to share an armrest or keep their knees out of her personal bubble. Worse, the young girl behind her had alternated between kicking the back of her seat and playing a game on her phone with the sound well above levels appropriate for public consumption.

By the time Cassie made it to baggage claim and pulled her suitcase off the carousel, a small tension headache had bloomed across her forehead, squeezing her temples. More than once, she had to remind herself to unclench her jaw or risk the simple headache turning into a migraine. It didn't help that the airport was packed, or that the same kid from the plane complained about wanting ice cream for dinner in a voice that somehow carried over the hustle and bustle around them. Her mother ignored her, much to the annoyance of everyone within earshot.

Twisting away before she said something she'd regret, Cassie stalked over to the small group of drivers crowded by the exit, each of them holding a sign with expressions ranging from bored to impassive. The man bearing her name fell into the latter category, his eyes dark and his gelled brown hair parted at the side. His pressed suit fit well enough to indicate it was tailored. If it wasn't already obvious he was waiting for her, she would've guessed he was from Apex. No one else was in his league.

When their eyes met, he nodded once and tucked the sign under his arm.

"Good morning, Ms. Quinn," he said, reaching out a hand to greet her.

"Good morning." Cassie mirrored his movements and furrowed her brows. "How'd you know it was me?"

The man smiled, then looked down at her suitcase. "May I?"

"Please," she said, unsure of what to make of him ignoring her question but relinquishing the handle on her bag when he reached for it.

"If you'll follow me."

The driver wound his way through the airport as if he could do it with his eyes closed. Most people stepped out of his way when he passed by, his broad shoulders carving a path like a knife through butter. Worried that if she lost sight of him, she'd be without a ride and her clothes, she stayed on his heels until he led her through a pair of automatic doors and out into the late-morning breeze.

Her skin soaked in the sun after the sharpness of the airport's fluorescent lighting, but honking horns and angry shouts made her head twinge. Exhaust fumes and cigarette smoke did nothing to alleviate the pressure, and she couldn't help being disappointed in her first breath of Tennessee air.

"Ms. Quinn."

Cassie turned to find the driver had already packed her bag into the back of a black Escalade and stood by the open rear door, waiting for her to slip inside. Not for the first time, Cassie wondered if it was smart to walk into the belly of the beast like this. The luxury SUV was sleek and shiny, like it had just been through the carwash, and the windows were so dark, she couldn't see inside. But if Apex wanted her dead, they wouldn't have gone to such lengths to recruit her.

There was arrogance, and then there was reimbursing a person for their plane ticket as they hurtled toward their demise.

"Ms. Quinn," the driver repeated, his voice neutral and his clean-cut face still impassive. "If you please."

Blushing, Cassie scurried forward and slid into the car, slamming to a halt when she realized she wasn't alone in the back seat. But before she could back out the way she came, the driver shut her door and walked around the front of the vehicle, slipped behind the wheel, and shifted into drive. And just like that, they pulled away from the curb while Cassie stared daggers at the woman beside her, as though she could make her disappear using only her thoughts.

But no matter how many times she attempted to blink away reality, Anastasia Bolton remained.

"Cassie," Anastasia purred. "It's wonderful to see you again."

Cassie fought back a groan of pain and displeasure as her head twinged at the sound of Anastasia's voice. It had been a month since she'd last seen the woman. It was still too soon to be trapped in the back of a car with her. Anastasia had not changed in that time. Her glossy hair fell in sheets around her shoulders while one manicured finger tapped the screen of the tablet she held in her other hand. Today, she wore a sleek grey pantsuit with a crimson shirt that matched her nails and the sharp heels glinting from her feet. She was not physically imposing, but Cassie felt herself leaning away from the woman to put as much distance between them as possible.

"Buckle up, please," Anastasia said. "Robert is an impeccable driver, but accidents do happen."

Anastasia delivered the sentence in a pleasant tone, but goosebumps still erupted along Cassie's arm. Searching the woman's face, she tried to decipher if it was a warning or a threat. While Anastasia was nothing if not loyal to Apex Publicity, she had gone out of her way to recruit Cassie to their cause, whatever that might be. Was she hoping to see their newest employee succeed, or was she waiting to watch her fail?

Anastasia's scarlet lips stretched into a grin, making it even more difficult for Cassie to determine the truth. Amusement lit up the other woman's eyes, and a flare of satisfaction flitted across her face as Cassie twisted to pull her seatbelt across her chest. Once it clicked into place, Anastasia nodded her head in approval.

"I trust your flight was okay?"

Cassie scoffed.

"You knew we would reimburse you. Why didn't you fly first class?"

Cassie shrugged. Truth be told, the option hadn't occurred to her.

"And your job?" Anastasia asked. "They let you have the time off?"

Technically, Cassie had two jobs, and they were both part-time. One was at the SCAD Museum of Art as a preparator, which was the only slice of relative normalcy she had left in her life. They had been more than accommodating of her schedule once Harris had told her boss how she was an indispensable part of the Savannah Police Department. When she'd been offered a part-time position as a consultant with the SPD, Cassie hadn't hesitated to accept. She had already been putting in the work. At least now she got paid for it.

While her trip to Tennessee was not officially on behalf of the SPD, Cassie didn't feel too bad about lying to the museum. Assistant Chief Adelaide Harris was not only her closest friend, but also her boss, and she was just as interested in finding out what Apex hid behind closed doors. If anyone got curious, Harris would cover for Cassie, no questions asked. Besides, the fewer people who knew about Apex—and that she was now working alongside them—the better. For both her and anyone else in her life. Not even her sister or her parents knew where she was at the moment.

"Are we really doing this?" Cassie asked, glaring at Anastasia.

Innocence widened the woman's eyes. "Doing what?"

Cassie gestured between them, as though that was explanation enough. "This. We both know it's bullshit. I'm not here by choice."

"You know as well as I do that there *was* a choice," Anastasia replied. "And you made yours. There's no point in needless cruelty. Apex Publicity has a vested interest in your well-being. I am merely checking in. Catching up."

"Like a couple of old friends," Cassie spat.

Anastasia lifted a shoulder and dropped it. "If that makes you more amenable, then yes."

Cassie shook her head and peered out the window, watching as the open interstate gave way to the clogged streets of downtown Nashville. Robert navigated the vehicle with precision, providing a smooth ride even when other drivers cut in front of him or slammed on their brakes. The clean air of the car and the tinted windows had done wonders for her headache, but she felt the ghost of it waiting in the wings to strike again. All she wanted was a bottle of water, a couple Advil, and for this nightmare to be over.

"And how's Jason?"

Cassie whipped her head around to stare at Anastasia, who grinned when Cassie provided the reaction she'd been looking for. Rage built in Cassie's chest, darkening her vision and causing her head to throb in time with her heartbeat. She counted back from ten, never taking her eyes off the woman next to her. A few tense seconds passed before Cassie's head cleared enough for her to think again.

"Apex has been interested in bringing me on board for a while now. They've gone to great lengths to get me to this point. And they've waited a long time to see me walk through the front doors of their building."

"Yes." Anastasia's eyes narrowed as she picked through the meaning of Cassie's words. "They have."

"But you're not the only person who has approached me."

Her grin faded. "I'm not."

"I wonder what would happen if I mentioned how dissatisfied I was? How much more willing I'd be to do what they asked if you were, for example, removed from the equation?"

A flash of anger crossed Anastasia's face, but she schooled it behind a look of bemusement. "I never considered you an arrogant person, Ms. Quinn. If you think you're more valuable to the company than I am, then you're in for a rude awakening."

That might be true, but Anastasia's reaction proved the threat was cause for concern. Apex wouldn't fire Anastasia if Cassie asked, but they could replace her as Cassie's handler, so to speak. She liked the idea that she had some sway over Anastasia, regardless of how small. Still, she'd rather keep the woman close—the devil you know, and all that.

"Be that as it may," Cassie said, "I'm here for a reason. You need me, or else you would've given up on me a long time ago. Blackmailing Jason was a desperate move."

"But it worked, didn't it?"

Cassie ground her teeth, then winced as her head throbbed again. "One job, and then you'll delete the video and any copies you've made."

A predatory smile spread across Anastasia's face, as though she enjoyed this little game they played. She tucked her tablet into her bag as the car pulled to a stop. "We can negotiate your terms once you've proven you're willing to work with us. Besides, you may feel differently once you become aware of what we're trying to accomplish."

"Don't hold your breath."

"We've made much more important and dangerous people come to heel, Miss Quinn. You are no exception."

Cassie leaned into Anastasia's space, drinking in the surprise on the other woman's face. "It's not smart to underestimate me."

Anastasia searched Cassie's face. A new smile bloomed across her lips when she found what she was looking for. "I knew I was right about you."

Cassie sat back again. "Right about what?"

Anastasia's grin got impossibly wider. "That you'll fit right in at Apex."

3

Cassie stood on the sidewalk and gazed up at the building before her while Robert pulled away from the curb and drove around the corner, out of view. Her tête-à-tête with Anastasia had distracted her from following their trek from the airport, so she didn't know where they were outside of somewhere in downtown Nashville. That should've worried her, but the hustle and bustle of the city's morning commuters pulled her attention away from any concerns over self-preservation.

Various professionals walked by in their suits and skirts, most likely on their way to lunch. Most of them didn't pay the Apex building any mind, but Cassie couldn't tear her gaze away. The sleek edifice was as modern as they came, all shining silver and glass. It wasn't the tallest building in the vicinity, but it demanded attention. Where many of the surrounding facades were straight out of the early twentieth century, built in a Classical Revival style, this one had been erected within the last decade. It was imposing and impressive, but somehow not garish. Every glint of the sun screamed prosperity and authority.

"Beautiful, isn't it?" Anastasia asked, stepping close. "We have buildings in New York, Los Angeles, Chicago, Dallas, and Seattle. But I think this one is my favorite. I've always loved Nashville."

"I've never been," Cassie said, regretting the words as soon as they left her mouth. She didn't want to give Anastasia any more information than she already had, even something that insignificant.

"Oh?" Anastasia said, turning to her. "We'll have to give you the grand tour, then."

"I won't be here long enough for that."

"We'll see, I suppose."

Anastasia cut across the sidewalk, forcing Cassie to follow and drive passersby out of their way. Pulling the door open, the other woman stepped to the side and allowed Cassie to enter first. Awe replaced anticipation as she took in the lobby. Like the building itself, it was modern, yet elegant. Gray, white, and black marble floors gleamed beneath her feet, making her wonder how many times a day they were polished. The gray walls and furniture should've made the space look drab, but pops of red in the form of the ergonomic chairs and vases of fresh flowers livened it up. A large sign behind the front desk read *Apex Publicity* in a stylish cursive font, the red of the first word matching the exact shade of crimson dotted around the room.

And, Cassie realized, Anastasia's shirt, shoes, nails, and lips.

She knew Anastasia was dedicated to the cause, but there was something sinister about the way she wore her loyalty on her chest like a badge of honor.

Before they could access the lobby, two security guards stepped forward to greet them. They weren't twins, but their matching uniforms and coordinated movements made them appear as though they shared one brain. A metal detector loomed behind them, tall and imposing.

"Good morning, Ms. Bolton," the one on the left said.

"Good morning, Gerald," Anastasia replied, smiling at him. She turned her attention to the other one and nodded in greeting. "Roger."

Roger tipped his head in return. "Morning, ma'am."

"Cassie, you may lead the way."

Gerald held his hand out, and after a moment, Cassie realized he was asking for her purse. She handed it over, then stepped through the metal detector, breathing a sigh of relief when she didn't set it off. It wasn't like she was sneaking any weapons inside, but guilt pulled at her. Maybe it had to do with the fact that she didn't want to be there. Or that she planned on bringing them down from the inside, one way or another. At least the scanner couldn't read intentions.

On the other side, Gerald passed her purse back with a nod, then watched Anastasia walk through the contraption while Roger peeked into her own purse. It didn't escape Cassie's notice that the man was much less thorough than Gerald. Somehow, she thought that said less about him than it did about Anastasia and her role in the company.

"This way, please," Anastasia said, leading Cassie across the lobby floor, past the main desk, and over to the security station.

A handful of people milled about, chatting on the couches or walking into and out of the elevators. They all dressed like Anastasia, wearing suits or skirts or dresses, most in varying shades of gray or crimson. Discomfort crawled down Cassie's spine. It was like a cult. While she felt underdressed in her leggings and t-shirt, she also felt a small burst of satisfaction at having chosen to wear blue and white that morning. Anything to break up the monotony.

Anastasia stopped in front of the security desk and turned to Cassie. "This is Bernie Griffin, the head security officer for Apex Publicity in Nashville. He's been with the company since we established this building. Bernie, this is Cassie Quinn, our newest recruit."

"Good morning, Miss Quinn," Bernie said, a genuine smile breaking across his face and making his gray mustache twitch. "You flew in from Savannah, right?"

Cassie startled, not liking that he already knew who she was and where she'd come from. Bernie looked to be about fifty or so, but his eyes were sharp and assessing, his back ramrod straight as he sat in his chair. Cassie guessed there was a reason he was the head security officer, and it wasn't because of his seniority. She had no doubt that if there was a breach, he'd be the first to tackle an intruder or throw himself into the line of fire.

"Yes," Cassie replied, taking Bernie's hand when he offered it to her. "It's nice to meet you."

"Pleasure is all mine. Shall we get started?"

"Get started?"

"Protocol," Anastasia said with a wave of her hand. "Nothing to worry about. You have the paperwork I sent over?"

Cassie pulled three pieces of folded paper from her purse, smoothing them out on the counter before handing them to Bernie. After she'd secured her plane ticket, she'd received the forms with instructions to have them prepared prior to landing in Nashville. Part of her wanted to see what would happen if she ignored the directions, but her desire to appear as though she were cooperating won out. It was better not to paint a target on herself so soon.

The forms asked for basic employee information, and while Jason hadn't liked the idea of her giving Apex any information, it was all but guaranteed they already had it on file somewhere. The company had been watching her for years, and they were resourceful enough to already know something like her middle name or her social security number.

The paperwork also consisted of an NDA and an employment agreement. She'd sent pictures of them to Harris and Lorraine to look over, and both women said there was nothing egregious in the wording. With no other choice, Cassie signed and initialed the forms in the appropriate spaces, promising herself that if she felt uncomfortable upon arrival, she could void them with a single rip down the center before handing them over.

But she wouldn't. Not with Jason's future on the line.

"Everything looks good," Bernie said. "If you'll step over here."

Cassie did as she was told, walking behind the desk and standing in front of a blank wall. She tried to smile when the camera went off, but there was no way it reached her eyes. A small line of sweat had formed along her brow, and her hands shook hard enough that she wished her leggings had pockets so she could shove them in there to avoid letting Anastasia know how much this process terrified her.

Without a doubt, this was the point of no return.

Bernie gestured for Cassie to rejoin Anastasia on the other side of the desk. "And that's it. Pretty painless, right?"

Cassie nodded, her mouth so dry she couldn't swallow to relieve the ache in her throat. Taking up her previous position once more, she ignored the way Anastasia's eyes sparkled like a hunter watching their target stumble into a hidden trap.

Cassie saw the ruse and still couldn't do anything to stop herself from falling into it.

"Here's your employee badge." Bernie handed over a small plastic card with a clip attached to the top. It was still warm from the printer. "Make sure you have that on you at all times. You'll need to scan it every time you come and go from the building."

Cassie stared down at the card. "Employee badge?" She looked over at Anastasia. "Not a visitor's badge?"

The sparkle in Anastasia's eyes grew brighter. "What paperwork did you think you were filling out?"

Cassie looked back down at the badge, still failing to swallow past her dry throat. It sported the picture he'd just taken, and she had been right—the smile on her face looked more like a grimace, and her eyes were wide with anxiety and trepidation.

"A visitor's badge will be too restrictive for your role here, Miss Quinn," Bernie explained, not noticing the tension between the two women. "This will give you full access to the first four floors of the building. You'll find everything you need at your fingertips."

"The first four floors?" Cassie asked. "I don't get the all-access pass?"

Bernie laughed, not realizing the question hadn't been directed at him. "Only a few people have that level of clearance. You'll need to work your way up to that, but it's nothing a bit of time and hard work won't solve."

"This is a lot of security for a publicity company," Cassie said.

"We have a lot of high-profile clients," Bernie explained. "It's for their benefit as much as yours. You can never be too careful these days."

"Bernie takes his job seriously," Anastasia said, flashing the man a wide smile that he returned. "And he's very good at it." She returned her gaze to Cassie. "Ready to get started?"

No, she thought, but she wasn't about to admit that out loud. Instead, she gave a sharp nod of her head.

"Wonderful. Follow me, please."

As Cassie turned away from the desk, Bernie called out after her. "Miss Quinn?"

Cassie met his gaze over her shoulder. "Yes?"

"Welcome to Apex Publicity. We're happy to have you on our team."

All Cassie could do was offer him another grimace as her stomach twisted at his words.

4

Cassie followed the echo of Anastasia's heels as she strode to the elevator bank. Everyone they passed greeted the woman with a smile or a nod, which Anastasia returned with an air of grace and authority. Cassie had known upon first meeting her in North Carolina that the woman was important within Apex's ranks, but seeing her interact with other members of the staff put Anastasia's position into perspective. It was a lot like realizing your neighbor was an honest-to-goodness rockstar, when all this time you just thought he was some guy who liked to sit on his porch and fiddle around on the guitar.

The looks Cassie received ranged from curious to delighted. It wasn't surprising that her reputation preceded her, but she was shocked to be recognized on sight. Did they have a bulletin board hanging in some meeting room titled *Apex's Most Wanted* with her picture tacked front and center?

As they stepped into a waiting elevator, Cassie couldn't hold her tongue anymore. "A lot of these people know who I am."

"Your work speaks for itself," Anastasia replied. She had pulled her tablet out of her bag and was tapping away on the screen, only looking up long enough to hit the button for the fourth floor. "As you said, we've been trying to recruit you for some time now. Whole meetings have been devoted to discussing the best course of action to make that a reality."

Cassie couldn't fight back a shudder at the mental image of half a dozen people crowded around a conference table discussing her personal and professional information. "Do they know what I'm capable of?"

Anastasia lifted her head, her brow already raised in beguilement. "You mean that you're a medium?"

It didn't escape Cassie's attention that Anastasia used the word she preferred, and not the one most people lobbed at her—*psychic*—to humiliate her or make her feel abnormal. Peculiar. *Unnatural.*

Shrugging, Anastasia returned to her screen. "Yes. You're not the first to work for us, and you won't be the last. In fact, you'll be meeting one of your peers in just a moment."

Before Cassie could inquire further, the elevator dinged, and the doors slid open to reveal the fourth floor. While not as opulent as the lobby, the richness of the carpet and the lavishness of the art on the walls spoke to the kind of image Apex wanted to present. She studied the hallway as though she had no preconceived notion of what Apex was capable of, and she had to admit, at least within the confines of her own head, that she was charmed.

But a good interior decorator didn't erase the reality that Apex had killed a man and threatened to frame Jason for it. And that was just the most recent offense she knew about. There was no telling what else she would discover while she roamed their halls.

Unaware of Cassie's line of thought, Anastasia strode forward at a quick clip, clutching her tablet to her chest as though it were all the armor she needed to go into battle. Cassie trailed a few steps behind, peering into every open doorway. Some were offices, while others were meeting rooms. In every instance, the people inside kept their heads down, focused on their work and uninterested in the newcomers or their destination. If nothing else, Apex had cultivated an army of workers dedicated to their various roles within the company.

Questions darted through Cassie's mind, wondering who these people were, what their jobs entailed, and which clients they worked with. It struck Cassie that for all she knew about Apex's true capabilities, she had little information about their public purview. Sure, they were a publicity company, but what did that *mean*? Their website was impressive, but the information it offered was abstract at best and nebulous at worst. Word of mouth did more for them than any advertising campaign ever could.

That's where Lorraine came in. At first, Cassie had felt guilty dragging Lorraine away from her administrative job at the Coastal State Prison into the tangled web that was her relationship with Apex Publicity, but the woman had been fierce in her determination to help in whatever way she could, even if it meant going toe-to-toe with a giant who could knock all of them from the board with a single swipe of its far-reaching hand.

Lorraine had been researching Apex for about a month now and had found little to help Cassie in her plan to expose the company's misdeeds. They were, after all, excellent at presenting a false narrative and playing with the public's perception. But Lorraine didn't give up easily, and she had promised Cassie new information soon.

Anastasia turned down several hallways before coming to a stop outside a conference room lined with glass walls that featured an oval table and enough chairs for a dozen people, all of which were sleek, modern, and ergonomic. Memories of having to complete a public speaking course in college resurfaced, and panic flooded her system at the idea of having to present her life story in front of a room full of executives.

"It's bigger than we need," Anastasia explained, stepping inside. "The other conference rooms were booked. We're still putting the final pieces together on your office, but soon you'll have a private space if you need to conduct meetings or work in silence."

"I don't want an office," Cassie said, refusing to step inside the room, as though she hadn't already crossed a dozen lines she'd promised herself she never would. An office felt permanent. Official. "I won't need it."

"Regardless, it's there if you want it," Anastasia said, not even sounding exasperated at Cassie's continued resistance to her current situation. "Are you hungry? I had some sandwiches brought up."

Cassie leaned forward to peek into the room, taking in the small assortment of subs sitting on a silver platter at one end of the table. Four water bottles, a small stack of plates and napkins, and a few bags of chips sat nearby. A growl emanated from Cassie's stomach, convincing her to cross the threshold of the conference room, even as her brain screamed that it was a mistake.

Anastasia busied herself with the blinds, obscuring their view of the hallway, but not bothering with the ones that hung from the windows overlooking downtown Nashville. Cassie stepped up to the vista, taking it in with wide eyes. They were only on the fourth floor, but it offered a pleasant panorama of the metropolitan area. The sun shining through the tinted windows was bright without being blinding, and for at least a few seconds, Cassie could forget where she was and why she was there.

A knock on the open door startled her, but she didn't turn around, wanting to take in the view for a few more seconds before facing the reason for her visit to Tennessee. She had already told herself she was past the point of no return, but once she agreed to take on a case, there was no turning back. If innocent people were involved, she wouldn't abandon them, in life or in death.

"You're late," Anastasia snapped, all manner of affability gone from her tone.

"By less than three minutes," a man answered. "Hardly a punishable offense."

Upon hearing the voice, Cassie whipped around, taking in the familiar form of the man before her. Agent Chris Viotto had changed. Still tall and lean, his mouth was set into a frown, and his green eyes didn't sparkle quite as bright. His boyish good looks remained, now hidden just under the beginnings of a beard.

When Chris turned his attention to Cassie, his demeanor shifted. His lips tipped up into a smile, and his eyes softened from cold emeralds to a warm sage. He didn't look surprised to see her, but he drank in her presence like she was a balm to his soul. Despite the confusion of their last meeting, she was relieved to see a familiar face in the middle of enemy territory.

"I assume you're capable of handling this meeting on your own?" Anastasia asked.

Chris' eyes dulled and his jaw tensed as his gaze left Cassie's. "You mean I won't get to bask in the glory of your presence for much longer? Whatever will I do with myself?"

"Doesn't matter to me." Anastasia grabbed one of the water bottles from the table before approaching the doorway. "As long as you do what you're told."

Chris didn't move out of her way as she approached him. Anastasia was several inches shorter, even in heels, but her presence was just as imposing. They glared at each other for the span of several heartbeats before Chris stepped back, allowing Anastasia just enough room to slip by. Out in the hallway, she glanced over her shoulder at Cassie, her face amicable once more.

"It was nice seeing you again. I look forward to witnessing what you do here. Please don't hesitate to reach out if you need anything at all."

Anastasia had barely finished her sentence before Chris shut the door behind her. The closed blinds kept Cassie from seeing the other woman's expression, but the hesitation before she continued down the hallway and out of earshot painted a picture of the woman stopping long enough to glare at the door before moving on.

When Chris turned back to Cassie, the smile on his face and the warmth in his eyes were back. He crossed the room in three strides and scooped her up into a hug so tight that her feet left the ground. When he set her down again, he kept his hands on her waist and looked at her with such earnestness, she thought she might've imagined all the glowers he'd sent in Anastasia's direction.

"You have no idea how glad I am to see you," he said, the words coming out in a rush, the flyaway hair around her face fluttering in the breeze of his excitement.

Cassie knew she was gaping at him, but no matter how much she tried, she couldn't snap out of her stupor. "What are you doing here?"

Chris' face fell, though it didn't lose any of its newfound warmth.

When Cassie had last seen him, he'd stopped Piper McLaren from putting a bullet in Cassie's head. Piper had been arrested for attempted murder, and Chris had gone back to Apex, playing triple agent in an attempt to take them down from the inside.

She hadn't been able to get a ton of information out of him at their last meeting, but during their brief reunion, he'd informed her that Apex wanted to use his FBI status for their own purposes. He'd agreed, working to avoid breaking any laws while he buried himself within their operation. He had already been doing for months what Cassie planned on doing now.

"I'm here to work with you." Chris' eyes darted to the pile of sandwiches on the table. "Are you hungry? The food is usually pretty good. They spare no expense."

"Work with me?" Cassie echoed, turning her back on lunch. "Why?"

"Apex knows we've worked together before. It made sense to bring me in. Anastasia isn't an investigator. They figured you'd need a partner for this, and I was available." Chris grabbed a plate and put two small sandwiches and a bag of chips in the center of it. "Seriously, you should eat something. It's important to keep your energy up. I promise it's not poisonous. Can't trust much in this building, but you can trust that."

Cassie met his gaze, which was steady and insistent as he stared her down. Realization dawned when she pulled apart the meaning of his words.

Can't trust much in this building.

He didn't want her asking too much about why he was there. He couldn't risk letting something slip. The only way Apex would find out would be if the room was bugged.

Nodding in understanding, Cassie turned to the plate of sandwiches and grabbed a couple for herself, along with a water bottle. The pair of them sat down on one side of the table and ate in silence for a few minutes, glancing up several times to meet each other's gaze, laughing each time they did. Cassie's heart filled with a giddiness she hadn't felt in close to a month. She might be in the belly of the beast, but at least she was no longer alone.

Cassie polished off one of her sandwiches before finding the right words that wouldn't give either of them away. "It's been a while. I don't even know what you've been up to since I last saw you."

"A lot," Chris said with a laugh. "I've been running around all over the place."

For Apex or the FBI, she wondered? Maybe both. Cassie itched to pick his brain, to see how much he knew of their operation and if he had gathered any evidence against the company since working for them.

"Do you want to get a drink later?" Cassie asked, trying for casual and unbothered. "Catch up, and all that?"

A slow smile spread across Chris' face. "I'd like that."

"Great. Anastasia suggested I get the *Nashville tour*." What seemed to be an abhorrent idea only a few minutes ago was turning into a possible highlight of this trip. Cassie felt lighter than she had in weeks. "Maybe you can be my guide."

"I know this great place—"

A sharp knock cut off the rest of Chris' sentence. Before either of them could do anything more than look to the door, it swung open, and a man stepped inside. He was short, pudgy, and wore round glasses that magnified both his eyes and the circular shape of his face. Thin, mousy hair covered his head, and his suit was wrinkled and at least one size too big. His scowl made his whole face sink in on itself, as though it had been etched into his cheeks from the time he was born.

But that's not what stole Cassie's attention.

A black shadow swirled around the man's shoulders, forcing him into a hunch. His neck bent like he bore the burden of Atlas, and he shuffled his feet as though he didn't have the energy to pick them up off the floor.

Yet, none of that compared to the overwhelming malevolence billowing from the shadow in invisible tendrils that stretched across the room until ice-cold fingers wrapped around Cassie's throat and squeezed. She shot up and out of her chair with such force, it rolled across the floor and into the wall of windows behind her, tipping over. But the sound came to her as though she were underwater, her vision darkening around the edges until her knees buckled.

5

Cassie flung out her hands and caught herself on the table in front of her. Chris was at her side, grasping her shoulders to keep her upright. He called her name several times, but it took her a moment to recognize the sound of his voice. The heaviness of the malevolent force pushed in on her from all sides, obscuring her hearing, clouding her vision, and making her feel as though she might implode.

But she'd dealt with worse and come out on the other side.

Dragging in a shuddering breath, Cassie used the pressure of Chris' hands on her shoulders and the feel of the table beneath her palms to ground herself. She imagined an invisible barrier pushing out from her skin to envelop her entire body. She had no idea if it was real or imagined, but that mattered less than the fact that it kept the most insidious spirits out of her head.

Mind growing clearer by the second, Cassie took in another couple lungfuls of air before straightening. Sweat had beaded along her brow, and she wiped it away with the back of her hand. As her pulse calmed to a more reasonable pace, she peered up into Chris' worried eyes and mustered a small smile.

"Sorry about that," she said. "Didn't mean to scare you."

"Are you okay?" he asked, still holding onto her shoulders. "What the hell happened?"

Cassie kept her gaze on the man before her and not the one on the other side of the room. She needed a few more seconds to ensure she would keep her footing before she allowed her gaze to lock with his. "This building is on the newer side compared to others in the area."

Chris shook his head. "What's that got to do with anything?"

"There are spirits and remnants of psychic energy everywhere I go. Most of the time, they're faded enough to blend into the background. I notice them like you might notice the smell of exhaust from a passing car or the shadow of a cloud covering the sun." Cassie swallowed, using the time between speaking to take stock of the returning strength in her muscles. "The spirits that stand out amongst all that noise are few and far between, but I see them everywhere. Most often in older buildings and areas with a longer history. The more people are attached to a place, the higher the chances they return there in death. Hospitals, graveyards, apartment buildings, historical sites—they're the ones I have to mentally prepare for."

"Mentally prepare for?" Chris dropped his arms and glanced at the silent man on the other side of the table. "What do you mean?"

"Spirits spend their afterlife wandering without much direction, flickering between the spirit realm and the realm of the living. They each have a purpose—solve their murder, pass on a message, exact revenge. But few are strong enough to do that on their own. They need to work through a vessel."

"Like you."

Cassie nodded. "Acknowledging their existence often gains their attention. They see me seeing *them*, and it gives them hope they may be able to fulfill their purpose. I don't like doing that unless I have the time and energy to help them. Otherwise, it feels like giving them a false promise."

The man on the other side of the room scoffed. "They're dead. It's not like you can hurt their feelings."

Cassie ignored him. "There are too many spirits that need my help. As much as I hate the idea, I have to pick and choose my battles for the sake of my own sanity. But it takes a lot of mental energy to stay vigilant. If a building is newer, I don't have to prepare against the same level of onslaught I'd feel if I entered a historic site."

"Okay," Chris said, his nod slow but understanding. "Then what happened? Why'd you almost pass out like that?"

"Because I wasn't prepared for *him*." Cassie finally met the eyes of the other man in the room. The shadow around his shoulders had settled like a shroud, but she could feel it waiting for her to lose concentration again. "Or, rather, the entity he brought with him."

"Entity?" Chris asked, his voice taking on a tone caught somewhere between fear and curiosity.

Cassie retreated to her upturned chair and set it back on its feet, pushing it across the floor and back to its proper place at the table. After she sat down and folded her hands in her lap, she looked back to the man. "Do you want to answer this one?"

"If I knew what it was," he sneered, "then you wouldn't be here, would you?"

Chris sighed and sat down next to Cassie. After giving her another questioning glance, he gestured for the other man to sit. "This is Don Carver, Apex's resident psychic at the Nashville headquarters."

"Medium," Don corrected and slid into a chair across from them. Cassie had to fight the twitch of her lips. "I don't get visions. Just talk to dead people."

"Don has worked at Apex for three years," Chris said. "I met him a few months ago. Hard to imagine, but he wasn't such a prick back then."

"Personality change," Cassie replied. "When did that happen?"

"As soon as he started investigating his latest case. That was, what? A little over a month ago?"

Don leaned back in his chair, clasping his hands over his stomach. "Give or take."

Cassie's mind whirled. A month ago, Anastasia had blackmailed her into joining Apex's ranks. Not long before that, Jason had been approached to solve the disappearance of a young boy from Camp Fortuna, a local rehabilitation center for troubled teens. It was also around this time that Ross Hughes, one of Apex's high-profile clients and someone with ties to Camp Fortuna, announced his presidential candidacy.

It had to be related, but could Cassie risk bringing up the connection without knowing more? Dismissing the thought, she kept her gaze locked on the man in front of her. The black entity clinging to his shoulders was still, its presence dulled by the mental shield she'd placed around her. It was comforting to know she could hold it at bay, but she wouldn't take that for granted.

"What's the case?" Cassie asked.

"Three years ago, a woman went missing." Don shrugged his shoulders as though that's all Cassie needed to know. "We'd like to find out what happened to her."

"Why?"

"Because it's our job."

"I mean, why is Apex interested in what happened to her? They're a publicity company, not a private investigation firm."

"I don't ask questions," Don said. "And neither should you."

Cassie scoffed. "You clearly know nothing about me."

"Carver," Chris snapped. "Need I remind you that you requested dismissal from this investigation and Ms. Bolton acquiesced? I know it's difficult for you, but being a pain in the ass isn't going to solve your problem. Or this case."

Don sighed and leaned forward, placing his elbows on the table and pinning Cassie with a glare. "About a month ago, I received paperwork for a new job. Information was basic to begin with. Woman disappeared three years ago. Like I said, I don't ask questions, so I don't know why we want to find out what happened to her. My job was to discover where she went and if she was still alive."

"Her name?" Cassie asked.

"Millie Abrahms. Twenty-nine. Unmarried, no children. One day she was there, and the next, she wasn't." For the first time, something close to panic or desperation filtered through the dullness in Don's eyes. "We had her home address. An upscale apartment. I went there. As soon as I walked inside, something dropped me to the ground."

"Some*thing*," Cassie said. "Not some*one*."

"You're a smart one, aren't you?"

"Less commentary," Chris said. "More information."

Don rolled his eyes. "Woke up and felt a presence nearby. Oppressive, dark, angry. Couldn't shake the feeling when I left. Haven't been able to since."

"When did your personality change?" Cassie asked.

"Days afterwards. A week, tops." He shook his head, as though trying to work through the fog of his memory. "At first, it was little things. Quick to frustration and anger. Quick to say something if someone annoyed me, first at my local coffee shop and then at home with my wife. Shit that normally didn't bother me now felt like it was personal. Like people were doing it on purpose, just to piss me off. And as much as I knew that wasn't true, I couldn't stop from reacting. I'd blow up. Every single time."

Cassie heard beyond the irritation in the man's voice to the panic just under the surface. She sympathized with him. She'd come across entities like this in the past. One of her cases with David involved the ghost of a serial killer, and she remembered with brutal clarity the way it had manipulated her emotions, even after a brief encounter. She couldn't imagine living with that presence for a full month.

"My wife knows what I do. She told me to talk to someone about it. I refused. Apex doesn't hire quitters, and they certainly don't keep them employed for long." Don took off his glasses and placed them on the table so he could rub at his eyes. "But then she threatened to move out. I love this job, but I love my wife more. And she's right. I haven't been sleeping. Haven't been eating. I feel like something inside me is pulling at my strings. All I want to do is solve this case. But I've hit a dead end." A sob escaped Don's mouth. "I can't take it anymore."

Cassie traded a glance with Chris, his face mirroring her thoughts. Whoever Don Carver was, he didn't deserve this. As much as Cassie didn't want to aid Apex, she couldn't refuse helping someone in distress, dead or alive.

"How does it appear to you?" Cassie asked.

Don swiped at his cheeks with the back of his hand, then returned his glasses to his face. "What do you mean?"

"The entity. What does it look like?"

Don furrowed his brows. "It doesn't look like anything. But I can feel it. Like a dark cloud hanging over me, wrapping me up in every miserable feeling I've ever had."

"It's never appeared to you in physical form?"

Don shook his head, then studied her. "You can see it, can't you?" When Cassie nodded, he looked like he had to force out his next question. "What does it look like?"

"Just like you described. A dark cloud draped around your shoulders."

"Anastasia said you were good." Don chuckled, but he looked more shocked than amused. "But you're a lot more powerful than I am. If anyone is gonna get to the bottom of this, it won't be me."

In her mind, Cassie had already agreed to help, but she didn't like how Don peered at her with such high expectations. It would mean even more disappointment if she failed, both to him and herself. "Your assumption is that the entity is Millie Abrahms?"

Don shrugged. "Your guess is as good as mine. But her body was never found. For all we know, she's still alive."

"Can we even assume the entity is related to the case?" Chris asked. "Could it be something different altogether? A strange coincidence that he picked it up at her apartment?"

"There's always a chance," Cassie said. "But I won't know more until I start my own investigation."

"I'll get you whatever you need," Don said, standing. "The sooner we figure this out, the sooner my life gets back to normal."

"Send whatever information you have over to my office." Chris mirrored the man's movements. Cassie pushed out of her chair, too. "We'll see if we can spot something you didn't."

Don narrowed his eyes at Chris' implication, but Cassie saw him bite back the words on the tip of his tongue. When Don looked over at Cassie, the clench of his jaw loosened, but the anger and annoyance stayed steady in his eyes.

Stepping around the table and reaching out a hand, Don said, "Thank you. I know you haven't solved it yet. But I've got a good feeling about this."

"I thought you said you weren't psychic," Cassie said, staring at his outstretched fingers for a moment. Black tendrils crawled down his arms, winding around his wrist like smoke. Ensuring her barrier was still in place, she reached out and clasped the man's hand. A sharp pain stung the tip of her fingers, and she gasped, pulling away in surprise.

Chris was at her side in an instant. "What was that?"

"Static electricity," Don said. "Sorry about that. I need to remember to pick my feet up when I walk."

Cassie couldn't tear her gaze away from her hand. There were no marks along her skin, but an echo of the current thrummed in her veins, causing a shiver to race along her spine. It had felt like more than a static shock. A hazy childhood memory of touching an electric fence surfaced in her mind. She remembered being surprised when it hadn't hurt and confused by the strange sensation that had coursed through her body. Like waves of energy crawling up her arms.

This had been ten times as powerful.

Cassie looked up to ask Don if he had felt the same thing, but he was already gone.

"You okay?" Chris asked.

"Yeah." She looked back down at her unmarred hand. "I'll be fine."

6

Cassie spent the rest of the afternoon getting the official tour of the building—at least the portion she could access. The four floors were much the same, with offices and meeting rooms taking up most of the space. Chris had no idea how many employees were stationed in Nashville, but he said the door was open for anyone the company employed, regardless of their hometown location. Apex also had a penchant for hiring contractors, which could've accounted for the additional space. Either way, it was no small operation.

There were seven floors total in the building. Chris had access to the fifth, but said it was more of the same. Curiosity made Cassie's skin itch, but she refused to acknowledge the feeling. Getting caught snooping wouldn't do her any favors.

For now, all she wanted was a drink.

There were several bars within walking distance of Apex, but Chris drove for fifteen minutes before stopping at a hole-in-the-wall Irish pub he claimed had the best burger and fries and the cheapest cocktail prices in the city. It didn't escape her attention that they were also far enough from prying eyes to have a conversation in peace.

Pulling open the door, Chris allowed Cassie to enter first. The smell of sizzling beef and raucous laughter hit her like a warm gust of air, easing some of the tension in her shoulders. Dim overhead lights and neon signs illuminated the space, but it only added to the atmosphere. This was the kind of place you could walk into after a hard day of work and find your preferred beverage waiting for you at the bar.

Chris led Cassie to the other side of the room. She slid into a seat against the back wall at a high-top table. From this angle, they could keep an eye on the entrance, the bar, and the door to the kitchen, watching as servers and patrons came and went. Between the classic rock spilling out of the overhead speakers and the animated conversations from the bar's regulars, no one would pay them any mind.

"Pick your poison," Chris said, once Cassie was settled.

"Something strong and sweet," Cassie replied.

He flashed a grin. "Like you."

Before Cassie could respond, Chris slipped through the crowd and up to the bar. There was a good crowd tonight, but the bartender looked like he'd been doing this job for a couple decades. No one went longer than a few minutes without a fresh libation, and while he offered more scowls than smiles, it seemed his demeanor didn't deter a single person in the establishment.

Less than two minutes later, Chris slid a red drink with a cherry garnish across the table to her, then pulled the other chair around so he could gaze out at the room. Between David and Adelaide, Cassie was used to the way officers operated. Don't ever put your back to the door, and don't ever let your guard down, even when you you're off duty. Situational awareness was paramount to the safety of yourself and others.

In a way, Cassie understood. It had become second nature to her as well, but on a different plane of existence. As she scanned the room, her gaze skipped over the shadowy ghost of a woman in the far corner, but she would remain aware of the spirit's location relative to their position. These days, she didn't often get ambushed or caught off guard, but that was only due to her constant vigilance.

Earlier today was one of the rare exceptions. The tips of Cassie's fingers tingled at the memory.

Turning to Chris, she asked, "How'd you find this place?"

"Trial and error." He put his Heineken to his lips and took a long sip. It looked like he needed the alcohol more than she did. "Spent a lot of the first few months drinking away my worries, only to realize they were still there in the morning."

Cassie peered around the room again. "You sure it's safe to talk here?"

"The safest we're gonna get. I've never seen another Apex employee come here. Not that I know them all. But it's not hard to pick them out of a crowd once you know what to look for. They're like robots or—"

"Cult members?"

"That's exactly what I was going to say."

"It's eerie." Cassie took a sip of her cocktail, enjoying the tartness as it burst across her tongue. "I thought Anastasia was in her own league, but that building was full of people like her."

"No one is quite like Anastasia."

"I can't tell if you're impressed or intimidated."

Chris shot her a glance, and there was a sparkle of mischief in his eyes. "A little of both, I think. She's a powerful woman. Good at her job. There's a reason she's made it into the inner circle. I'd be an idiot not to take that seriously."

"Inner circle?" Cassie asked. "You know that for sure?"

"I don't know anything for sure, but it's an educated guess. Anastasia's well-connected, respected, and feared. Doesn't matter which doors she walks through, whether they're in Nashville, New York, or Los Angeles. People defer to her."

"Good to know," Cassie said. "Any other insights you want to share?"

"I'm hungry. Do you want something?"

"Oh." The sudden detour caught Cassie off guard. "Sure. Whatever you recommend."

Chris slid from the table again. When he made it to the bar, he caught the man's attention and leaned in close to pass along their order. The guy nodded once, then pushed through the doors of the kitchen to relay the information. When he returned to his position behind the bar, Chris ordered them another round and made his way back to Cassie with their drinks in hand.

"You trying to get me drunk?" Cassie joked. She wasn't even halfway done with her first one.

"Trust me, you'll need it."

Cassie studied Chris for a moment, comparing this version of him to the one she'd first met in North Carolina. In many ways, he was the same—good looking, jovial, a little mischievous. But in others, he was a shell of his former self. Hints of his usual nature shone through here and there, but they were cast in a never-ending shadow that clung to him as tightly as the entity had surrounded Don Carver.

She took another long swig of her drink, the burn of the alcohol chasing away the memory. "We didn't have much time to talk when I saw you last. Fill me in on what's been going on."

Chris drained his first beer and picked up his second before he spoke. "After what happened in Charlotte, I couldn't get Apex out of my head. Mannis warned me to drop it. I didn't."

Cassie remembered Agent Mannis as a level-headed older man who knew more about Apex than he let on. He'd told them both not to go looking for trouble. It was advice Cassie had adhered to for as long as she could. Chris, it seemed, had ignored it altogether.

"Mannis doesn't spook easily, but I could tell he wouldn't touch Apex with a ten-foot pole. At first, it was just morbid curiosity. The company was a powerhouse, and their client list was impressive. People in every industry, from politics to Hollywood to computer science and everything in between. But what really caught my attention was what *wasn't* there. Hardly anyone talked about them."

Cassie had come to the same realization. "Their website is basic. Flashy, but vague. Not many articles about them, either. If they're mentioned, it's in passing. No one's written a profile on the company or the CEO."

"Exactly." Chris shook his head. "I started asking some questions. I thought I was being discreet. Subtle. But then Apex came knocking."

"They found me on a business trip in New Orleans," Cassie said. "It wasn't Anastasia. Someone new. He didn't like that I told him no."

"They didn't like that I told them no either." Chris wiped the condensation from his beer until it was free of any moisture. "The

Agency relegated me to desk duty. And I started getting written up for the stupidest shit. Had all sorts of interpersonal problems. Even Mannis distanced himself from me. But I could handle a little bullying. It was a pain in my ass, but it told me what I needed to know. Apex was hiding something, and they didn't like when people poked their noses where they didn't belong."

Cassie held her breath, knowing the other shoe was about to drop.

Chris scanned the pub before he spoke again. "Did you know I have a sister?"

"No, I didn't."

A wry smile found its way to Chris' face. "Her name is Christina. We're Irish twins. Real original, right? Naming both your kids Chris, I mean."

"Are you close?"

The smile fell from Chris' lips. "Real close. Always have been. We didn't fight like most siblings. A couple squabbles here and there, but we always had each other's backs." A sigh left his mouth, sounding like it contained the weight of all his woes. "She married her high school sweetheart, Ben. They'd already been together ten years at that point. A week after their second wedding anniversary, she found him dead on their bedroom floor. Aneurism."

Cassie couldn't hold back the gasp that left her mouth or the tears that pricked at her eyes. "That's awful."

"They had a little girl, Jessi, and Christy didn't know it at the time, but she was pregnant with their son, Jonah." Chris washed away the emotion in his voice with another swig of beer. "I can only imagine what she must've felt when she found out. Happy to have this one last gift from him but devastated she'd have to raise them on her own. That neither one of them would ever really know their father."

Cassie knew they were on a train barreling toward the obvious conclusion. The brakes had been cut and there was no stopping what came next.

"My sister is the strongest, bravest, most loving person I know. If I were in her shoes, I'd want to watch the world burn. But even through all the tears, I never once heard her turn bitter or angry. She's a better person than I am."

There were no words that could comfort him in that moment, so Cassie placed her hand on his arm and squeezed.

The sigh that left his mouth was just as world-weary as the first. "I did everything I could to help. Whatever they needed, I found a way to get it for them." Chis looked at her out of the corner of his eye, his lips tipping up into a sheepish smile. "They're part of the reason my love life is in shambles."

"But you wouldn't trade it for the world, would you?"

"No," he said, shaking his head. "I wouldn't."

"You're a good brother," Cassie said. "And a good uncle."

His face fell again, and when he swallowed, it looked like shards of glass had lodged in his throat. "Apex made it pretty clear what would happen to them if I didn't comply." He rushed on, as though these words had been building in his chest from the start and he could no longer hold them back. "There are certain risks that come with this career, and I'm willing to pay all of them. But my sister didn't sign up for that. Jessi isn't even ten yet. I couldn't—I didn't have a choice. I didn't know what else to do. I—"

"You did the right thing." Cassie waited until Chris looked at her, his eyes shining and his gaze desperate for the support her words provided. "My sister and I are still trying to rebuild our relationship after years of barely speaking to each other, and I wouldn't have hesitated to do the same thing. They forced your hand. This is on them, not you."

Chris nodded, tearing his gaze away and blinking rapidly. After a moment, he croaked, "Thank you."

"Does anyone else know?" Cassie asked. When Chris shook his head, her heart broke for him. "Thank you for trusting me. I know it's not easy."

"It is with you." When he looked at her again, his eyes were rimmed red but free from any tears. "It's always been that way, ever since we first met. I don't trust people easily, but I've always trusted you. It's a nice feeling. One I could get used to."

Cassie became aware of the fact that her hand still rested on his arm. She squeezed once, then slipped her fingers around her glass to give them something else to do. "I trust you too," she said, then took a deep breath before proving how much she meant that. "The only reason I'm here is because Anastasia has a doctored video of Jason committing murder."

Chris returned his gaze to the room, watching the crowd while he gathered his words. "I'm surprised he's not here with you."

"I made him stay home. I didn't want this getting more complicated than it already was. He can be a little overprotective."

"Can't say I blame him."

Silence stretched between them. Cassie drained her first drink and grabbed the second before finding her footing again. "You've been working for Apex since then, right? Have you found anything we can use against them?"

Chris shook his head. "They don't trust me yet. Most of the information they had me track down through the federal database seemed pretty innocent. I'm sure it all leads somewhere, but I don't have enough of the puzzle pieces to put together a full picture. The biggest lead so far is this case you're working on."

"You think it's that important?"

"They've been working on it for a while. Don isn't the first psychic they put on the case."

"Medium," Cassie said without thinking.

Chris rolled his eyes, but he was grinning again. "He's not the first *medium* they put on the case. They weren't happy when he wanted to drop it from his workload. But a few days later, Anastasia approved it, saying they found someone to replace him. Not long after that, she told me I'd be working with you. Made it very clear I was to keep an eye on you."

"She knows our history. She trusts you to keep me from causing trouble for them?"

"She trusts the threat on my family's life."

Now it was Cassie's turn to feel like there was glass in her throat. "I won't do anything to jeopardize their safety. Or Jason's. We have to be smart about this."

"I hate to say it," Chris said, "but I think the best thing we can do right now is solve this case. See where it leads."

Cassie tossed back the rest of her drink, enjoying the way the alcohol lifted the weight off her shoulders. But it didn't calm her nerves or quiet the worry in the back of her mind. "Then I guess there's only one thing we can do right now."

"What's that?"

Cassie held up her empty glass. "Get another round."

7

Lorraine jumped when Jason's cell phone rang.

She could feel the long day in her back, feet, and the pressure building behind her eyes. It was always a struggle to remember to drink enough water and eat enough food, but now that she was creeping toward thirty, she could feel the effects of her inattention on her body. The couch she was sitting on in the middle of Jason's office wasn't helping matters, either.

She had always been an organized person, capable of handling multiple projects at once, keeping schedules, and finding solutions to problems that stumped her peers. Not everyone thrived on turning chaos into order, but Lorraine gained a deep satisfaction when she walked through the door into her office to find everything on fire, knowing she had the capability to douse each individual flame until everything was cold and calm again.

The job at the Coastal State Prison had been a godsend when Lorraine had first landed it. Her mother's cancer diagnosis had sharpened her resolve in a way innate passion never could. While she wished she could've gotten a job in the field of computer science after graduating from Georgia Tech, it was more important to spend time with her mother. Her own happiness meant nothing if she couldn't share it with the woman who had sacrificed everything for her.

At first, the job kept her interest—challenged her, even. The fact that she was overqualified to be the warden's administrative assistant should've bothered her, but she'd needed the money and stability. In the beginning, she had found ways to become essential to the operation. Reorganizing and digitizing their filing system had taken months, and now the prison ran like a well-oiled machine. She'd even increased the administration office's efficiency in scheduling personal and vacation days, not to mention the program she'd written to decrease the number of payroll errors.

But now there was nothing left to improve, and she found her patience with Warden Wickham waning with each passing day. In those first few months, he'd been kind and gentle with her. When he'd started getting a little too familiar, she put her foot down, not allowing any excuse to misinterpret friendliness for interest. After that, he'd distanced himself, which had suited her just fine. But now, he went out of his way to make her life more difficult. A part of her wished he would just fire her and get it over with. But she couldn't afford to lose her job. Her mother might be in remission, but the hospital bills never stopped knocking on their door.

But then Cassie had arrived in a ray of sunshine, asking if Lorraine would be interested in doing research for Jason's business. While they couldn't pay her much, the extra money would go a long way to ease some of her monetary stress. Her mother had always been frugal, avoiding brand-name products and repairing clothes with a couple stitches instead of buying new ones, but now that she was unable to work, they'd had to cut back even more.

More than that, though, Lorraine felt like she was finally helping people. She saw the worst humanity had to offer at the prison, but she was powerless to do anything about it. Now, with Cassie and Jason, she could help victims and their families find the justice they deserved. She didn't have to sit back and accept the world as it was anymore.

That's not to say it was easy. Over the past few months, Lorraine had averaged about four hours of sleep each night and consumed caffeine in its various forms in lieu of proper meals. Her mother had noticed she'd dropped a few pounds she couldn't afford to lose, so Lorraine had stashed protein bars in her purse, center console, and desk drawers in the hopes of alleviating some of her mother's worries. Her body was still sluggish most days, but her mental vigor had been renewed, as had her determination to help Cassie and Jason solve their problems, big and small.

Taking a bite out of an outdated granola bar, Lorraine watched as Jason picked up his cell phone and placed it against his ear. Cassie would be on the other line to update them on her progress.

Just thinking of the name *Apex* made Lorraine cringe, but it was nothing compared to the tension Jason held in his shoulders. She hadn't known him for long, but it wasn't hard to see how much he cared about Cassie—and how much he worried about her. Lorraine couldn't blame him. Cassie had the weight of the world on her shoulders thanks to her eerie abilities. Lorraine could see how he struggled with not being able to relieve that pressure in the woman he loved.

Jason got up from his chair and walked around his desk, crossing the room, and sitting down on the cushion next to Lorraine. She folded the wrapper over her half-eaten granola bar and shoved it back into her purse, then lifted her water bottle to her lips to wash away the dryness left behind by her impromptu appetizer. She'd have to remember to grab something on the way home if she didn't want her rumbling stomach to wake her up in the middle of the night.

"You're on speaker now," Jason said, hitting a button on his phone and holding it out between them.

"Hey, Lorraine," Cassie said from the other end of the line. "Doing okay?"

"All good here," Lorraine said, the answer automatic. "How are you?"

Wind buffeted the phone, and Cassie waited until it passed before she answered. "About as good as can be expected."

"Where are you right now?" Jason asked.

"Outside my hotel room. I didn't want to call you while I was in there in case the room is bugged."

Lorraine bit the inside of her cheek. Sometimes she felt like she was in the middle of a blockbuster movie, talking about bugged rooms and seeing spirits. Cassie and Jason took it all in stride, as used to it as you could get, she guessed. But sometimes she had to pinch herself to make sure she wasn't dreaming. How was this her life?

"What have you been up to today?" Jason asked.

"Not a whole lot. Anastasia picked me up at the airport, which was about as pleasant as you could imagine. Then she took me to Apex's Nashville headquarters so I could turn in my paperwork and get my employee badge."

"Employee?" Jason asked. "Not visitor?"

"Yeah." Cassie's tone was clipped, and Lorraine couldn't stop herself from shifting in her seat. "For all intents and purposes, I'm an Apex Publicity employee now, albeit one they keep on a short leash."

"What do you mean?" Lorraine asked.

"I have access to four out of the seven floors. Chris has one more than me. He says it's more of the same."

Jason stiffened at the mention of Chris' name. "Agent Viotto is there?"

If Cassie caught the coolness in Jason's voice, she didn't let on. "Anastasia brought him in to work with me on this case."

Before Jason could ask more about Chris, Lorraine steered the conversation in a more important direction. "What kind of case do they have you working on?"

"Missing persons. We met with another medium named Don Carver who gave us the basics. I'll get more information about the case tomorrow. Today was more about getting a lay of the land."

Lorraine had already pulled out a notepad and jotted down the medium's name. "Anything else you can tell us about Don Carver?"

"Only that he had a dark entity attached to him. It was powerful. Caught me off-guard at first."

"Are you okay?" Jason asked, leaning forward as though he could reach through the phone and comfort her.

"I'm fine," Cassie said, and even Lorraine could hear the impatience in the other woman's voice.

"You think it's related to the case?" Lorraine asked.

"Most likely. He picked it up while working this job. Caused his personality to change, too. And he's not the first who'd been affected. That's why Anastasia wanted to bring me on board. She thinks I can figure it out."

Jason ground his teeth together, and Lorraine winced at the sound. "And if you can't?"

"That's not an option."

"Let us know when you find more information about the case tomorrow," Lorraine said. She had no interest in witnessing the squabble building before her, even over the phone. There had been a lot of tension around the office over the last couple of months. "I'll do what I can on my end."

"I appreciate that." Cassie paused, as though she didn't want to say what came out of her mouth next. "Chris is convinced Anastasia is part of the inner circle. He says no matter where she goes, everyone defers to her. There's no way she'll betray Apex, but she might still be our best source of information. If she lets something slip, it could be what we need to take them down."

"Be careful talking about her in that building," Jason said. "I wouldn't be surprised if they've got it bugged."

"That's what Chris said, which is why we went out for a couple drinks tonight."

If Jason ground his teeth together anymore, they'd be dust in his mouth by the time this phone call was over. "You went out for drinks?"

"Just a couple of old friends catching up," Cassie said, sounding as casual as she could, as though she could sense Jason's reaction. "Easiest way to talk without being overheard. Not that he had much for me."

"Are you sure we can trust him?"

"Yes. He hates Apex as much as we do. You're not the only one they're blackmailing."

"What do they have on him?"

"Not him. His sister and her kids. Apex threatened their lives. He's just as motivated as we are to take them down."

Jason hesitated. "If you're sure—"

"I understand you're trying to look at this from every angle, but I know Chris." Cassie took a deep breath, and her voice was steadier than it had been a moment ago. "He's a good man, and he's doing the best he can right now. He's been open and honest with me every step of the way. He doesn't want to rock the boat until he knows we can nail them to the wall, but when the time comes, he'll be there with us."

"You can't know that—"

"It doesn't matter. He's the only ally we have right now. I'm choosing to trust him."

Jason dragged a palm down his face, his agitation coming off him in waves. But he didn't say anything.

"I might've found another lead," Lorraine said, clinging to the scrap of good news she'd stumbled upon earlier that day.

"Oh?" Cassie asked, sounding both interested and distracted at the same time.

"A disgruntled former employee that goes by the username Omega14782. I don't have much information right now, but I wanted to mention it in case you hear something around the office."

"That's good," Cassie said, sounding more distracted now. "Let's me know when you find more."

Lorraine flipped through the notebook in her lap until she came across her notes from earlier. "Of course. I'm not sure how reliable he is yet, considering I found him posting on some conspiracy theory forums, but out of everything I've seen so far, he appears to be the most informed about what Apex is capable of. I sent him a direct message, and we're just waiting to hear back now."

The other line remained silent.

Lorraine leaned forward to look at the phone's screen. Still connected. "You there?"

Jason exchanged a glance with Lorraine, worry replacing the agitation in his eyes. "Cassie?"

"Yeah, I'm still here. Sorry, I thought I saw something."

Jason sat up straighter. "Like what?"

"I'm not sure—"

"Describe it to me."

Cassie sighed. "It was nothing. Look, I've had a long day. A long couple of months. I need to go to bed so I'm fresh tomorrow. The sooner I can solve this case, the sooner I can come home."

"Cassie—"

"I'm fine," she said, though there was more exhaustion in her voice than annoyance now. "Thanks for your help, Lorraine. Let me know if you find anything else. I'll talk to you guys tomorrow, okay?"

"Okay," Jason replied. "I hope—"

But the line had already gone dead. Lorraine avoided Jason's eyes as he picked up the phone and shoved it in his pocket. "I'll look into Don Carver," she said, hoping that would reassure him a little bit. "Maybe it'll give us some insight into the company to learn about some of its employees and their backgrounds."

"Add another name to your list, too."

"Who?"

Jason tried and failed to keep his voice neutral as he said, "Agent Christopher Viotto."

8

The hairs on the back of Cassie's neck now stood on end and wouldn't let her appreciate Lorraine and Jason's small victory.

Cassie had been excited to talk to Jason all night. When he'd answered, the deep timber of his voice had caused a pleasant shiver to course through her body, and she couldn't ignore the ache in her chest from how much she missed him.

But the feeling had been overshadowed by her exhaustion and frustration—and something looming in the shadows. While Cassie's anxiety was manageable these days—thanks to a healthy dose of medication and therapy—it was never truly gone. Her fears lived under her skin like worms burrowing through the soil, invisible to the naked eye but ever-present. She'd been on high alert and overstimulated by all the new environments and situations, and she could feel the toll it had taken on her body. Sore feet, tight muscles, aching joints, and a tightness in her chest that wouldn't go away without a hot shower and a good night's rest.

Jason meant well whenever he checked in on her. His compassion was one of the reasons she'd fallen in love with him. Years ago, she would've relished having someone at her side, ensuring she was always safe and comfortable. But lately, his overprotective nature had felt more stifling than supportive. She had finally found her place in the world, her life's purpose, and she didn't want anyone or anything to hold her back—even out of love and devotion.

A flash of movement out of the corner of Cassie's eye caught her attention again. Years of conditioning herself not to react to these kinds of situations kept her from turning to look at the figure, but she tracked the motion from her peripherals. If it was a ghost, she didn't want to make eye contact for fear of adding more to her plate.

But if this was a person, the situation would be a whole different beast. In the distance, she could hear partygoers enjoying their warm April evening from her place in the courtyard outside her hotel, but once she got up to her room, the insulated walls and thick glass windows would allow her to sleep in peace.

A few people milled about, coming and going from the hotel or walking to the nearest bar. No one paid her any mind, and she reveled in feeling invisible among the passersby after the intensity of her visit to Apex, where she had been the center of everyone's focus.

When she had first sat down on the bench, she'd been grateful the streetlamp closest to her was out, basking her in just enough darkness that she could remain hidden until those walking by were practically on top of her.

Now, every shadow felt like a threat.

The courtyard was small, but there were a few large trees and dozens of bushes that came up to her waist or higher. The movement had come from the tree closest to the corner of the hotel. It wouldn't be difficult for someone to walk up the sidewalk, squeeze through one of the bushes, and hide behind the tree to watch their victim.

Cassie sucked in a deep breath and exhaled with deliberate slowness. When she felt her heart rate return to normal, she twisted in her seat and peered at the tree. The wind rustled the leaves around her, but other than a couple people passing by, there was no other movement. The smell of the spring breeze carried with it the hint of sizzling meat. Otherwise, the night was quiet and serene.

Then why did the hair on the back of her neck still stand at attention?

Cassie had learned years ago to trust her instincts. It wasn't always obvious whether it was women's intuition or preternatural instinct, but nine times out of ten, it helped her solve a case or keep herself safe. She wasn't about to ignore it, not even when she wanted nothing more than to run up to her room and lock the door behind her.

Standing on shaky legs, Cassie took a moment to brush invisible dirt from her pants and gather her bearings. Her heart was steady, but her mind was racing. No matter how much she'd worked on fighting against her intrusive thoughts, she still struggled to maintain a clear head in potentially dangerous situations. After going through the kind of trauma she'd experienced, no one would blame her for this type of vigilance.

But the last thing she wanted to do was give in to her fears.

Cassie took a step forward, aware of every molecule around her. The slight humidity in the air caressed her skin, adding to the goosebumps that had erupted along her arms when the breeze had swirled past her. Shouts and laughter in the distance made her ears perk up, and a conversation from behind her had her turning to watch as a man and a woman passed by, her arm looped through his as their heads bent toward each other like they couldn't stand the distance between them.

Twisting back toward the tree, Cassie took several more measured steps forward. Tilting her head up, she sniffed the air, differentiating the smells and cataloguing each one. Burgers or steaks made her mouth water, though she wasn't hungry, and the ozone in the air indicated incoming rain. Soil from the nearby flowerbeds invaded her nostrils, and it took her a moment to move past the scent and pick up a different fragrance. Sweet and pungent, Cassie furrowed her brows as soon as she recognized the smell.

Violets.

She'd always thought the flower was beautiful, with its silky-smooth petals that came in a variety of shades, including the richest royal purple she could imagine. But something about it always reminded her of death, like the initial delicate aroma couldn't quite mask the smell of decay beneath the surface.

Looking around the courtyard, she couldn't see a single bloom. A shiver raced down Cassie's spine like it did whenever she brushed up against the supernatural world. No matter how much experience she had with the spirit realm, she'd never get used to the uncanniness of dealing with the afterlife.

Squaring her shoulders, Cassie took one more deep breath, ignoring the floral scent that dug its way deeper into her nostrils, and exhaled with one sharp gust.

Marching forward with her phone in one hand, unlocked and ready to dial the police, Cassie didn't hesitate as she circled wide and peered around the other side of the tree. After all the scenarios that had gone through her mind, she hadn't expected this one.

There was nothing there.

Empty air, smooth soil, and rustling leaves greeted her. The scent of violets had disappeared from everything but her memory, and the hairs along her neck had settled back into their resting position.

Leaning across the bushes that separated the courtyard from the sidewalk, she peered up and down the street. There were no ghostly manifestations and only a single woman walking away from her, taking in the night air at a leisurely pace.

Huffing out a relieved and exasperated laugh, Cassie turned back to the hotel and made her way inside, stopping long enough to ask the front desk clerk when the streetlamp in the courtyard would be fixed. After being assured it would be in operation by tomorrow evening, Cassie rode the elevator up to her floor and stepped inside the room she would call home for the foreseeable future.

Her anxiety from earlier was now a shadow of what it had been a few moments ago, but Cassie made sure to lock the deadbolt and flip over the swing bar to ensure no one could enter. After a second's hesitation, she also texted Jason, so he'd know she was safe in her hotel and would talk to him tomorrow after a good night's rest.

Feeling a sense of relief for the first time that day, Cassie went about her nightly routine before crawling under the covers and giving in to her unconsciousness, knowing that the real work would begin in the morning.

9

Cassie had been having the same recurring nightmare for well over a month. She was so familiar with the scene set before her that she could close her eyes and recount every single detail even when she was awake. From the way the fog swirled in the faint breeze to the weight of an invisible hand that pressed against her throat, constricting her windpipe and cutting off her air supply. She had long ago learned to breathe through the panic.

The goosebumps that erupted along her skin were just another piece of background noise that lent reality to her nightmare, but not much else. The smell of dirt and rain with a hint of smoke assaulted her senses, gathering in the back of her throat until she wanted to cough to dispel it.

But it was the shuffle of footsteps that caught her attention, as it always did. When it had first become obvious the dream would be sticking around for the long-term, Cassie had dreaded going to sleep each night. She'd done everything within her power to fight off the nightmare, whether it was staying up for days on end or talking to her doctor about sleep aids that might be able to stop her from dreaming altogether.

Now, Cassie accepted her fate. She didn't look forward to experiencing the same dream every night, but she'd stopped fighting the inevitable, choosing instead to look at it as an opportunity to discern new information from it.

Like always, the figure approaching her was lit from the back, their silhouette against the fog the only part of them she could discern. Now that Cassie had lived through this moment so many times, her brain was able to remain detached and analytical, surveying the scene as though through a magnifying glass, attempting to discover a detail that had previously gone unnoticed.

More frustrating was that she didn't know *why* she was still having the nightmare. The figure's identity was uncertain, but Cassie had always found familiarity in it. After her run-in with Piper McLaren, she'd been certain the person before her was the podcaster who'd threatened her life. Considering this moment had played out in real life, Cassie didn't know who else it could be.

Then why did she keep having the same dream?

Behind her, Cassie could feel another figure approach. She didn't fight the invisible force that turned her on the spot. Already receding into the fog, all Cassie saw was a glimpse of a muscular arm she now recognized as Chris Viotto's. He'd saved her that day, appearing out of nowhere to distract Piper long enough for Cassie to get the upper hand.

Chris had put a bullet in Piper's shoulder, and she'd been hauled off to the hospital before ending up in jail for assault with a deadly weapon. Interesting that she was once again working with Chris. Was that why she kept having the same dream?

Was her subconscious trying to tell her she'd missed something?

As soon as the force released her, Cassie turned to face the first figure. The gun was raised, a finger already on the trigger. She tried to discern whether it was Piper. But like every other time she tried to force her mind to work beyond the scope of her dream, she hit an unsurmountable brick wall.

No matter how hard she tried, the dream wouldn't reveal its truths before she was ready.

But something new happened now. The figure froze instead of pulling the trigger. A subtle wind brought with it the cloying scent of violets, and the gray and white fog surrounding her turned black. It was so glacial, Cassie was sure the soft clouds had grown talons and dug their claws into her skin as though trying to pull her soul from her body.

Crying out, Cassie twisted left and right, which only drove the sensation deeper. But the noise broke the spell, and the figure raised the gun in front of her another half inch before pulling the trigger. The sound caused Cassie to crash back into consciousness, where she could feel she was in the middle of her bed in a hotel in downtown Nashville.

But instead of the relief that came with waking from the same nightmare, all Cassie experienced was cold dread. Try as she might to open her eyes and sit up, she could do nothing more than lie there in bed, frozen with fear and paralyzed from the top of her head to the tips of her toes.

A weight sat on her chest, so solid and real she would've thought Apollo had climbed on top of her in the middle of the night. She ached for his comforting presence and Bear's steadfast breathing at the foot of her bed. Despite her earlier frustrations, Cassie would've given anything to have Jason wrap his arms around her and drag her closer to his chest.

As the pressure deepened and it grew harder to breathe and concentrate, Cassie gained enough movement to squeeze her eyes shut even tighter. This was not the first time she'd experienced sleep paralysis, though it had been years since it last happened. And it had never felt so intense and real.

Doing her best to calm her breathing, Cassie took the time to tune in to each part of her body, starting with her toes. She imagined wiggling them, first on her right foot and then on her left, concentrating until she felt one of her big toes twitch. Unable to lift her lips into a smile, Cassie resigned herself to doubling down on her efforts.

She moved her internal sensor upward, finding her ankles, then her knees, and finally her hips. Drawing her legs up until her feet were flat on the bed, Cassie kept her eyes screwed shut while she sped through the rest of her checklist, feeling for her shoulders and elbows and wrists. When she was able to lift her arms and wiggle her fingers, she moved her head from side to side and opened her eyes, feeling in complete control of her body once again.

Sitting up, Cassie had just taken her first full breath of stuffy hotel air when she noticed the figure standing at the foot of her bed, curled forward as though it had been studying Cassie while she slept. Adrenaline flooded her system, but Cassie reined in her reaction as she took in the woman's sallow skin, greasy hair, and a sliver of her milk-white eyes.

Over the years, Cassie had gotten accustomed to imagining what a spirit would've looked like while they were still alive. Despite the woman's translucent, gray appearance, it was obvious she'd been a brunette. Her hair fell to her shoulders in strands, but Cassie could see the soft waves that would've framed her face.

A tank top and pair of leggings adorned the woman's body, loose and comfortable around her thin frame. A stain sat in the middle of the woman's chest, though it didn't look like blood. Light filtering through the window illuminated her ashen skin, catching on a series of scars along the inside of her wrist.

Cassie didn't bother to look away. Rage rolled off the spirit in waves, visible in the form of black smoky tendrils. They moved independently of the woman, reaching out and curling back at a whim.

Opening her mouth to ask the woman her name, Cassie barely got the first syllable out before the figure lurched forward, arms outstretched like she wanted to wrap her hands around Cassie's throat.

Slamming back onto the bed, Cassie drew in a sharp breath and imagined an invisible shield encasing her body, as thin as glass and as strong as diamonds. A millisecond before the woman touched Cassie's skin, the armor snapped into place with an inaudible *click*. Holding her breath, all she could do was watch as the figure hurtled herself at Cassie's prone body.

But when the woman hit the invisible shield, a groan escaped her decaying mouth, and she dissipated into a cloud of black smoke, fading from sight within a matter of seconds.

A cloud of black smoke, just like the entity she'd seen around Don Carver's shoulders.

10

Cassie's morning went from bad to worse.

She didn't see the entity again, but she felt the woman's presence through every step of her morning routine. A heavy pressure made her shoulders sag, and it was more difficult than usual to pick up her feet to walk from one end of the room to the other—even after two cups of strong, bitter hotel coffee.

Cassie was no stranger to exhaustion, but this weight had burrowed its way into the center of her being and attached itself to her soul. Keeping up her psychic barrier stole most of her attention, so she didn't think twice when she tripped over her bag or hit her elbow on the bathroom doorframe more than once.

But that was just the beginning.

She'd been looking forward to a hot shower after her rude awakening. She'd managed two minutes under the warm spray before it switched between ice-cold and volcanic in a matter of seconds and stayed that way the entire rest of her shower. The scratchy hotel towel set her teeth on edge, and she didn't notice the puddle of water on the floor before she slipped and almost cracked her head on the bathroom counter.

With a racing heart, Cassie slowed her movements to a crawl. She got dressed without incident, donning a pair of green pants and a cream shirt, but when she went to put her makeup on, she dropped her brand-new bottle of foundation on the tile floor and spent the next ten minutes meticulously cleaning up shards of glass.

Breathing a sigh of relief when she plugged the hotel hairdryer into the outlet unscathed, Cassie switched it on and enjoyed five seconds of warm air before there was a loud pop. Both the dryer and the lights over the mirror went out. Resetting the outlet did nothing to alleviate her problem, and by that point, she was done trying to have a normal morning.

Cassie grabbed her purse and went down to the front desk, enduring shocks from every doorknob and elevator button she touched. Keeping her annoyance in check was harder than usual as she explained the situation to the concierge, but the man behind the desk was apologetic and promised everything would be in order by the time she returned that night. All she could muster was a grateful nod as she made her way outside and into the back of the car waiting for her at the curb.

During the drive to the Apex building, Cassie still felt that weight on her chest. It didn't so much as shift in pressure no matter how many breathing exercises she did. The only thing that worked was fortifying her psychic armor, building it up layer by layer until she could take a full breath without wanting to rip someone's head off.

Still, she was hyperaware of every person who walked too close, each choking whiff of exhaust, and all the insincere smiles she received as she strolled through Apex's front door. Gerald and Roger manned the metal detector again that morning, and it took three unsuccessful swipes of her employee badge before she gave up and allowed Roger to scan it for her. She didn't miss the pinch of his brows as she snatched her card back and marched off to her destination.

Forgoing the elevators, Cassie endured another static shock from the entrance to the stairwell before climbing to the second floor and yanking open the door with more force than necessary. Anger and adrenaline fueled her every move, building inside her like a balloon ready to burst. She'd long forgotten her earlier exhaustion. She felt like she could run a marathon and still have the energy to go three rounds in the ring against an opponent twice her size.

Thanks to Chris' tour from the day before, Cassie knew where Anastasia's office was and had met the woman's personal assistant, Charlotte. Today she wore red slacks with a silver shirt, and with her long black hair, Cassie couldn't help but think she looked an awful lot like her boss. Unlike Anastasia, however, Charlotte had kind eyes and a sweet smile that Cassie suspected wouldn't last for long. Either she'd lose her sense of innocence, or Anastasia would find someone a little more ruthless to fill the position.

"Good morning, Miss Quinn," Charlotte said, spotting her as soon as she turned the corner. "What can I do for—"

"I need to speak with her," Cassie said, forcing the words out between clenched teeth. Everything about Charlotte bothered her this morning, starting with her bright smile and cheery disposition and ending with her overwhelming floral perfume. "It's an emergency."

"Oh." Charlotte's eyes grew wide. They'd had a lovely conversation the day before, and even through the haze of her ire, Cassie could feel the other woman's surprise at her brusque manner. "I'm so sorry, but she's with someone right now. If you'll have a seat—"

Cassie was moving before she realized what was happening. Behind her, Charlotte protested, but Cassie burst through Anastasia's closed door, stopping short when she saw Chris sitting across from the woman, his hands gripping the armrests of his chair like they were the only things tethering him to the earth. His horrified expression was at odds with Anastasia's smug smile.

Both their faces morphed into surprise when Cassie strolled inside without a cursory knock. Charlotte scurried in after Cassie, wringing her hands and looking like she was about to cry.

"I'm so sorry, Ms. Bolton. She wouldn't listen—"

"That's quite all right, Charlotte." Anastasia leaned back in her chair and plastered a neutral expression on her face. "Agent Viotto and I were just finishing up."

Clenching his jaw, Chris stood without sparing Anastasia a second glance, his pink shirt at odds with Apex's unspoken dress code. On his way past Cassie, he caught her eye and gave her a tight smile, but she didn't have the patience to consider what she might've interrupted.

As soon as the door clicked shut, Anastasia motioned to the chair Chris had vacated. "Please," she said, her voice amicable, "have a seat."

Cassie crossed the room, sparing a single glance at the walls of bookshelves, tasteful paintings, and verdant houseplants before stopping on the other side of Anastasia's vast wooden desk. The office was classy without being opulent, but something about the décor suggested this was the image Anastasia preferred to present rather than one which embodied her true spirit.

Ignoring the woman's request, Cassie placed her hands on the polished expanse of Anastasia's desk, reveling in the small frown that marred the other woman's face as her fingerprints smudged the glossy surface. As she leaned into Anastasia's space, Cassie was aware she was being aggressive and rude, but she couldn't muster the energy to care. Her limbs moved of their own accord, even as her mind questioned why.

"You knew what would happen, didn't you?"

Anastasia's frown turned into a confused pursing of her lips. "Pardon me?"

"You knew," Cassie repeated, her chest heaving with restrained anger. "You knew that if Don Carver and I were in the same room, the entity would pass from him to me."

Anastasia adjusted her expression, but Cassie could see the way her eyes lit up with interest. "It was one of my working theories, yes, but I had no way of knowing that for sure."

"Bullshit."

Anastasia lifted a single perfect eyebrow, but Cassie couldn't tell if it was in surprise or amusement. "Think what you will about me, Miss Quinn, but I have no interest in seeing you brought to harm. In fact, that goes against everything I'm trying to accomplish here."

"No. You just treat me like a science experiment instead."

Huffing out a laugh, Anastasia motioned to the chair on the other side of her desk once more. "Please, sit. You're worked up. I understand why. But let's have a civilized conversation. You're not acting like yourself."

Grinding her teeth together, Cassie's gaze flicked to the corner of the room where dark smoke gathered amongst the shadows, the tendrils rippling and dancing with aggravation. She had the urge to crack her neck and all her knuckles, just to feel some release of pressure.

But as much as Cassie hated to admit it, Anastasia was right.

Backing up until her knees hit the chair, Cassie sank into the comfortable leather. It was soft and pliant, molding to her body like it already knew the shape.

Anastasia studied her as Cassie licked her dry lips. The other woman's expression was full of curiosity instead of scrutiny, and even a hint of concern. That, above all else, told Cassie how out of character she'd acted.

"I take it you had a rough morning," Anastasia said.

"You could say that."

"If you tell me about it, I may be able to help."

Cassie tried to hold back her scoff and failed, and the flash of dismay on Anastasia's face was enough for her to relent. "Yesterday, when I shook hands with Don, he shocked me."

"In what way?"

"A static shock. A strong one." Cassie shifted in her seat, ignoring the way the smoke in the corner corporealized with each passing minute. "Nothing out of the ordinary happened for the rest of the night. This morning, the entity showed up, and I spent the last hour living Murphy's Law."

"Anything that can go wrong, will go wrong," Anastasia said, more to herself. "What happened? Are you hurt?"

Cassie tamped down on a flare of annoyance, knowing Anastasia was more interested in keeping her safe because she was useful to Apex. "I'm fine. The most I endured was a temperamental shower, a small power outage, and a hairdryer that gave up the ghost after about five seconds."

"Gave up the ghost?" Anastasia said, a hint of humor in her voice.

"So to speak."

"You keep looking at the corner of the room. Should I be concerned?"

"She won't do anything to you."

Anastasia sat up straighter in her chair. "The entity is a woman? You're sure?"

Cassie remembered the surprise on Don's face when she revealed she could see the insubstantial apparition clinging to him. How would he react when he found out she was now able to see the figure in full? "Yes, I'm sure. I first saw it as a black shadow wrapped around Don's shoulders. This morning, when I woke up, there was a woman standing at the end of my bed, studying me. She lunged but disappeared back into smoke when she hit my psychic barrier."

"You're capable of producing a psychic barrier?"

Cassie clamped down on her tongue in response to revealing that bit of information. "After that, my morning went to hell."

"What does she look like?" Anastasia pulled a notepad from one of her drawers and grabbed a pen from the cup on her desk. "Can you describe her to me? In as much detail as possible, please."

Knowing this could only help the woman find peace, Cassie forced her wandering gaze back to the corner of the room. Appearing as she had that morning, Cassie described the woman's attire, including the stain on the front of her shirt, her transparent and ashen skin, the greasy tresses hanging over her face, and the small sliver of white eyes that shone through a small gap in her hair. She made sure to mention the scars on the inside of her wrist. Anastasia took detailed notes, asking for clarification here and there.

All the while, the entity stared at Cassie in hungry desperation.

"You're not the first person to be affected," Anastasia said, setting her pen down. "But you are the first to see it in any form. That must be significant." The woman studied Cassie for a moment, as though debating whether she would be open to receiving the olive branch she was about to offer. "It transfers from psychic to psychic. Like reverse osmosis."

Cassie had to search her high school memories for the definition of the term. "Meaning it passes based on who has higher concentrations of, what, psychic power?"

"That's our current understanding."

"Don said he picked it up while he was at Millie Abrahms' apartment."

Anastasia stood, glancing over her shoulder as though hoping she might spot a glimpse of what so many others had felt but never seen, and walked over to her door. "I'm sorry to say that Don lied."

Cassie stood and turned her back on the entity, despite all her instincts telling her to keep it in sight. "Why would he do that?"

"You'll have to ask him." Anastasia pulled open her door and stepped to the side, a clear dismissal. "He's waiting for you in the conference room with Agent Viotto. Charlotte can show you the way."

In response, Charlotte stood and plastered a cautious smile on her face. As Cassie left the office and the entity behind, Anastasia called out after her.

"And Cassie?"

"Yes?"

"Next time, be sure to make an appointment. We have zero tolerance for impromptu social gatherings. As much as we love having you here, you are not above reproach when it comes to how Apex Publicity's employees are expected to conduct themselves."

And then, without waiting for a reaction, Anastasia shut the door in Cassie's face.

11

Cassie wanted to tell Charlotte she could find her way to the conference room without help, but she didn't want to get the woman into any more trouble. Following Charlotte into the elevator, Cassie prayed it wouldn't come to a sudden stop or drop three stories without warning. The other woman pressed the button for the fourth floor and then folded her hands in front of her, avoiding eye contact.

Breathing a sigh of relief when the elevator stopped without incident, Cassie stepped through the doors and turned to the other woman. "I can take it from here," she said, plastering a smile on her face. "I'm sorry about earlier. I wasn't myself."

"It's quite all right, Miss Quinn," she said, but her formality gave her true thoughts away. "It happens to the best of us."

"Yes, well..." Cassie couldn't finish her sentence. What would she say? *Yes, well, it's possible I'm dealing with a disgruntled spirit who's altering my emotions and causing me to act out of character.* "Thank you for your time."

With a nod, Charlotte pressed the button that would return her to the second floor and looked everywhere but at Cassie until the elevator doors closed between them. Cassie couldn't blame the woman for her annoyance, and she found that it was easier to keep her own anger at bay now. Perhaps the entity had retreated for the time being.

Spinning on her heel, Cassie retraced her steps from the day before until she found the door to the conference room. The blinds were shut, but the door was ajar, as though waiting for her to arrive. With a steadying breath, she stepped inside and closed it behind her, taking those extra few seconds to gather her wits and prepare for the conversation she was about to have.

Facing the table in the center of the room, Cassie first took in the spread of bagels, cream cheese, doughnuts, and juice at one end. The smell of coffee was sharp and pleasant, and she made her way over to the machine. Something told her Apex's choice of grounds would be ten times as strong and enticing as what she'd had at the hotel.

"Morning," Chris said, placing a thin file folder in front of him where he sat on the other side of the table. "How are you doing today?"

It was a loaded question, and Cassie knew he was asking about their run-in earlier. She was more curious now to know what she'd walked in on, but with Don Carver sitting in a neighboring seat, she had to set that aside for later.

"I've been better," she said. She held up her fresh coffee. "I'm hoping this will solve most of my problems. How are you?"

"Ready to get started," Chris said.

Cassie cocked her head at the distance in his voice. Whatever had happened between him and Anastasia was still sitting with him.

Meanwhile, Don's entire demeanor had changed overnight. Cassie half-expected to see black shadows draped across his shoulders, but he was absent of any additional supernatural energy, invisible or otherwise. With squared shoulders and bright eyes, Don met her gaze with a smile he wouldn't have been able to muster yesterday.

"Coffee helps," he said. "The more alert you are, the better. A sharper mind means you can keep it at bay for longer." He barely took a breath between sentences. "I'd also suggest eating extra calories because you'll be burning a lot more energy. I'm not mad that I lost a few pounds, but it wasn't exactly doctor-prescribed, was it?" He tipped his head back and laughed at his own joke, even going so far as to wipe away a tear at the corner of his eye. "The real trick is to keep it off, right? I think I'll start walking every day. I heard that's one of the best things you can do for your health."

Cassie gaped at the man, the steam rising from her coffee the only movement in the room. "You seem to be in a better mood."

"I feel like a weight has been lifted from my shoulders." Don chuckled. "I guess it has, right?"

Cassie felt anger rising from the pit of her stomach like a volcano ready to erupt. Taking a sip of her scalding-hot coffee was the only thing that distracted her long enough to tamp down on the emotion. She'd regret burning her tongue later, but for now, the pain was worth the price if she could keep it together for a few more minutes.

Don sobered and cleared his throat. "I wanted to thank you, Cassie, for what you did yesterday. You saved my marriage. Maybe even my life. I'd lost touch with my sense of self, and there's nothing I can say or do to truly express what that means to me. If you need anything, please don't hesitate to ask. I am forever in your debt."

"You lied to me." Cassie kept her tone neutral as she stared down at him. "You didn't pick up the entity from Millie Abrahms' apartment. Someone else did, didn't they?"

Don had the sense to look embarrassed, but he didn't avoid Cassie's gaze. "Yes."

Chris startled. "What? Who?"

"Jamie Meyers. Then it passed on to two others before it attached itself to me."

"You knew what would happen when we shook hands," Cassie said.

"I did." This time, Don looked away. "I'm sorry about that. Truly. I wouldn't wish that thing on anyone, least of all someone as kind and compassionate as you. But—" He cleared his throat. "But I couldn't live like that anymore. I was desperate. I know what I did was wrong, and I hope someday you'll be able to forgive me. But if you can't, I'll understand."

"The static shock," Chris said, several steps behind the conversation. "That was the entity traveling from you to Cassie? That means—" His gaze snapped to Cassie's. "Are you all right?"

"I'm fine." Cassie pulled out the chair across from him and sat down. Grabbing a doughnut from the tray next to her, she kept a firm grip on her coffee, relishing the warmth that bled through the paper cup and into the palm of her hand. "Rough morning, but nothing I can't handle."

The way Chris turned to glare at Don made her wince. "You—"

"Don't blame him," Cassie interrupted, watching in amusement as Don shifted his chair a little farther away from Chris. "It was a shitty thing to do to someone, but he wasn't exactly in his right mind."

Chris grimaced before asking his next question. "Are you?"

"What? In my right mind?" When Chris nodded, Cassie had to laugh. "For now. I'm having trouble keeping my anger in check, so the sooner we can solve this case, the better."

"Point taken," Chris said, flipping open the folder in front of him. "This is everything we know about Millie Abrahms."

"That's an awfully thin folder," Cassie replied.

"It's just my personal notes," Don said. "I figured we could start with those. There are copies of all the relevant files, but I've collated the appropriate information."

"We'll see about that," Chris mumbled. "Millie Abrahms, twenty-nine, unmarried, no children."

"At least that part was true," Cassie said.

"Text messages to her fiancé indicate she left to visit an out-of-town friend, but she never told him who it was. When they found her phone, there was no record of her reaching out to anyone else."

"Could it have been a surprise?" Cassie asked.

When both Chris and Cassie looked to Don, he shrugged. "Maybe. Your guess is as good as mine."

"Could've been a cover story," Cassie said. "An affair?"

"Always a possibility," Chris said, flipping to the next page. "With Millie missing for three years, we can't discount murder. There's a reason a person's significant other is—"

Chris broke off, his face going slack as he stared down at something on the page.

"What is it?" Cassie asked.

"Millie's fiancée is Arnold Warren."

Cassie shook her head, not recognizing the name. "Who's that?"

"Kentucky's governor." When Chris locked gazes with her, she saw realization mixing with trepidation darkening his eyes. "And Ross Hughes' main opponent for the presidential candidacy."

12

"Am I missing something here?" Don said, looking between Cassie and Chris with a furrowed brow. "Why is that important?"

Cassie searched Don's face for a few seconds, but the question seemed genuine. Did he not know what Apex had their hands in, or did he not care?

Cassie weighed how much she wanted to tell this virtual stranger and decided to start slow. "A few months ago, I worked a case related to Ross Hughes' family."

"What kind of case?" Don asked.

Cassie didn't miss the way Chris shot her a warning look. "That's not important," she said. "At least, not as important as the fact that Apex is the driving force behind Hughes' presidential candidacy."

"I'm not following."

Chris leaned back in his chair and twirled a pen between his fingers, his gaze distant and contemplative. "Not a lot of state senators get a crack at that title. Hughes has a lot going for him. His father is a senator, so he's got a legacy name behind him. Not to mention deep pockets. He's been popular in the state of Tennessee, and after the news about his biological parents came to light, he's been in national headlines."

When Don looked confused, Cassie jumped in. "Jack Hughes adopted Ross as a teenager. Prior to that, Ross had gotten into some trouble with his foster parents and the like. Once Jack adopted him, he straightened up. Decided to get into politics. Not too long ago, his biological parents stepped forward, and the country found out his parents had been addicts and convicted criminals. Ross essentially reconnected with them under the scrutiny of the public eye—which I doubt was his choice—and he spent a good deal of money helping them with their rehabilitation. It's a rags-to-riches story for Hughes, and both the media and the nation have become more than a little obsessed with him."

"You can thank Apex for that," Chris added, clicking the end of his pen in a staccato rhythm. Cassie ignored the way it set her teeth on edge. "They've been working with him for quite a while. Lawrence Grayson was their frontrunner for the presidential campaign, but Hughes has proven to be a better option. The reason state senators don't often run for president is because no one knows who they are outside their state, but Hughes is a household name. Apex made sure of it."

"What do you know about his opponent?" Cassie asked.

"Arnold Warren." Chris' gaze traveled to the ceiling as he riffled through the information in his head. "Governor of Kentucky. Promising candidate. Someone who turned down Apex's services, as far as I'm aware."

"And his fiancée went missing three years ago," Cassie said. "Coincidence?"

Chris tossed his pen down on the table and glared at it like it had affronted him. More than likely, he was thinking the same thing Cassie was. "Maybe, maybe not. But I can think of a much more logical reason we've been assigned this case."

Don furrowed his brows again. "Why?"

"Apex wants to dig up Warren's skeletons. They must think he was involved. Maybe he killed her. Or maybe he knows who did."

Cassie sagged in her chair. If Apex wanted to solve Millie Abrahms' disappearance, it wasn't to provide her family with answers or seek justice for a crime that had been committed. It was a means to an end, ensuring Ross Hughes made it all the way to the top with the fewest obstacles standing in his way.

Chris retrieved a laptop from underneath the table and set it in front of him. Opening it up, he offered them a sardonic grin. "Guess it's time to huddle up and get down to business."

When Cassie stood to join them on the other side of the table, Don popped up out of his chair with such force, it teetered first to one side and then the other before settling back down. As he skirted around the other side of the table, he wore a look of trepidation and remorse.

"Where are you off to?" Chris asked.

"Just remembered I have some paperwork to fill out," Don said, not meeting his eyes. "If I find anything else, I'll send it over. Good luck!"

And with that, he was out the door.

Chris shook his head. "What the hell was that about?"

Cassie took up Don's abandoned seat and slid close enough to Chris to see the computer screen. "He doesn't want to get too close to me. Just in case."

Chris' mouth turned down when he realized what she meant. "He doesn't want to risk picking up the entity again."

"Probably wouldn't happen." She leaned forward and pulled the file folder closer. "Anastasia thinks it jumps to the most powerful psychic in the room. But I doubt he wants to put that theory to the test."

"Gotta say I prefer this version of Don to the one we've been dealing with lately, but that doesn't make him any less of a coward."

Cassie shrugged. "Can't say I blame him. I just wonder—" Cassie broke off, heat creeping into her cheeks.

"You wonder what?"

"If anyone can tell." Her blush deepened. "I could see the shadow hanging around Don when I first met him. I wonder if others will be able to see it on me. Or, if they're not psychic, will they be able to tell that I'm, I don't know"—she searched for the right word—"tainted?"

Cassie startled when Chris laid a hand on her arm, forgetting for a split-second that the entity couldn't pass to him. "You're not tainted. You're the same as you've always been." He cracked a grin as he let go.

"Besides, I like seeing you all fired up. I think even Anastasia was a little scared."

"That woman feels nothing but greed and pomposity." Cassie looked down at the folder in front of her and flipped through it, scanning the contents. "Don was light on notes, but there's some interesting information in here."

"Anything useful?"

"A little background on Millie. She was living in Nashville at the time of her disappearance. Had a two-bedroom apartment all to herself. She'd been dating Arnold for a couple years before they got engaged. She disappeared a couple months after that. Don says the governor was pretty heartbroken about it."

"Not sure I trust Don's judgement," Chris muttered, his fingers flying over his keyboard.

"Their relationship was public but quiet. Some speculation as to why she still lived in Nashville when he was in Frankfort, but it seems like he was a competent governor without any major scandals. Not until Millie went missing, anyway."

"Did anyone suspect he did it?"

"A few tin hats did, for sure. But otherwise, it seems Arnold was open to discussing it. The police said he was cooperating, and they had no evidence to suggest he was involved in any way."

Cassie got to the end of Don's notes and sighed. "We need to start over from scratch. Talk to everyone again."

"Not sure they'll be happy about us digging up the past," Chris said. "Not that we have a choice."

"Depends on if they've moved on or not. Some people are grateful to realize they're not the only ones who care about what happened to their loved ones, even if that person is a stranger and a couple years behind the times."

Chris' fingers hovered over the keyboard as he cast a glance at Cassie. "I hate to bring all this to the surface, especially after everything Millie's parents have been through."

"It's not easy losing a child," Cassie said. "Harder still to wonder what happened to them."

"Bad enough when you outlive one of your kids." Chris turned the laptop screen toward Cassie. "Worse when you outlive both of them."

She stared at the laptop, taking in the coroner's report for someone named Maxine Abrahms. "Accidental overdose. This is Millie's sister?"

"Yep." Chris pointed to the date at the top of the report. "She died two years to the day after Millie went missing."

13

A knock on the door made Cassie jump. When the person on the other side opened it, Cassie's face fell into a scowl as Anastasia's brightened.

"Sorry to interrupt," she said. "I need to borrow Agent Viotto for an hour or two."

Chris' frown matched Cassie's. "We're in the middle of something. Can it wait?"

"Unfortunately, it can't." Anastasia's smile stayed in place, and her tone was apologetic, but her gaze sharpened as she stared Chris down. "I promise to return you to Cassie as soon as possible."

It seemed Chris knew there was no arguing. With a sigh, he slid the computer to Cassie and stood. "Sorry about this. I'll be back as soon as I can."

"It's okay," Cassie said, but she was just as annoyed as he was. Would every day be like this, where Anastasia pulled rank? Cassie didn't need him to solve the case, but it was a hundred times easier to have a partner, especially one who worked for the FBI. If nothing else, it was nice to have someone to bounce ideas off of.

Glancing from Anastasia to Chris and back again, she tried to determine what was going on between them. Chris appeared on edge but resigned. Anastasia seemed haughty, which wasn't out of character—but what did she need Chris for now, and what had they been discussing earlier that morning?

"Cassie, I forgot to tell you." Anastasia slid past Chris and placed a heavy black credit card on the table in front of her. "This is for you to use as you wish. Feel free to put all your expenditures on there, including food, clothes, or anything of the sort. One of the perks of working for Apex. And your office is ready. It's the one on the corner just down the hall. Can't miss it."

Cassie's scowl deepened. The last thing she wanted was to spend Apex's money, considering she wasn't sure where it came from and who had to die for her to receive it. And she wouldn't step foot in her office if she could help it.

If Anastasia could tell which direction Cassie's mind had moved in, she didn't show it. "There's an amazing ramen shop a couple blocks over. I've eaten a lot of noodles in my day, but that one is far and away the best I've ever had. Outside of Japan, of course."

Cassie's stomach growled at the thought, even as she recoiled from the familiar tone in Anastasia's voice. The woman acted like they were best friends, like her beloved publicity company wasn't blackmailing Cassie's boyfriend and threatening the lives of Chris' family. Like she had no idea Apex had murdered a man in order to bury his connection to their presidential hopeful.

"That sounds nice, but—"

"Great," Anastasia interrupted, beaming. "Robert will be out front in a half hour to take you there."

And before Cassie could argue, Anastasia swept out the door and down the hall.

Chris paused in the doorway. "The ramen really is phenomenal."

And then he was gone, too.

Cassie did a little more digging while she waited for Robert to arrive, but all the articles she found about Millie Abrahms' disappearance had basically the same information, and nothing they didn't already know. But Maxine was more of a mystery. There were only two articles about her death, both of which didn't outright name her, and the authorities concluded it as an open-and-closed accidental overdose.

But Cassie had long given up on believing in coincidences.

When her time was up, Cassie made her way down to the ground floor of the building and into Robert's waiting SUV. With a neutral expression and a pleasant greeting, the man drove her the few blocks it took to get to the ramen place without her needing to instruct him to do so. The weather was nice enough that she could've walked, but perhaps Anastasia wanted to keep her on a shorter leash than that.

"Thank you, Robert," Cassie said, placing a hand on the door. "I appreciate you taking the time to drive me to lunch when I'm sure you have much more important clients to attend to."

"Nonsense. You're my only client for the duration of your stay in Nashville. It's no hardship at all." Robert ignored the way Cassie blanched and reached into the back seat to hand her his card. "Please call me whenever you need my services. I'm available twenty-four hours a day, seven days a week."

Cassie took the plain business card with a smile she hoped looked grateful and not apprehensive. Considering Apex was swimming in money, it meant nothing for them to hand her a credit card and personal driver, but instead of feeling like she was living in the lap of luxury and freedom, she just felt the noose tightening around her throat.

Slipping the card into her purse, Cassie jumped out of the SUV and walked up to *Love, Ramen*, taking in the bright façade and whimsical sign featuring a cute cat eating noodles with a pair of chopsticks. Inside, the décor was just as colorful, and the air was friendly as the hostess approached her.

The woman was petite, with shiny black hair and a wide smile. "Are you Cassie?"

Startled, Cassie stared down at her for a moment before she found her words. "Yes?"

"Right this way." The woman grabbed a menu and led her through the restaurant. There weren't many patrons yet, since it was on the earlier side for lunch, but the woman stopped at an occupied table and placed the menu across from a man who sat studying his own. "Your server will be right with you."

Before Cassie could call her back, the man at the table stood and reached out to shake her hand. "By the look on your face, Anastasia didn't mention you'd be meeting me for lunch, did she?"

Cassie took the man's hand as she studied him, realizing she was dining with none other than Ross Hughes, Tennessee state senator and current presidential candidate. He was a tall man with broad shoulders and dark, wavy hair peppered with hints of silver. His nose was a little large for his face, but his eyes were kind and expressive. She'd seen pictures of him before, but he was much more captivating in person. His aura of humility wrestled with his commanding presence.

"No," Cassie said, slipping into her seat. "She didn't."

"I apologize for that. I was nervous about how you'd react to me asking you to sit down for lunch, and I think she took matters into her own hands."

"She does that a lot."

Hughes winced, though he still had a smile on his face. "That she does. She's the most requested publicist at Apex for a reason, and while I don't always agree with her strategies, I can't say they've steered me wrong yet."

"First time for everything," Cassie mumbled.

Hughes looked like he wanted to say something, but their server arrived and took their orders, returning less than a minute later with their drinks. The senator made eye contact with the waiter while he thanked him for his sweet tea, and Cassie had to wonder how much of his geniality was for show and how much was real.

"Why were you nervous?" Cassie asked, taking a sip of her water and watching the man across from her.

Hughes fiddled with his chopsticks. "Anastasia told me you were involved in the case in Savannah." The senator's gaze flicked around the room, but there was no one nearby. He'd probably chosen a seat in the back against the wall for that very reason. "I appreciate your discretion about my connection to Douglas."

"It's not like you did anything wrong, right?"

Hughes met her eyes, but she couldn't quite read the expression there. "Of course not. But politics is about reputation and perception. My father adopted me, so I'm not related to Douglas by blood, but our association with him could be enough to tarnish the Hughes name. I'm not just talking about myself here. My father is also in the public spotlight. This could devastate our family."

"Is that the most important part of the story?" Cassie asked, folding her arms. "How it affects *you*? What about Douglas' victims? Some will never be discovered, and others have had their stories buried beneath flashier headlines. That's what you're paying Apex to do."

Hughes cocked his head to the side. "You act like you don't work for Apex."

"I don't. Not by choice, anyway."

Their server chose that moment to arrive with their meals, setting two bowls of steaming noodles down in front of them with a flourish. The pair were momentarily distracted by the mouth-watering aroma emanating from their food, and Cassie dug in without preamble, relishing in the warmth and spiciness of the broth.

After a couple minutes of quiet slurping, Hughes broke the silence. "I need to apologize to you, Cassie. What I said—it wasn't okay. And you had every right to call me out on it."

Cassie set her chopsticks down and dabbed at her mouth with her napkin. "Go on."

Hughes chuckled and leaned forward on the table, bracketing his bowl with his elbows. "The most important part of Douglas' story is not my family's reputation. It's the people he hurt and whether their names will be honored and remembered. What he did wasn't just a tragedy. It was horrific, and trust me when I say I've spent plenty of sleepless nights thinking about his victims." He sighed, and for the first time, he looked unsure of himself. "This isn't an excuse, and I don't want you to think less of me for saying it, but I think it's human nature to center ourselves in other people's stories. It takes a truly selfless person to ignore how an event will affect them. And I'll admit that after my initial shock wore off, I was scared about how this could skew people's perception of me and my father."

"Because you're running for president."

Picking up his chopsticks, Hughes stirred the noodles around his bowl but didn't take another bite. "Yes ... and no. Like anyone who runs for president, I feel as though I have something to bring to the table. Perhaps it's arrogant to say this, but I think I can do some good in that position. Maybe accomplish some things no one else can."

"Good luck with that," Cassie said, a wry smile blooming across her face. "It's not easy these days."

"You're right about that." Finally taking another bite, he chewed and swallowed before speaking again. "My father built his legacy on his political career, and I followed in his footsteps. It's all we have. And while I don't think my children want to continue the family business, Douglas' legacy will affect them too. Kids can be cruel. So can adults, for that matter."

"I'm not denying the information about your brother could be damning," Cassie replied. "He's done enough damage. But this goes beyond what he did. It's not just about the murders. It's about the coverup, as well."

Hughes had been fiddling with his chopsticks, but his head snapped up at her words. "What do you mean it's about the coverup? What coverup?"

Cassie searched the man's face for any hint of dishonesty, but she couldn't find it. Either he was an excellent actor, or he really didn't know the full extent of the story. "How much do you know about Apex and the services they provide?"

"As much as any other client, I suppose. My father suggested I use them. They have an excellent track record, and they were already familiar with my career and situation."

Cassie nodded, fiddling with her own chopsticks now. "Maybe it's time to start asking more questions."

"What kind of questions?"

Cassie set her chopsticks down and folded her hands in her lap. There was no telling how much she could trust Ross Hughes, but he made a better ally than an enemy. If she could get him on her side, it might go a long way.

"Questions about how far Apex is willing to go to accomplish their goals," she said. "Or why they were so quick to give up on Lawrence Grayson once he no longer proved useful. Maybe ask if there's any possibility whether Apex knew about Douglas' proclivities prior to recent events, and if the scandal surrounding Savannah's mayor could have anything to do with covering it up. But the biggest question I'd ask is why Apex hired me to solve the disappearance of a woman who was once engaged to your biggest competition."

With every question Cassie posed, Hughes' eyebrows drew closer together. "Arnold Warren?"

"Anastasia didn't tell you that, did she?"

The waiter returned to refill their drinks, and as soon as he left again, the hostess seated a young couple at the next table over. Hughes eyed them for a moment before posing a question of his own.

"I'd like to continue this conversation in a more private setting. Would you be open to having dinner with me and my family tomorrow? My wife is making meatloaf, and trust me when I say you'll be asking for the recipe by the end of the night."

Unease crawled up Cassie's spine and sat between her shoulders, but she shrugged it off as she offered the man her widest smile. "That sounds amazing. I'd love to."

14

Lorraine had already consumed three cups of coffee by the time she made it to her desk outside the warden's office, and she couldn't wait to pour herself another. The office machine was old, but she kept it in pristine working condition. As long as the person responsible for buying coffee that month got the good stuff, it made a halfway decent cup.

April was Claudia's turn, and she always bought the best money could buy. They didn't have much in common, considering the woman was at least twice Lorraine's age, but they both loved their coffee. For Lorraine, it was less about the taste and more about the caffeine it provided, but she knew a good cup when she tasted one.

Returning to her desk with her mug near overflowing, she heard her phone buzzing from her purse on the floor. Considering it was just shy of eight in the morning, she could count on one hand the number of people who would call her at this hour. One of them was her mother, and that thought was enough to have her digging through her bag until her fingers closed around the device. Jacqueline Krasinski was in remission for her breast cancer, but Lorraine couldn't help worrying every time her mother called. It didn't help that her mom had fallen down a few days ago and suffered a nasty bruise along her hip and thigh. She'd refused to go to the hospital, but there had been a limp in her walk ever since. Lorraine had caught her wincing whenever she sat down, but there was no talking sense into the woman.

Pulling her phone out and reading the name on the screen, she blew out a breath of relief. The other two people who could be calling this early in the morning were Jason and Cassie, and it was the former whose name appeared on her phone. He knew her working hours, so if he was calling this close to eight, it must be important.

Last night, they'd finally gotten in touch with the one person who'd been vocal about the company, but information was still scarce. Jason was supposed to reach out to one of his contacts to see if they could find something she couldn't.

Before she could answer the call, however, a man walked through the door and stopped in front of her desk. A *tsk* emanated from his mouth, and Lorraine glanced up to meet the gaze of former Mayor Blackwood. A trickle of apprehension washed over her, and she had to fight back a chill.

"I don't think the warden would be happy to see you on your phone instead of working, Miss Krasinski." The sneer on his face ruined the mild admonishment in his voice. "He has a reputation to uphold, after all."

Lorraine fought back a snort. The warden had a reputation all right, but it wasn't one he appreciated. Maybe he didn't mind being known as a hard ass, and he certainly didn't care that he was a misogynist, although he would've just played it off by saying he was an advocate for *traditional family values*. No, the rumors of embezzlement, fraud, coercion, adultery, and harassment were what really got on his nerves. It was hard to be perceived as an upstanding citizen with good Christian morals when those whispers followed you wherever you went.

Not that anyone confronted Warden Wickham with those sorts of allegations. Not since Detective David Klein, anyway. He was the only person Lorraine had ever seen stand up to Wickham and get away with it. Everyone else was either too scared, too naïve, or too involved in whatever he had going on to do anything about it.

The man standing in front of her fell into the latter category.

"I had a phone call," Lorraine responded, infusing her voice with saccharine sweetness. "I was just silencing it." Her phone buzzed one more time to indicate Jason had left her a voicemail. "What can I do for you, Mr. Blackwood?"

The man's left eyebrow twitched, and it gave her a great sense of satisfaction knowing that he missed his title as mayor of Savannah. "I'm here to see Preston."

"Warden Wickham isn't in yet. If you'll have a seat, I'm sure he'll only be a few minutes." She turned to her computer and logged in with a flurry of fingers on her keyboard.

"I wanted to speak to you as well," Blackwood said, his voice having returned to its usual oily slickness.

"What about?" Lorraine asked, not bothering to look up.

"Your mother," he replied, aiming his words right at her heart. "How is she doing these days?"

Lorraine's hands froze, and she lifted her head until she met his gaze. It wasn't a secret that her mother had cancer, but how would Blackwood know that? And why would he care? The man stopped in to see Warden Wickham at least once every couple of months, and this morning, he had already spoken more words to her than he had all last year.

"She's great," Lorraine said, forcing her voice to remain calm and even. "Thank you for asking."

"Of course, of course." The way Blackwood looked at her made Lorraine's body go tense. "Cancer is such an insidious beast. Invisible and devastating. It's hard to fight what you can't see."

"That's what the doctors are for." Lorraine wanted nothing more than to return to her computer, but she refused to be the first one to look away. "Besides, she's in remission now."

"That's wonderful news. I hope it remains that way. There's nothing worse than losing a parent. And you only have the one. What a tragedy that would be."

Lorraine wasn't the kind of person to push back against bullies. She'd rather keep her head down and do her job, trusting that one day they would get what was coming to them. But Blackwood had crossed a line.

"Mr. Blackwood, I would imagine you have enough to worry about without fussing over my mother. Is your wife still visiting her sister? When will she return, do you think? Or don't you know yet?"

Blackwood stiffened, and the anger in his eyes was enough for Lorraine to recoil. She'd never liked the man much, even though he'd shown promise when he'd first become mayor. It didn't take long, however, to discern the true predator lying beneath the surface of his shiny veneer. Even still, she hadn't thought of him as a violent man. Not until this moment, anyway.

Placing his hands back on her desk, he leaned forward until he towered over her, and it took every fiber of her being not to shrink back in response.

"I know who took those pictures. And I know what you get up to in your spare time, Miss Krasinski. The warden has mentioned how your performance has slipped since you started working for Jason Broussard. It would be a shame if you lost your job. I don't think the private investigation business pays well enough to bring you on full time. And your mother's treatment didn't come cheap, did it? Imagine if the cancer returns or she has a nasty accident. What would you do then?"

It took a moment for Lorraine to find her words. Blackwood was never this direct. He must have been desperate. "Jason isn't the person you should be angry at," she said. "He's not the one who ruined your life."

"I know he took the pictures."

"But do you know who paid for them?" Lorraine asked.

Blackwood's jaw clenched, and he didn't say a word, but she knew as well as he did that Apex was behind the scandal. Lorraine wanted to hear him say it out loud. She wouldn't trust the man to become their ally in taking the company down, but maybe he knew something they didn't.

Blackwood straightened and said, "I have just one question for you, Miss Krasinski. What's more important to you: your job, your mother, your peace of mind, or Jason Broussard's reputation?" As Warden Wickham strolled through the door, Blackwood slid a card out of his pocket and placed it on the desk in front of her. "I know you'll make the right choice."

All Lorraine could do was stare down at the card in shock and apprehension. She didn't stir when Wickham ordered her to prepare his coffee, nor when Blackwood rapped his knuckles on her desk twice before following the warden into his office.

Lorraine liked Jason, and she felt a certain sense of loyalty to Cassie because of David, but none of that compared to the love and affection she felt toward her mother. In a daze, Lorraine stood and made her way to the kitchen, contemplating how she could keep her mother safe without betraying the two people who had given her a sense of purpose.

Despite her conviction to remain loyal to Jason and Cassie, she knew the choice between them and her mother was no choice at all.

15

Cassie stepped out of the black SUV with a polite wave to Robert and watched as the man pulled away from the curb and back into traffic. As he turned the corner down a side street, she wondered where he went and what he did when she wasn't in need of him. Did he have a hobby, or perhaps another job? Then again, maybe they were paying him well enough that he simply waited in his car to be summoned. She couldn't decide if she found that horrifying or humorous.

Taking a deep breath, Cassie closed her eyes and took a moment to recenter herself. She'd eaten most of her ramen, and her stomach was full to bursting. While she'd never admit this out loud, Anastasia had been right about the restaurant. Those were the best noodles she'd ever eaten. Maybe one day she'd get a chance to go to Japan and draw a comparison.

While her lunchtime company had been an unwelcome surprise at first, Cassie had enjoyed her conversation with Senator Hughes. She was convinced he either didn't know the extent of Apex's machinations or he believed the end justified the means. That wasn't an excuse by any stretch of the imagination, but the man she'd shared a meal with had been humble and genuine.

Then again, those were the kind of people who could be the most dangerous.

"Good lunch?"

Cassie jumped at the sound of Chris' voice and spun to find him leaning against the outside of the building, his hands deep in his pockets. A small smile lit up his features at her reaction, but it didn't reach his eyes. Out here in the natural lighting, she saw for the first time how tired he looked. The bright sunshine didn't hide the bags beneath his eyes or the way he'd been running a hand through his hair all day.

"I've had worse," Cassie said. Then, with a shrug, "Still trying to think of when I had better."

Chris chuckled. "Yeah. First time Anastasia sent me there, I avoided her for two full days because I knew she would be all superior about introducing me to the place. Now I eat there at least once a week."

"Bet she didn't waste the opportunity to lord it over you."

"She never does."

"Wish you could've joined me." Cassie crossed the sidewalk and stood in front of him. "Would've been nice to have a little backup when the server sat me down with Senator Hughes."

Chris' eyes bugged. "Damn, I knew Anastasia was up to something, but I didn't think she'd do that. Are you okay? Did he do anything?"

Cassie was shaking her head before he finished his sentence. "He was a perfect gentleman. In fact, he was a lot more down to earth than I expected."

"Do you trust him?"

"Not sure." Cassie blew out a breath, ruffling the hair that framed her face. "He thanked me for not shouting the truth about Douglas from the rooftops, but I can't tell how much he knows about what Apex is up to. Could be a really good actor. Could have his head buried in the sand."

"Or anything in between." Chris crossed his arms and stared up at the sky in contemplation. When he met Cassie's gaze again, he looked a little bit more like himself. "We should err on the side of caution. Find out what he's aware of before we tell him too much about what we know."

Cassie bobbed her head. "I had the same thought. I hinted that Apex—and his father—knew about Douglas all along. He seemed shocked. Then he invited me over for dinner."

Chris stiffened. "That could be dangerous."

"It's dinner with his wife and kids," Cassie said, rolling her eyes even though she'd had the same thought. "If he has ulterior motives, it's not to do me any harm. We can have a more honest conversation if we're not out in public. Besides, it'll be nice to see what he's like around his family."

"Fair enough."

Cassie eyed Chris, noticing that while he'd relaxed since they'd been talking, there was still a stiff set to his jaw. "What did Anastasia want to borrow you for?"

Chris ran a hand through his hair, making it stick up even more, and avoided Cassie's eyes. "There was some paperwork I forgot to fill out. And she wanted access to some files on a potential client. All routine stuff."

It wasn't hard to make out the hesitancy in his voice. "What else?"

Hanging his head with a sigh, he finally looked at her. "She also thought I needed a friendly reminder not to get too close to you."

Cassie felt like she was wading through molasses to get to the true meaning of that statement. "Too close to me?"

"Anastasia's not stupid. She knows the last thing you want to do is work for Apex. It doesn't take a genius to figure out that you're looking for any weakness you can exploit. And she thinks I'm one of them."

"That makes no sense. She put us together on this case. Why would she be worried about us teaming up?"

Chris shrugged. "She knows the threat against my family's life is enough to keep me in line." The look of pain that crossed his face made Cassie want to give him a hug. "I'm sorry. I'll help you in any way I can, you know I will, but I can't risk anything happening to my sister and her kids."

Cassie placed a hand on his arm and gave him a reassuring squeeze. "You know I would never ask you to do anything that would endanger your family. They've still got that video of Jason, too. We both have to be smart about this. But I don't think we should give up. Not until we've exhausted all our options."

"I know." Chris dragged a hand down his face and smirked. "You'd think I'd be better at this double agent stuff."

"I'm kind of glad you're not," Cassie said, dropping her hand and crossing her arms. It was warm today, but the breeze held a little chill. "What do we do now? What's our first step?"

"Well—" Chris' gaze flicked to a spot just behind Cassie as a car door shut. His look of confusion morphed into annoyance, and then transformed into cool disinterest. "First, I think you'll have to deal with your new guest."

"My guest?" Cassie asked, turning around. "I'm not expecting—"

Before she could get the whole sentence out, her gaze landed on Jason standing on the sidewalk with a duffle bag over his shoulder and an apologetic grimace on his face.

"This a bad time?"

16

As if existing in a dream, Cassie remembered this moment in bits and pieces, hazy around the edges and colored with emotion rather than fact.

Jason stepping forward to embrace her.

Cassie stepping back, shaking her head.

His look of surprise and hurt.

Her frustration and anger bubbling to the surface.

Then her decision to walk away and save him the pain of seeing her explode.

Jason had begged her to come back so he could explain. Even Chris called after her. She continued down the sidewalk as if she knew where she was going. The weight of Robert's business card sat heavy in her pocket, but she ignored it. The fresh air and exertion would clear her mind faster. So would surrounding herself with something she loved. Something that could take her mind off her gut reaction to Jason's unannounced arrival.

That was how she'd ended up standing in front of the Tennessee State Museum.

Modern with a nod to the classical, its sweeping expanse of

windows reflected the afternoon sun, and the fountain out front added ambient noise that—at least in part—distracted from the nearby traffic. It was an imposing building, and she wanted nothing more than to get lost inside it for hours on end.

As she ventured through the exhibits, she let her mind go to that place that existed only when she was in this kind of environment. It was peaceful, outside of time and space, and she felt like a neutral observer passing through the annals of history. Instead of fighting to stay in the present moment, she allowed her thoughts to wander, appearing and disappearing at random, like ripples on the surface of a lake. There was no point in chasing them, not when the next wasn't far behind.

She ended up in one of the temporary exhibits, showcasing the history of the state through the art of photography, stopping in front of the faded image of two women dressed in nineteenth century garb.

If the size and intricacy of their dresses were any indication, the two women came from a wealthy family. The one on the left had fair features, with light hair and pale eyes which stood out even amidst the sepia tone of the photo. Her dress was dark, perhaps green or navy, and she wore a wistful smile as she peered into the distance. Cassie thought she looked like an angel or a saint—delicate and vivacious, as though life had never once treated her poorly.

The other was her opposite, with dark hair swept back into an intricate up-do and a severe part down the middle. Her dress was also dark, with ruffles along her collar and hem that were too fine and frilly for the melancholic expression she wore. Unlike her companion, she glared into the camera, challenging the viewer to a game neither would ever win. Her eyes held several lifetimes worth of pain and anger.

A small plaque to the right of the photograph indicated they were sisters, and Cassie zeroed in on the way the dark-haired woman was a step or two closer to the camera, as though ready to throw herself in danger's way should her sister fall into any trouble. It made Cassie think of Laura and how they'd protected each other over the years. A sense of longing and malaise flooded her system, and Cassie had to look away from the image to regain her balance.

It wasn't lost on Cassie that she had ended up in front of this photograph. Millie and Maxine Abrahms looked nothing like the two women in the image hanging on the wall, but something about the dark-haired woman called to her. The fierceness in her eyes and the strength of her stance made Cassie want to reach out and comfort her. To tell her that she didn't need to carry the weight of the world on her shoulders.

A bitter-cold breeze enveloped Cassie in that moment, and she shivered so violently, her teeth chattered. When she looked up to the ceiling, she expected to see an air conditioning vent, but there was nothing there.

Moving out of the cold spot, Cassie made her way around the room, taking in other photographs even as her mind stayed with the one depicting the two sisters. A boy and his horse made the corner of her mouth tip up in amusement, while a dark-skinned soldier missing an arm caused her heart to squeeze in despair. Love and heartbreak were at odds with each other as she toured the exhibit, and while she couldn't say she was at peace, at least she had calmed down since seeing Jason.

She knew her extreme reaction was due to her connection to the entity. She'd kept up her mental barrier as well as she could, but it was impossible to create a flawless shield and maintain it every second of the day. Even now, she sensed the spirit nearby, waiting for an opportunity to make her move.

Passing through another cold spot, Cassie ignored the next few photographs, focusing instead on locking down her emotions. It was only when she heard a thud and the shattering of glass behind her that she stopped. Multiple gasps echoed around the room, and Cassie spun to find one of the framed photographs had slipped from its hook on the wall.

A security guard arrived within seconds, steering people back and calling for someone on her radio. After ensuring no one had been hurt by flying glass, the woman asked if anyone had seen what had happened. Most people shook their heads no, but a small child pointed to someone standing off to the side as though desperate to remain invisible but too curious to walk away.

"She broke it," the boy said.

His mother hushed him. Then, looking up at the security guard, said, "I'm sorry. He has a very active imagination."

The crowd had shifted when the boy pointed, and it was only then that Cassie realized the figure was a woman with ashen skin and stringy hair. It took a lot of energy to affect objects and people in the real world, and yet the entity did so time and again without so much as flickering in and out of existence.

Had her rage made her that strong?

Cassie's gaze slid to the photograph sitting face-up on the ground amidst the debris. It was another faded image, but it didn't contain a single person or animal. Instead, it was nothing more than a field full of flowers.

Cassie searched the crowd for the entity again, wanting to know why she'd destroyed this particular photograph, but the figure was gone. In her place was nothing more than empty air.

Stepping closer, Cassie tried to pick apart the photograph, but the security guard held up her hand.

"Please stay back," she said, her tone gentle but authoritative. "I don't want anyone getting hurt."

"I'm sorry," Cassie replied. "I was just wondering which one it was."

"It's titled *Mountain Violets*," the woman said, hooking a thumb over her shoulder at the plaque on the wall. "One of the first we hung in this gallery. Must not have been installed properly."

"Right," Cassie said. "Thank you."

Cassie backed up until she was out of the crowd, but she couldn't escape their murmurings.

"Why would someone do that?" one woman asked.

"Do you think the kid actually saw what happened?" a man whispered.

"God, someone needs to lay off the floral perfume. I'm getting a headache."

"Did they turn up the AC? I'm freezing all of a sudden."

When the lights flickered, another round of gasps replaced the low murmur of the crowd and cast them in darkness for no more than a second or two. In that short span of time, Cassie felt a cool breath on the back of her neck, like a lover leaning in close to whisper sweet nothings. When she whirled around to see who had touched her, no one was there. But another cold spot made her tremble, and when the lights blinked out again, she knew she had to get out of the museum before she caused something more destructive to happen than a fallen picture and a few pieces of broken glass.

Cassie fought back panic as she retreated from the room and wound her way through the museum and out the front door. The museum squeezed tight around her as though it would never let her go.

Hurrying out of the shadow the building cast, Cassie didn't stop until she was next to the fountain, soaking up the April sun until it melted away the goosebumps that had erupted along her arms. She continued to shiver, but that was more from her experience than the cool breeze that caressed her neck, so different from the breath she had felt moments ago.

Cassie was no stranger to spiritual disturbances, and she didn't scare easily. But this entity lived somewhere inside her, too deep for her to extract it on her own.

Closing her eyes, Cassie focused on the warmth of the sun and the bubbling of the fountain. She reached out and touched the water, smooth and cool against her skin. She took a deep breath to clear her mind of panic, inhaling the aroma of fresh-cut grass on the breeze.

WITH THE ENTITY AT HER BACK PLAYING WITH HER EMOTIONS, CASSIE could feel her grip on reality slipping. She wasn't the kind of person to walk away from an important conversation without saying her piece, yet she hadn't let Jason explain why he'd shown up in Nashville unannounced. What if something was wrong? What if he hadn't had another choice? She'd just walked away like whatever he had to say wouldn't be enough.

Guilt gripped her chest, and she slipped her fingers from the fountain to rub at the spot around her heart. It had been an overreaction to abandon him like that. But even as she fought to replace panic with composure, the sensation of being watched crept over her like a cluster of spiders.

17

Cassie took a deep breath and tuned into the world around her—both the natural and the spiritual. Sometimes it was difficult to separate the two, and she couldn't tell if the eyes on her were from a person or a ghost. She remembered the feeling from the courtyard outside her hotel, and the sensation intensified. There was no doubt in her mind it was the same person.

Was it the entity messing with her head again? Focusing on the weight of a gaze on her back, Cassie treated it like a thread of gossamer ribbon. In her mind's eye, she could see it sparkle and shine in the light, leading back toward the museum and around the corner. Like a bug caught in a web, she was careful not to disturb it.

Cassie straightened her shoulders and turned on her heel, as though she'd regained her balance and had decided to continue her walk from before she'd taken a detour inside the museum. Her senses remained vigilant while she strolled and looked up at the trees and down at the flowers. The ethereal strand she followed pulled taut but didn't break, and she quickened her pace in response.

People milled about the museum's exterior, chatting or staring at their phones. A few took in the day's beauty, but most were distracted. She searched every face, trying to discern whether she had seen them before, but none stood out. A few spirits also milled around the museum, trailing behind a loved one or standing in the middle of the sidewalk, confused as to why everyone passed them by. The sun made it harder to see their forms, and more than once she had to veer off course to get a closer look, hoping they didn't notice her attention.

The string gave a delicate tug, but it was enough to snap her concentration and, with it, the connection to whoever watched her. Speeding up, Cassie strode toward the corner of the museum with purpose, not hesitating before rounding the bend to the other side. She walked so fast and with such purpose, that she crashed into a young mother and son, nearly sending the two of them to the ground.

"I'm so sorry," she said, steadying the woman and hoping she hadn't done any damage.

"No, no, it's okay," the woman said. "I wasn't paying attention either. Are you okay?"

Cassie looked beyond the woman, sure this hadn't been the person watching her. But while the street wasn't empty, she couldn't discern who might've been stalking her.

"Miss?"

"Sorry," Cassie said, pulling herself from her distraction. "Yes, I'm all right. Sorry again."

The woman gave her a polite smile and stepped out of the way, continuing toward the museum while her son looked over his shoulder at the strange woman who seemed to be going out of her mind. Annoyed, Cassie swept her gaze along the street one more time, but it was no use. The sensation was gone, once again escaping like sand through her fingers.

There was no way to be sure, but this didn't seem like the entity messing with her mind. If it was something or someone else, then who? And what did they want? Perhaps the more important question was, how dangerous were they? Cold dread pooled at the base of her spine, and she had to fight the urge to sprint back into the museum.

Intent on heading back the way she had come, Cassie turned on her heel and ran into another person. Only this time, she recognized the hard plane of his chest and the strength of his arms as they steadied her. His scent, light in the open air, brought her back to a place of comfort and joy, even as she remembered he was supposed to be back home in Savannah, helping Lorraine find enough evidence to bring down Apex once and for all.

"Cassie," Jason said, breathing her name like a sigh of relief. "You scared me. You weren't answering your phone. Why did you run off like that? You could've—" He cut himself off. Taking a deep breath, he started again. "I was worried about you."

"I'm sorry," Cassie said, all her earlier anger gone from her body, replaced with exhaustion. "I just needed a minute."

"I'm sorry for surprising you like that. I should've called and given you a heads up."

Cassie wasn't quite ready to talk about it yet. "How did you find me?"

Jason's smile was warm. "When I saw there was a museum within walking distance, I figured you'd end up here. I was just coming down the sidewalk when I saw you heading over this way. Were you looking for someone?"

"Kind of." The last thing she wanted to do was tell him how she thought someone might be stalking her. "An entity has attached itself to me. She shows up at, uh, interesting times."

"An entity? Is that different from a regular ghost?"

"It feels different." Cassie leaned back against the side of the museum to take some pressure off her feet. "She's strong. Took a picture right off the wall in one of the galleries inside. She's been affecting my mood, my reactions."

"That's why you walked away."

"Part of it. I didn't want to say something I'd regret. Especially since it wouldn't have been me. Not entirely."

"Not entirely. But partially?"

Cassie shrugged. There was no point in lying and ignoring her feelings. They'd have to talk about it sooner or later. "You've been overprotective lately." Jason opened his mouth to argue, but Cassie held up her hand. "Let me finish. I know it comes from a good place, but it's been rubbing me the wrong way. You're loyal to the people you love, and I know you show that by being protective of them. Trust me, I'm glad to be in that camp. I'm lucky to have you in my life."

When Cassie didn't continue, Jason nudged her with his elbow. "But?"

"But it makes me feel weak. I know that's not your intention, but I've spent so much of my life being afraid that I don't like to be reminded how dangerous the world is. Trust me, I know exactly the kind of monsters that go bump in the night. I finally feel like I've gotten my feet on solid ground, like I can take care of myself without spiraling into a panic. But I haven't forgotten what it feels like to fight for my life. And I don't need you to remind me to be scared. I need you to support me. And when you don't, it feels like you're holding me back. Like you don't trust me or my instincts or my abilities."

Jason was silent for a long time, and Cassie didn't dare look at his face. She was having trouble holding back tears, and her heart was like a drumline in her chest. Despite the cool wind, her hands were clammy, and she had to rub them down the front of her pants to dry them off.

"I understand what you're saying," Jason said, his voice trailing off for a moment. He cleared his throat before he continued. "I'm sorry I've made you feel that way. But I hope you believe me when I say that it has nothing to do with you or your abilities. God, Cassie, you're the strongest person I know. Sometimes I forget everything you've been through because you're so fearless. The things you do and see on a daily basis would send most people running, including me. I don't envy your position, but I do envy the way you've picked yourself up and found your purpose in life. Most people aren't strong enough to do that after what you've been through."

Cassie had to swallow several times before she could speak. "Thank you for saying that."

"You're right, though. My natural instincts are to put myself between anything and anyone that wants to hurt someone I care about. I'm not trying to make excuses, but I spent a long time keeping people safe. My sisters. My mother. My unit. Survivors of the worst kinds of crimes. Even my job at the museum was about protecting people."

Jason took a deep breath, like he didn't want to admit what came next. "The truth is, I'm the one who feels weak. And helpless. I'm worried about you. I'm worried about *me*. And Lorraine and Adelaide. My family. *Your* family. Apex wants you, and they're willing to use me as a bargaining chip. Who knows if they'll stop at that. There are a lot of people in our lives that we care about. And I'm just not built to stand by and do nothing."

"But you weren't," Cassie said. "You were helping Lorraine. You were talking to your contacts. You *were* helping me, just from a distance."

"I know." Jason reached out to take hold of Cassie's hand, and when she didn't pull away, he lifted it to his lips and placed a gentle kiss along her knuckles. "Lorraine got in touch with the former Apex employee and connected us. Cassie, he knew you were in Nashville. It spooked me enough that I jumped on a plane without even thinking. I figured you had enough on your plate. It was time for me to pull my weight."

"You do pull your weight," Cassie said, finally meeting his eyes. They were glossy from unshed tears, and she saw hope and anxiety warring with each other. "It's dangerous for you to be this close to Apex's headquarters."

Jason shrugged. "They already knew where I was. It doesn't make that much of a difference."

"It will if they figure out what you're doing here."

"I'll be careful," he said. Then, at her disbelieving look, added, "I promise."

"They probably already know you're here."

"But they don't know why. They might think I just wanted to be closer to you. Which I do." Jason flashed her a cheesy grin, but when Cassie didn't laugh, he squeezed her hand. "I'll stay out of your way, but I want to be close in case you need me, okay? Not because I don't trust you, but because I don't trust Apex." His gaze flickered away for a moment. "Or Agent Viotto."

Cassie scoffed. "He's the only one on our side." She chewed the inside of her lip. "What about Lorraine? You just abandoned her?"

"I left her a voicemail. I'm hoping I'll hear from her soon. She doesn't need me there to help her with research. I'm much more useful as a pair of boots on the ground."

Cassie couldn't argue with that. "Okay. But if Apex catches wind of what you're doing, I want you to promise you'll go home where it's safe and let me deal with this."

"I promise," Jason said.

But Cassie didn't miss the way he wouldn't quite keep her gaze.

18

Cassie said her goodbyes to Jason as he left to check in at his hotel. He'd had the same thought she did—it was smarter for him to stay elsewhere in case Apex was keeping an eye on her and the room they'd paid for.

Meanwhile, she returned to Apex headquarters. Chris had been waiting for her in the lobby, and she didn't even get the chance to swipe her card through the terminal before he'd whisked her back outside and into a car. She half expected Robert to be behind the wheel, but when Chris opened the passenger-side door for her, she realized he'd be driving.

The plan was to travel north to Frankfort, Kentucky to speak with the governor, Arnold Warren. Chris had elected not to give the man a head's up that they were coming, given the three-hour drive would be more than enough time to prepare for their arrival. They wanted to see what he was like when he was under pressure and scrutiny.

As any law enforcement agent could attest to, there was a reason they questioned a missing person's loved ones first. It's not just that they might have the most relevant and up-to-date information. More times than not, the spouse or partner committed the crime, and they couldn't count Warren out of that category.

After their initial discussion of the plan, the car fell silent, and Cassie passed the time watching the trees whip by as they zipped up I-65. Chris kept the music low, but she could make out the classic rock guitar riffs and drumbeats. She could even hear him singing along under his breath. The warmth of the afternoon sun made her eyes droop, and despite the commotion from earlier that morning, she felt herself slipping into a state of relaxation.

To Cassie's dismay, Chris chose that exact moment to break the silence. "So. You want to talk about it?"

Cassie blinked at him slowly and yawned. "Talk about what?"

Chris cut her a look from the corner of his eye. "Come on. You really gonna make me say it?"

She shrugged. "No use in only one of us feeling uncomfortable."

Chuckling, he drummed his fingers on the steering wheel until he found the right words. "You weren't expecting Jason to show up like that, were you?"

"What gave it away?"

"Let's see, the shock on your face," he said, ticking off the reasons on his fingers, "you asking him what he was doing there, and you storming off down the street without any explanation."

She winced, thinking of how she'd reacted. "Yeah, sorry about that. I was feeling a bit overwhelmed. Didn't want to say something I'd regret. Especially given my current, uh, volatility."

Chris didn't laugh. "You okay though?"

"Sure, yeah. I'm fine."

"You want to talk about it?" he repeated.

"You sure *you* want to talk about it?" Cassie joked. "I didn't think we were those kinds of friends."

Chris frowned. "What kind?"

"The kind that talked about me and my boyfriend's relationship troubles."

"Maybe we haven't been in the past," Chris said, sounding quiet and unsure, "but that doesn't mean we can't. It's up to you. I don't want to pry. Just thought you could use a shoulder to lean on."

Cassie's chest squeezed at the realization that he was trying to be a good friend and she was the one who had drawn a line in the sand. Sighing, she faced forward and let her head tip back against the seat. "I'm sorry. I appreciate your concern. He just caught me off-guard showing up like that. I don't want him any closer to Apex than necessary."

"Did he say why he showed up unannounced?"

The real reason Jason was in town caught in her throat. Why get Chris' hopes up if they weren't sure they would ever track down the disgruntled former employee, let alone convince them to help take down Apex?

"He's a bit overprotective."

"Can't say I blame him," Chris said, trying to lighten the mood. "You do tend to get into some interesting situations."

Cassie scowled. "I tend to get myself out of them, too."

Chris held up one hand, keeping the other firmly on the steering wheel. "Didn't mean to imply that wasn't the case." He was smiling, but when he glanced at her, his eyes were serious. "Any reason it's bothering you so much?"

"Just makes me feel like he doesn't trust me. Like he doesn't believe in me."

Cassie had said as much when she spoke with Jason, but it felt different when she said it out loud to Chris. Like it was more real, more concrete. There was no doubt in her mind Jason supported her in every way he could. But if that was the case, why did it feel like his every action was intended to hold her back?

"I don't really know the guy, but I don't think that's true." Before Cassie could argue, Chris continued. "And that doesn't mean your feelings aren't valid. If that's how he's making you feel, then he needs to change the way he shows you how he cares. Otherwise, you guys are going to hit a brick wall you might not be able to climb over."

Cassie eyed him, studying his tone and taking in every detail of his expression. She wasn't naïve. He'd been flirting with her the day before. But his advice seemed genuine. "Thank you for saying that."

"See? Told you I could be that kind of friend."

Cassie rolled her eyes, but she laughed. "We'll see how long you can keep this up. We still have a long way to go on this case."

The rest of the ride was filled with playful banter and random anecdotes. Every once in a while, Chris would turn up a song he liked and bang his hands against the steering wheel like he was playing the drums at a rock concert. It was the lightest and most carefree she'd seen him since they met in North Carolina, and his breezy attitude was contagious.

But by the time they arrived at the governor's downtown office, they both had arranged their faces into expressions of cool indifference. Cassie let Chris take the lead, knowing he had a more domineering presence. For her part, she stood by as his silent partner, daring anyone to question why they were there.

Unsurprisingly, an FBI badge could get you through most doors, and that's how they ended up in a waiting room outside Warren's office, staring down his assistant, who tapped away at his keyboard until he finished his thought. After what felt like minutes, he looked up and greeted them with a lukewarm smile.

"Good afternoon," the man said, looking them both up and down with what Cassie could only describe as a scrutinizing glower. But whatever conclusion he came to was kept hidden behind his placid face, perfectly framed by a tousle of copper curls. "What can I do for you?"

"Agent Viotto with the FBI." Chris flashed his badge. "And this is my associate, Miss Quinn. We're here to speak with Arnold Warren."

The man looked unimpressed. "What is this regarding?"

"That's for Warren to know."

"*Governor* Warren is a busy man. Without an appointment, I can't let you in. I apologize for the inconvenience. Hopefully, you didn't have to travel far to get here."

"We did, actually. When will he be available? We can wait."

Holding Chris' gaze for a moment, the man turned his attention back to his computer and tapped out a few keystrokes. "Looks like his next available opening is on Monday." After a dramatic pause, he said, "Four weeks from now."

"That doesn't work for us."

"I can look in June if you'd like?"

Chris placed his hands on the desk between them. "What's your name?"

"Matthew," the man said, with an air of disdain.

"Matthew. Have you ever heard of Apex Publicity?"

The man stilled, staring up at Chris with unblinking eyes. His gaze flicked to Cassie's, as if asking if Agent Viotto had said what he thought he'd just said. All Cassie did was raise an eyebrow in expectation. Matthew returned his attention to Chris.

"Yes. Of course." All of Matthew's former insolence had been wiped clear.

"Excellent. We're here on their behalf. They would like me to speak with *Governor* Warren as soon as possible. Do you think you could find an opening before next month?"

"I applied as an intern at their Chicago office," Matthew said, as though in a daze. "I didn't get it."

Chris straightened, a beaming smile on his face now. "I can always put in a good word for you if you're looking for a new job."

Matthew's eyebrows shot into his hairline. "You would?"

"Of course." Chris' shrug was aloof, even a bit smug. "All I need to do is drop by Anastasia Bolton's office. She's always on the lookout for new prospects."

This time, Matthew's jaw dropped. "You know Anastasia Bolton?"

All Chris did was smile wider. "I believe you were going to find us an opening?"

"Right," Matthew said. "One moment."

And instead of searching the calendar on his computer, the man stood and strode toward a heavy oak door set into the far wall. Knocking twice in rapid succession, he disappeared inside, letting it click shut behind him with a sense of authority.

Cassie turned to Chris. "How'd you know that would work?"

"I've been with Apex long enough to know their name opens a lot more doors than my badge." He shrugged. "Sad but true."

Before Cassie could respond, Matthew poked his head out from Arnold's office. His mask of indifference had slipped back into place, but it was warmer than it had been when they'd first arrived.

"Governor Warren will see you now."

19

Chris motioned for Cassie to walk ahead of him as they entered the governor's office. The room was spacious, with tall windows that let in plenty of natural light, and all the wood furniture was a deep cherry red. Family photos and a couple coin displays dotted his desk and floating wall shelves, but otherwise, the place looked like it had gone unchanged for close to a hundred years.

The room had bright, shiny wooden floors that matched the paneling on the walls, but the carpet in the center of the room had seen better days. Bookshelves set into the walls were lined with volumes from various decades, the degree of fading along their spines the only indication of their age. A pair of chairs sat in front of an unlit fireplace with a small table between them, a book open and face down in the center as though the governor had just stepped away from it a moment ago.

The governor sat behind his desk, gazing up at them with a cautious look in his eye, even as the smile on his face grew wider. Matthew stepped out of the room as Cassie and Chris entered and shut the door behind them with a *snick*. As he did so, Arnold stood and stepped around his desk.

He was a tall, lean man who looked like he'd been born to serve in this kind of work. Most people would describe him as all-American, with a square jaw, sparkling blue eyes, and a mop of sandy hair, deep silver along his temples, parted on the side. A pair of reading glasses perched on his nose made him look more approachable, like an old professor greeting a former student.

"Miss Quinn," Arnold said, shaking her hand. Then, turning to Chris, "Agent Viotto, I presume."

"That's correct," Chris said, meeting the man's piercing gaze in kind.

"Matthew tells me you're here on behalf of Apex Publicity. I must admit, that's a bit of a surprise."

Cassie raised an eyebrow. "Why is that?"

"They were interested in representing me. I declined." A sardonic smile lit up his face. "I get the impression not many people do that."

"No, they don't," Chris responded, a little impressed. "Mind if I ask why?"

Arnold pulled his glasses from his face and set them on his desk before leaning against it and crossing his arms over his chest. He looked at ease, even as he hesitated before finding the right words. "We had different ideas regarding the look and feel of my presidential campaign."

"You don't have to mince words with us," Cassie said. "Despite our association, we're not Apex's biggest fans."

Arnold looked startled at Cassie's admission, but after a moment, he uncrossed his arms and placed his hands in his pockets. "I don't agree with their aggressive approach to campaigning. I'd rather let my character speak for itself. They seemed to think that wasn't good enough to win."

Cassie was much more willing to give him the benefit of the doubt, but that didn't mean he had nothing to do with Millie's disappearance. Still, Cassie thought, wouldn't he have hired Apex to bury the story if he had been involved?

"You probably dodged a bullet there," Chris said. "But now you might have to worry about a different target on your back."

Arnold bobbed his head, pinching his lips together in thought. "They've put their considerable resources behind my opponent,

Senator Hughes. I assume that's why you're here?" Cocking his head to one side, Arnold glanced between Chris and Cassie. "If you're here to intimidate me or attempt to buy me out, it won't work. I'm dead set on running for office."

Cassie shook her head. "It's nothing like that. Apex hired us to investigate a case they're interested in solving. We're here for the truth, regardless of whether it benefits Apex."

"The truth," Arnold said, drawing out the words. "About Millie."

"That's right," Chris replied. "We'd like to ask you some questions, if you don't mind."

"And if I do?" Arnold asked, an edge entering his voice for the first time.

Chris shrugged. "Then we'll leave. But we'll continue to investigate. It's in your best interest to give us your side of the story. Like Cassie said, we're here for the truth. Nothing more, nothing less."

Arnold glanced down at his feet, and Cassie didn't miss the pained expression that flitted across his face. But when he looked up again, there was a determined set to his jaw. "I have nothing to hide. If there's a chance you can discover what happened to her, I owe that to Millie and her family." He pointed to the chairs across the room. "Please, have a seat. Can I get you anything to drink?"

"We're okay," Chris said, taking a seat and waiting for Cassie to do the same. Arnold dragged a third chair from the corner of the room and sat it in front of them. Chris waited for him to settle in before he placed his phone on the table between them. "Do you mind if I record this conversation? Purely for our own records."

Arnold looked dubious but nodded. "I don't have anything to say that isn't already out there somewhere on the internet. The case is three years old, after all."

"It's important to get as much information from primary sources as possible," Cassie said. "As you can imagine, we don't trust Apex's records. We'd hate to miss something because we were misinformed."

Arnold studied her for a moment. "You're not an agent, but you're an investigator?"

"Yes," she replied, resisting the urge to shift in her seat under his scrutiny. "From Savannah. Apex hired me as an independent contractor."

"And let me guess," Arnold said, with a derisive snort, "they're hoping to uncover some skeletons in my closet?"

"That's the idea," Chris replied. Then, leaning forward, he said, "But this is just as good of an opportunity to make them look like fools for thinking you were involved in Millie's disappearance. Not to mention waste some of their resources in the process."

Arnold chuckled. "Well, who am I to argue that?" Sobering, he crossed one leg over the other and glanced around the room before meeting Cassie's eyes. "It's hard to admit, but some of the details of those first few days have been lost over the years."

"Just do the best you can," she said, nodding in encouragement. "Anything you can remember will be helpful."

Arnold waited for Chris to hit the record button on his phone before he cleared his throat and spoke. "Millie and I had been together for a little under three years. We met through mutual friends and hit it off." Arnold's face softened as he strolled down memory lane. "She was a vibrant woman who knew what she wanted and wasn't afraid to be herself. There's a lot of pressure on the spouses of politicians, especially the wives. You have to dress a certain way, look a certain way, be intelligent and successful—but not more so than your husband. Millie was a firecracker when we were alone, but she knew how to play a crowd. Everyone loved her, and she soaked up the spotlight. I was going to wait for our three-year anniversary to ask her to marry me, but she found the ring and put it on right then and there. When I came down for breakfast, she held up her hand and said, 'Yes.'"

A little laugh escaped Cassie's mouth. "Were you mad she ruined the surprise?"

"A little," Arnold said, chuckling. "But I was so relieved, it didn't last long." After a brief pause, his face fell. "A few months later, she went missing."

"Before we get to that," Chris said, "can you tell us what your relationship was like? Did you ever fight?"

"All couples fight," Arnold said, maintaining eye contact with Chris. "And if they tell you otherwise, they're lying."

"What did you fight about?"

"Money. I grew up in an upper-middle class household. Millie was from the working class. They didn't struggle, but they had to pinch pennies at times." He gestured to one of the nearby coin displays. "I chose a stressful career path. I find solace in curating collections, and I consider myself a proficient numismatist. She thought it was a waste of money."

"How did you argue?" When Arnold gave him a blank look, Chris clarified. "Yelling? Throwing things? Storming out of the house?"

Arnold shifted in his seat and uncrossed his legs, only to cross them the other way. "Yelling, mostly. Sometimes I would leave and drive around the neighborhood. She hated when I did that. But I didn't want to say or do anything I'd regret."

"Do you have a temper, Governor Warren?"

Scowling, the man leveled Chris with an annoyed look. "No more than the average person. I get angry and defensive. I'm not going to deny that. But I don't lash out at people. I'm not a violent man."

"What about Millie?" Cassie asked, watching the governor's facial expressions. "Did she yell a lot? Ever throw anything? Hit you?"

"She had a set of pipes on her, that's for sure," Arnold said. "Knocked over a vase on purpose once, but I wouldn't consider that throwing objects."

Cassie waited for Arnold to answer her last question, and when he didn't, she prompted, "Did she ever hit you?"

Arnold sighed. "She slapped me once. Immediately regretted it and apologized. I never held it against her."

"Why did she slap you?" Chris asked.

"I called her a bitch," Arnold said, rubbing his jaw, as though he could feel the ghost of her handprint. "I also regretted that one immediately."

"What was that argument about?" Cassie asked.

"That one was about my work schedule. For someone who didn't grow up wealthy, she could be condescending toward my constituents who need the most help. But we talked about it. Worked through it. Came to see each other's point of view."

Satisfied with his answers, Chris moved on. "Tell us about the night she went missing."

Arnold took a deep breath and squared his shoulders, as though preparing for the onslaught of memories this conversation would unearth. When he spoke, his voice was monotone, like he'd repeated these details a hundred times in the past, and now, it was just rote.

"She came along with me on a work trip over the weekend. I had every intention of spending as much time with her as I could, but things got busy. It felt like everything that could go wrong did go wrong. I came back to our hotel room one night, and she'd left a note saying she was going back home."

"To Frankfort?" Chris asked. "Or Nashville?"

"Nashville," Arnold said. "She stayed over at my house on the weekends, but she liked having her own apartment back home, closer to her family. Especially her sister. I couldn't visit her in Tennessee a lot, but she didn't seem to mind the trip north."

"What'd you do when you found the note?" Cassie asked.

"Called her," he said. "She didn't pick up. I thought she was mad at me, and I didn't blame her. I left a voicemail, apologizing. Told her I'd come home early, and we'd spend some quality time together. But I never heard back."

"What happened next?"

Arnold's gaze lifted to the ceiling, and Cassie saw his eyes glaze over with the torments of the past. "I had no choice but to stay another night at the hotel. Work stuff," he said with a wave of his hand. "The next morning, I got a text saying she was going to a friend's house. I asked who and where, but she never answered. At that point, I was starting to get worried. It's not like this was the first time I'd worked too much and ignored her. But we were in a good place. We'd just publicly announced we'd gotten engaged. I could tell she was frustrated because I'd promised her a romantic weekend, even if I'd only be available in the evenings. But she wasn't one to run off and ignore me."

"When did you realize something was wrong?"

"When I still hadn't heard from her once I got home. I called her sister. Maxine didn't like me very much," Arnold said with a wince. "Rather, she didn't like my chosen profession. But we were cordial. I asked if she'd seen Millie or heard from her, but she hadn't. Which was strange. The two of them were close. If she went off to stay at a friend's house, she would've told Max."

"You don't think she left her house willingly?" Chris asked.

Arnold dragged a hand down his face with a groan. "I don't know. I've been over that weekend so many times, from so many angles, I don't know what to think anymore. The police found her phone in her car a few days later. I was the only one she texted about her trip out of town. She never told me who she was going to see."

Chris scrolled through his phone until he found the information he was looking for. "There was no evidence of foul play. Yet you think she was kidnapped?"

"I have no other explanation for what happened," Arnold said, his voice growing strained. "But there was no phone call. No ransom demand. I don't think this had anything to do with me. But why would anyone want to kidnap her?"

"Lots of reasons that don't have to do with ransom."

Cassie winced at the pained look on Arnold's face. "We're not jumping to conclusions," she said, throwing an annoyed look in Chris' direction. "But we need to look at this from all angles."

Arnold bobbed his head up and down. "I know. I thought I had accepted what had happened to her. Even started dating again recently. But it still kills me inside, not knowing."

"Any chance she ran away?" Chris asked, his voice harsher than Cassie thought was necessary. "She could've sold your ring for money. Disappeared."

Arnold scoffed. "Without telling her sister? I doubt it."

"Maybe Maxine was in on it. If not at first, then later."

Scowling now, Arnold glared at Chris. "I doubt she would've ended up the way she did if that was the case."

"Do you know what happened to Maxine?"

"Overdose. I don't know much more," Arnold said. "Her family doesn't speak to me anymore, though they're more than happy to take advantage of the fact that I've been making payments on Millie's apartment."

Cassie's eyes widened. "You have? How come?"

Arnold shrugged. "At first, it was in the hopes that she'd come back. I didn't want her to be somewhere unfamiliar after everything she'd been through. After that, I thought it was a good idea to keep everything as it was, in case the police wanted to search it again. Maybe they'd find something new."

"And now?" Chris asked. "Three years later?"

The other man shrugged. "Habit, I guess. And maybe I haven't moved on as much as I thought I had."

"Can we visit the apartment?" Cassie asked.

"Sure," Arnold said, though there was much less energy in his voice than when they'd started this conversation. "I'll call the property manager and have him let you in."

A knock on the door interrupted them. Matthew stuck his head inside. "Sir? Your brother is here."

With a sigh, Arnold got to his feet. "I'm sorry, but that's all the time I have." He shook Chris' hand and then Cassie's. "Please, if you discover anything new, let me know."

"We'll be in touch if we need to speak to you again." Chris stopped the recording and pocketed his phone. "Don't go anywhere."

Arnold walked over to the door and opened it wider. "You know where I live, Agent Viotto. The whole state does. Couldn't disappear if I tried."

Cassie and Chris exited the room as Arnold's brother entered. He looked just like the governor, though he was a few inches taller and a little stockier. Before the door closed, Cassie heard him ask who they were.

"From Apex," Arnold replied. "They're working on Millie's case."

Cassie peered over her shoulder to gauge the other man's reaction, only to find him staring daggers at her as he closed the door between them.

20

It felt strange to turn back around and head toward Nashville, but at least the meeting with Governor Warren had been productive. From what she'd read online in various newspapers, all of his details matched what he'd relayed to the police and press three years prior. Her intuition hadn't sent up any red flags, but the fact that it had been quiet in general was more cause for concern.

Just because he was telling *his* truth didn't mean it was the *whole* truth.

As plausible as Governor Warren's story was, it would be easy to poke holes in a few different areas. The fact that Millie had left early from their trip was enough for an eyebrow raise at the very least. As far as they knew, no one had seen her since she'd left their hotel. While Arnold's whereabouts were accounted for during work, the middle of the night was wide open. He could've slipped out in the early morning hours, found Millie and killed her, and then returned to his colleagues like nothing had happened.

Cassie had a hard time believing Millie had left Arnold out of revenge, especially since she apparently told her sister everything. It was much more plausible that she had been kidnapped, but if not for ransom, then something worse.

The next step in their investigation was to meet with Millie's parents and get their side of the story. Unlike Governor Warren, Chris had called ahead to see if they were willing to talk. Much to Cassie's surprise, the Abrahms were more than happy to speak with them about everything that had happened.

Now, they walked up the front sidewalk to a quaint little house half an hour outside of Nashville. It had peach shutters and accents that stood out against the slate-gray siding. The manicured lawn accentuated the precisely placed plants and shrubs out front.

Before Chris could raise his fist to knock on the door, it swung open to reveal a man about the age of Cassie's father. His tan slacks and checkered vest over a long-sleeve shirt gave the impression of a grandfather dressed up for Christmas day. Salt and pepper hair, a short, silver beard, and a pair of spectacles hanging from a chain against his chest only served to reinforce the image.

Despite the reason for their visit, the man's green eyes shone with warmth and appreciation. "Agent Viotto and Miss Quinn, I presume," he said, stepping back and opening the door wider. "I'm Lloyd. It's a pleasure to meet you. Please, come in."

With a smile, Cassie followed the man inside, Chris on her heels. The house smelled of oranges and vanilla, and she took a deep breath, letting the scent relax the nerves that had taken over her body. She didn't know what had set her off, but she had to work to unclench her jaw and fists.

The man led them down a short hall and to the left, into a spacious office with a pair of leather couches and mahogany furniture to match. Lloyd gestured to one of the sofas. "Make yourselves comfortable. Can I get you something to drink?"

"Water would be great," Cassie said, her tongue sticking to the roof of her mouth. "Thank you."

"Not a problem," he said. "Back in a jiff."

When Lloyd was out of the room, Chris and Cassie exchanged a look, and she was glad to see he was as put off by the man's chipper demeanor as she was. It was one thing to welcome guests into your home with a warm smile, but he seemed excited for them to be there. Maybe they didn't get many visitors these days. Empty nest syndrome must have been ten times worse when both your kids had met tragic ends.

The man returned with a pair of glasses filled with water and set them down on the coffee table between them. Cassie didn't waste any time taking a sip as she and Chris settled onto one of the couches while Lloyd sat down on the other. The three of them waited no more than five seconds before a woman entered, carrying a tray full of little sandwiches.

"Wasn't sure if you'd be hungry at this time of day," she said, "but figured it wouldn't hurt to be prepared."

"Thank you so much," Chris said, his voice caught between surprise and appreciation.

"Nora's an excellent cook," Lloyd said. "Even if it's just chicken salad sandwiches."

Cassie watched as the woman blushed and settled next to her husband, who placed a hand on her knee. Millie's mother looked a few years younger than her spouse, but perhaps that was because her dark hair didn't have a speck of gray. The laugh lines around her eyes and mouth grew deeper when she gave them a small smile. Her deep blue eyes looked a little more hesitant than her husband's, but just as hopeful.

"We just wanted to say thank you." Lloyd leaned forward to emphasize his gratitude. "So many people have given up on Millie's story over the years, we were starting to think no one cared but us. Then Apex came along and gave us hope for the first time in what felt like forever."

Nora nodded her agreement. "I know you've run into a lot of obstacles, but every time we meet with someone from Apex, they're so sincere. I know they just want to find the truth."

Cassie caught Chris glancing at her out of the corner of her eye, but she didn't meet his gaze. As much as it pained her not to tell everyone she came across what Apex was capable of, she couldn't bring herself to crush the hopes of this poor couple.

"I'm sorry the road has been so long," she said. "And that we've hit so many snags along the way. But Agent Viotto and I are determined to get to the bottom of what happened to Millie."

"Do you mind if I record this conversation, purely for our own records?" Chris asked.

"Please, go ahead," Lloyd said.

Chris set his phone on the coffee table and hit the button. "Cassie and I just got back from a trip to Frankfort, where we talked to Governor Warren. We got his side of the story, but we'd like to get yours, too."

Cassie didn't miss the way Nora pursed her lips or how Lloyd's mouth turned down into a frown. Glancing between them, she said, "Something tells me you're not a fan of the governor."

"We don't like to talk ill of anyone," Lloyd began.

"But he wasn't good for our Millie," Nora finished. "Even before she disappeared."

"Why do you say that?" Chris asked.

Lloyd looked to his wife. "I can count on one hand the number of times Nora and I fought the entire time we've been together." When he turned back to Cassie, there was a wistful smile on his face. "We've been married for close to forty years now."

"Congratulations," Cassie said, feeling warmth seep into her bones.

"Thank you," Nora replied, patting her husband's hand where it still sat on her knee. "But Millie and Arnold fought so often. It felt like she called us up once a week to complain about him. I told her, 'Honey, it shouldn't be like this. He should be your sanctuary. Your refuge.'"

"But it felt like every time she called us, she was trying to convince herself she should stay." Lloyd shook his head. "I knew they weren't going to last."

"But they got engaged," Cassie said. "Maybe they'd worked out some of their issues?"

"It's possible," Nora said, twisting her fingers in her lap. "She'd been calling less often about him. At first, I took that as a good sign."

"And then?"

Nora's chin wobbled as she looked Cassie in the eye. "And then she disappeared."

Silence hung in the air like a weight around their shoulders. Cassie could feel Lloyd and Nora's despair like it was her own, and all she wanted to do was curl up into a ball and cry herself to sleep. She couldn't imagine what it would feel like to lose a child, let alone two within such a short amount of time. How could they possibly go on after that? How could they—

"When did you find out something was wrong?" Chris asked.

Cassie snapped out of her spiral, and she took another sip of water to regain some balance.

"Max called us after Millie left Arnold's hotel room and came home. We didn't even know she was out of town."

"Was that unusual?" Chris asked. "For her not to tell you her travel plans?"

"A little," Lloyd replied. "But since she wasn't going far—driving instead of flying—and it was just for the weekend, she probably didn't feel the need."

"It's not like we had plans," Nora said. "Millie was responsible. Put together. We never worried about her."

Cassie had no trouble reading between the lines. "What about Maxine? Did you ever worry about her?"

Lloyd let out a little chuckle, tinged with bitterness. "All the time. She was our wild child."

"We loved them both," Nora was quick to say. "But Max caused a lot more headaches than Millie ever did. You'd think with her being the older one, she would've been more responsible."

"But Max cared about her sister more than anyone in the world," Lloyd said. "They were very close."

Cassie sat up a little straighter, her earlier nerves turning to frustration. "Was Max worried when she couldn't get ahold of Millie?"

"Yes," Lloyd said. "At first, we thought she was overreacting. Like I said, Millie was the responsible one. But when we couldn't get ahold of her either, we started to panic." He swallowed back the emotion that had started to clog his throat and affect his voice. "Then they found her car."

Chris leaned forward and asked, "What do you think happened?"

The Abrahms exchanged a look. After a brief hesitation, Nora nodded, and Lloyd turned back to Cassie and Chris. "Governor Warren has been kind to us since Millie's disappearance, especially in keeping up with the rent for her apartment."

"We sometimes go there," Nora said. "Just to feel close to her."

Lloyd nodded. "We appreciate what he's done to keep Millie's story in the public eye, but with him running for president—" The man shook his head, looking for the first time like a disappointed, angry father. "We don't want Millie's story to be part of his platform. He's not her family. We are."

Cassie fought to find the right words for her next question. "Do you think Max's death had anything to do with Millie's disappearance?"

Nora pursed her lips. "Maxine didn't take her sister's death well. None of us did, but Max went off the deep end."

Heat crawled down Cassie's spine and settled into her gut like a sleeping dragon. "How so?"

"Like we said, she's always been the wild child," Lloyd answered. "She struggled with depression. Had to be hospitalized a few times. Then she started getting more into drugs. She overdosed about a year ago."

Unlike when they'd spoken about Millie, Cassie didn't catch any chin wobbles or glistening eyes. The dragon in her stomach lifted its head, smoke curling from its nostrils in warning. She ignored it. "You think she did that to herself? That she was just grieving, and it was an accident?"

The Abrahms looked startled at Cassie's veiled accusation. "That's what we were told. It's not like it was out of character for her. She had worse luck in relationships than Millie. Her boyfriend was no good for her. If anyone should be held responsible, it's him."

Cassie shot to her feet, bumping the coffee table and causing water to slosh out of Chris' untouched glass. The dragon in her stomach was awake now, pacing back and forth and spewing molten lava in every direction.

"I'm so sorry," she managed to say. "I need some air. Chris, you can finish up on your own, right?"

Before he could open his mouth to answer, she left the room in a whirlwind of fury and yanked on the front door, stepping out into the sunshine and letting the breeze stoke her fire until she felt like she would combust.

And then, just like that, it was gone as quick as it had come.

21

Cassie fumed on the entire ride over to Millie's apartment, and somehow Chris knew not to push her into talking about what had happened before she was ready. The farther they got from the Abrahms' house, the easier it became to let go of her anger and return to herself.

Because that wasn't her. It was the entity.

Cassie spoke slow and steady, as though testing her ability to string together a coherent sentence. "Whoever's attached herself to me, she's not happy with Lloyd and Nora Abrahms."

Chris glanced at her, as if making sure it was safe enough for him to talk. "Do you think they're hiding something?"

"Not sure," Cassie said. "But it's clear who the favorite daughter was."

Chris eased off the gas to take a turn onto a quiet street with several small apartment complexes. "Maybe Millie didn't like the way they were talking about her sister."

As Chris pulled into the driveway of their destination and put the car in park, Cassie turned to him with what she hoped was a serious but not alarming expression. "I'm going to be honest here—I don't know how this is going to go. It could get weird."

Chris pinched his eyebrows together. "Weird?"

Cassie took in the innocuous façade before her. The dark bricks were clean and solid. The front windows were all covered with drawn drapes, and while Millie's apartment had been vacant for several years, the curtains fluttered as if Cassie had just missed someone peeking through.

"This is where the entity first attached herself to someone," Cassie explained, feeling a strange mix of trepidation and excitement. She wanted to know what came next, but she was scared to see what would be revealed as she opened the next door. "It's a place of power for her. Whatever I've experienced so far will be nothing compared to this place's potential. So, yeah, it could get weird."

"Noted." Chris pushed open his door and stepped out into the fading afternoon light. "I can handle weird. Not a problem."

Cassie smirked. "You sound real convincing there, Agent Viotto."

"I'm a professional, Miss Quinn," he said, sticking his nose up. "It's what I do."

With the mood lightened, Cassie led the way through the unlocked front door of the building, climbing the stairs toward the second floor. As she drew closer to Millie's apartment, she felt Chris' hand on her lower back, urging her forward. Furrowing her brows, she glanced over her shoulder, but he was still several steps below her.

"What?" he asked, looking up at her from his vantage point.

"Nothing," she said, even as the spectral touch pushed her closer to their destination. "I just think she really wants us to go inside."

Chris joined her on the landing. "Good. That means we might find something useful."

All Cassie could do was nod, swept away in the storm of emotion that at once chilled her to the bone and lit all her nerve endings on fire. Sliding the key out from under the mat where the property manager had left it for them, Cassie slipped it into the lock and turned it, the thud of the deadbolt sounding like a gunshot in the hallway. The scrape of the doorknob under her hand was like the gun cocking once more.

"All good?" Chris asked. He'd said it in a low whisper, but it still made her jump.

"Yeah," she answered, a little louder than he had, if only to drive the deafening silence away.

Chris waited until Cassie stepped over the threshold before he followed her inside, closing the door behind them with a soft *click*. This time, Cassie didn't jump, but her heart beat a frantic rhythm in her chest. She felt so alive. So close to the truth. Like it was right there, waiting for her to reach out and grab it.

"It's clean," Chris said.

The comment pulled Cassie from her thoughts. They had stepped into a combined dining and living room, tiled in gray and white linoleum squares. The couch was beige, as were the curtains. It looked like the resident had just stepped out to run to the store. A modest television sat on an entertainment stand, filled with books and movies and knickknacks. Photographs hung on the wall, and a small pile of mail sat on the dining room table. From where they stood, Cassie could just see into the kitchen, with its white cabinets and gray countertops. There were no dishes in the sink or the aroma of a fresh-cooked meal. It smelled empty, but not forgotten.

"Warren must hire cleaners to come in every so often," Chris said. "No hope of finding physical evidence then."

"We're not here for physical evidence," Cassie said, feeling a pull toward the hallway that led to the back. She ignored it and walked into the kitchen, pulling open a few of the cabinets. "All her dinnerware is still here."

Chris followed her and pulled open the refrigerator door. "Fridge is empty, though. Except for a few bottles of water. Might be for the cleaners." He pulled open the freezer next. "Nothing in here either."

Cassie was about to look under the sink—why, she had no idea—when a loud beeping made them both jump. Chris went as far as putting his hand on his weapon before his attention zeroed in on the origin of the sound. Cassie followed his gaze to the microwave, which had just gone off like someone's meal was ready.

Stepping forward and pushing the button to open the door, Cassie confirmed what she already knew. "Empty."

"Why'd it go off?"

"No idea."

"Do you smell that?"

She did. As soon as she'd opened the microwave, the scent had hit her like a slap to the face. "Violets. It's been following me around since the entity attached itself to me."

"What do you think it means?"

"Not sure yet," Cassie said. "But I'd bet my reputation and a significant amount of money that it's important."

The slamming of a door had Cassie and Chris running out into the living room, and this time Chris did pull his weapon. Cassie shot him a questioning look, but he just shrugged. "Makes me feel better."

"It won't do you any good against what's in here."

"You do your thing," he grumbled, "and let me do mine."

Cassie smirked, but it fell away when they heard a door slam again. This time, she could tell it came from the back of the apartment, where there were two bedrooms with a bathroom between them. Cassie took a step toward the sound, but Chris' hand shot out and grabbed her wrist.

His eyes were wide. "Are you sure?"

"Let me do my thing," she said, slipping out of his grasp.

The truth was that Cassie felt off-kilter. It wasn't because she was dealing with an unknown entity—she was used to that by now—but because they were on a precipice. Her instincts were at war with each other, goading her into looking over the edge and backing away before anyone could get hurt.

But she wouldn't solve this case by burying her head in the sand. Taking a deep breath, she squared her shoulders and stalked into the hallway.

It was carpeted in lush gray that reminded her of storm clouds after they had released their moisture in a torrential downpour. A light flickered on overhead, helping illuminate their way, and she heard Chris swear under his breath. Sometimes she forgot other people weren't ready to expect the unexpected like she was.

Two of the doors in the hallway were open, one leading to the bathroom and one leading to a bare-bones bedroom that she assumed was the spare. The other door, which had been closed, swung open, creaking on its hinges.

"I will never, ever get used to this," Chris whispered.

Cassie ignored him, drawn forward by the promise of answers and something more ethereal. It was strange that she had yet to see the entity in its corporeal form here where it should be strongest, but perhaps it was expelling too much energy controlling physical objects to appear.

Stepping through the door, Cassie felt the temperature drop several degrees. Goosebumps erupted along her skin. Like the rest of the apartment, it appeared untouched. The bed was made and everything had been put in its place. But unlike the rest of the space, it felt desecrated.

Maybe because the cold breeze and thick scent of violets wafting around the room made her think of a graveyard.

Chris stopped at the doorway, his gun pointed to the floor as he took in the scene before them. "Looks the same as the photos the police took after she disappeared. One of her neighbors remembers seeing her come back that night, so they know she was here." He shuddered. "Is the AC on or something? It's freezing."

"That's not the AC." Cassie glanced his way and laughed when he blanched. "Don't worry, you can stay there and guard the door. I'll look around, see if I can spot anything."

"I'm not afraid of a little cold air," Chris said, though he didn't step into the room.

Cassie closed her eyes and imagined the space in her mind, picturing the bed and nightstand, the dresser and wardrobe, the bookshelf and trunk. She reached out her hands at the same time she felt around with something less corporeal. Everywhere had energy signatures, some as faint as a slight buzz at the nape of her neck, and some as strong as a punch to the gut. This room was a cyclone of energy pulling her in every direction until she felt dizzy and had to force her eyes open.

When she did, she realized she'd been spinning in a circle, and now she faced the bookshelf, which held about a dozen novels, a few non-fiction tomes, and some fake flowers. On the center shelf was a picture of two women, cheek to cheek, smiling up at the camera. She picked it up, knowing they looked nothing like the two sisters from the painting, yet her mind wandered back to the moment where she'd felt like she could read the thoughts running through their minds. On the left was Millie, eyes bright and smile wide, and on the right was Maxine, her lips tipped up into a sardonic smile even as her gaze remained clouded in dark shadows.

"What'd you find?" Chris asked from the doorway.

She walked over and handed him the photo. "I was drawn to this."

"Millie and Max," he said, looking at the frame in his hands. "They look happy. Wonder how long ago this was."

"Millie doesn't have an engagement ring on her finger," Cassie said. "But otherwise, it could've been from any time in the last few years leading up to her disappearance."

Another cold chill chased its way down Cassie's spine, and she looked past Chris to the figure that had appeared at the other end of the hall. The woman had manifested as she always did, with her head bowed and her face hidden by a curtain of hair.

"Millie?" Cassie whispered.

Chris followed Cassie's gaze over his shoulder, as though he'd be able to see her standing there. "She's here?"

Cassie ignored him. Once again, the entity didn't move a muscle, didn't bother looking up and meeting her gaze. Anger and frustration and pain radiated off it in waves, so thick and cloying that it made her dizzy. And though she hadn't known Millie in life, those emotions felt too strong and overwhelming to belong to her.

Sucking in a surprised breath, Cassie asked, "Maxine?"

The spirit's head snapped up, meeting Cassie's eyes for the first time. Max's were shadowed, just like they had been in that picture, though now they were as gray and colorless as her skin. As their gazes collided, Cassie was overcome with relief at having finally determined the entity's identity. But was it her own relief or Max's?

The feeling was short-lived. A second or two later, Max's jaw unhinged, and she let out a frustrated wail that sent another wave of cold barreling toward them. It was so strong and sudden, Chris sucked in a surprised breath, dropping the picture and clasping his gun with both hands.

Then Maxine charged.

One second, she was standing there at the end of the hallway, and the next, she was flying toward them, hair whipping out behind her as her mouth grew larger, as though she wanted to consume them whole. Cassie had no idea if Max was capable of hurting Chris, but she didn't want to take the chance. Shoving him against the wall, she took the brunt of Max's force, barely reinforcing her psychic barrier in time.

Max didn't manage to get inside Cassie's head, but the blow made her cry out in shock and pain, and she stumbled back until she hit something solid. Pain lanced up her back from where she'd run into the dresser, and only when it dissipated did Cassie realize Chris was squatting in front of her, calling her name and asking if she was all right.

"I'm fine," she groaned, not remembering when she fell to the floor. "She just surprised me."

"We should get out of here," Chris said, standing and offering his hand.

Cassie took it, getting to her feet and assessing her injuries. She might have a bruise on the small of her back tomorrow, but otherwise she was fine. In fact, she felt better than fine—she felt normal. The pressure that had sat on her shoulders since she'd entered the apartment was gone, as was the chill that had clung to every surface of the room.

"I think she's gone," Cassie said. "I don't feel her anymore."

"Better safe than sorry," Chris said. "At least we know it's Maxine and not Millie now." He scrubbed a hand over his face. "How that helps us, I have no idea."

"It means Max is the one who stuck around with unfinished business, not Millie." Cassie noticed another picture frame on the floor, face down from where she'd knocked it off the dresser. Bending to pick it up, she said, "She's more powerful here. She's connected to Millie's death somehow."

Chris groaned. "Now we've got two cases to solve." When he noticed her staring at the photograph in her hands, he leaned over to get a better look at it. "What's that?"

"Mountains," she said. "At sunrise. Looks like Millie was geared up to do some hiking."

"Looks like it could be here in Tennessee," Chris said, leaning closer. "Are those violets over there on the left?"

Cassie brought the photograph closer to her face, stomach swooping with excitement and anticipation. "Looks like it."

"What do you think it means?" Chris asked.

With a sigh, Cassie tore her gaze away from the photo to meet his eyes.

"I have no idea."

22

It had taken Lorraine a good ten minutes to convince herself to get out of her car and do what she'd set out to do. After her run-in with Blackwood, she'd had a normal day at work. Nothing had gone wrong at all, and Warden Wickham had stayed out of her hair for an entire eight hours. There was no doubt he knew the proposition Blackwood had come to her with. In fact, she was sure he was keeping his distance for now, showing her how easy life could be if she did as she was told.

But Lorraine was tired of being the good girl.

The sweetheart.

The one who never rocked the boat.

She was tired of being tired. And afraid. And ashamed.

As much as she hated to admit it, she'd felt trapped ever since her mother was diagnosed. She was mad at the cancer for what it had done to her mother and for what it had taken away from her. It wasn't often that she allowed herself to think of how different her life could've been if her mom hadn't gotten sick, but lately, she couldn't keep those scenarios from taking over her every waking thought. It made her bolder.

Which was why, after dinner, Lorraine had told her mother that she would be meeting a couple of friends and not to wait up for her.

Jacqueline's entire face lit up with excitement for her daughter, since Lorraine rarely went out. In fact, she'd asked a million questions, and Lorraine had to keep her answers short so as not to reveal her lies. These days, she only had two friends, and neither were in town at the moment.

Lorraine had listened to Jason's voicemail on her lunch break, away from the warden's prying eyes. She'd been disappointed by Jason's choice to head to Nashville, but not surprised. He'd been champing at the bit ever since Cassie left. Something told Lorraine the other woman wouldn't appreciate him showing up unannounced, but it wasn't her business to call him up and talk him out of it. Not that he'd asked for her advice.

But at least Lorraine had been tasked with stopping by Cassie's house to take care of Apollo and Bear. Silver linings, and all that.

With Cassie and Jason too far away and too busy to help her, Lorraine turned to the one other person in a position to help her. She and Assistant Chief of Police Adelaide Harris weren't close, but Lorraine trusted the woman to give her sound advice, not just as a police officer, but also as a friend. Or, at least, a friend of a friend.

Armed with confidence that was shaky at best, Lorraine walked up to the front of the Savannah Police Department and through the front doors. The sun had already crept below the horizon, but she'd called ahead to see if Harris was still in her office. Turned out that she was as much of a workaholic as Lorraine and didn't like to go home until her desk was clear.

The officer at the front desk checked her in and told her to wait while she retrieved Adelaide. A few minutes later, she appeared from the back wearing a tan pants suit, charcoal dress shirt, and high heeled boots that were as practical as they were stylish. As always, her hair was drawn back in a slick ponytail, and she wore a pleasant smile on her face.

"Lorraine," Harris said, reaching for her hand. "Good to see you."

"Thank you for meeting me," Lorraine said, trying not to wince at the surprising grip of Adelaide's handshake. "I know it's late and you probably have better things to do."

Harris waved a hand. "I could use the break. I was glad to hear from you."

"You were?"

Harris shrugged and turned on her heel, leading Lorraine down the long hallway and to her office. "I know we don't talk often, but Cassie and Jason have nothing but incredible things to say about you and your work." Waiting for Lorraine to enter before closing the door, she walked around her desk, gesturing for Lorraine to occupy the seat across from her. "It means a lot to all of us that you're as dedicated as they are. You've been extremely helpful."

Feeling her cheeks starting to blush, Lorraine sank into her chair and clutched her bag to her chest, looking everywhere but at Harris. Her office was modest and organized, not quite barren, but not homey. For someone who spent such a considerable amount of time there, she hadn't put her own personal touches on it.

"Thank you," Lorraine replied. "That means a lot, especially coming from you."

Smirking, Harris studied Lorraine for a moment before asking, "I hope you know you're welcome here any time, for whatever reason. But with that said—why *are* you here? You were vague on the phone."

Lorraine could feel her blush deepen. "Sorry about that. I wasn't sure how much I could—or should—say. This is all kind of new territory for me."

Sitting up a little straighter, Harris asked. "Are you in trouble?"

"No," Lorraine was quick to say. "Well, yes. Maybe?" Groaning, she put her face in her hands. "I don't know."

"Why don't you start from the beginning? I usually find that's the easiest route."

Sighing, Lorraine uncovered her face and met Harris' gaze with a sheepish smile. And then she proceeded to tell her everything that had happened that day, starting with Blackwood's appearance at her desk and his less-than-veiled threat, and Warden Wickham's unusually pleasant behavior. She had to backtrack once or twice to explain in more detail about her mother's illness and how she had first met David at the prison a little over a year ago, but Harris was a quick study and kept up with the narrative.

"I see," she said, once Lorraine was finished. "That's quite a lot to consider."

"What should I do?"

"I don't think that's the real question here."

Furrowing her brows, Lorraine cocked her head to one side. "I don't understand."

"Considering you're here and not on Blackwood's doorstep, I assume you have no interest in throwing Jason or Cassie under the bus, right?"

"Of course not," Lorraine said. "I could never do that to them."

"Exactly," Harris said, nodding as if the answer were obvious. "It's not a question of *what* you should do, but *how* you should do it. You've already decided you're not going to give into Blackwood's demands, so what you really came here for is help in figuring out how to do that—how to keep Jason, Cassie, *and* your mom safe while showing Blackwood and Wickham you're not a pushover. Maybe even giving them a taste of their own medicine."

Lorraine's laugh was a little startled. "Yeah, I guess you're right. But I don't even know where to start."

"Like I said, I always like to start at the beginning." Harris spun in her chair to face the wall of filing cabinets behind her. She riffled through the top drawer of one and pulled out a folder before turning to the bottom drawer and retrieving a second. Slapping them both on the desk between them, she said, "This is everything I have on both Blackwood and Wickham. Well, everything that can be substantiated, that is."

Lorraine's jaw dropped open.

"Unfortunately, it's nothing we can arrest either of them for or we would've done it already."

"I don't want to get them in trouble," Lorraine said, but she couldn't tear her eyes from the folders, wondering what kind of information could be inside. "I just want to keep my mom safe."

"Might be hard to accomplish one without the other. Blackwood was good at covering his tracks—until he wasn't. Wickham is not as subtle, but he's got a lot of powerful people in his pocket. You don't need to be careful when you've got friends like his."

"Are those my only two options? Either get them both arrested or worry about what they might do to us?"

Harris drummed her fingers on her desk for a moment. "Not necessarily. Cassie has already vouched for you, but I hope you'll humor me when I ask you this." She paused, waiting until she had Lorraine's full attention. "I know you're worried and you've got a lot on the line right now, but I need to know if I can trust you."

Lorraine considered the question, really taking a moment to think about her response. On the one hand, she'd do anything to keep her mother safe. On the other, she had a moral code she couldn't ignore. It's what had brought her to Harris' desk to begin with. There had to be a way to protect her mom and make sure Blackwood and Wickham could no longer bully people into doing their dirty work for them.

Finally, Lorraine squared her shoulders. "Yes. You can."

Harris nodded her head like it was the answer she'd expected all along. "Good. I've got some more information at my house. Let's just say it's less substantiated but a lot more damaging. David always had his eye on Wickham, and I had my misgivings about Blackwood, although neither of them had given me cause to look into them deeper. Not with everything else we had going on, especially with restructuring the department."

"And your promotion," Lorraine added.

Harris smirked. "That too. But this is as good of a reason as any, and I'd love for you to come over some night and look at what I have. Considering you've worked with Wickham for a while now, you've probably got some insight. Maybe together we can find a way to get them off your back, at the very least."

A weight lifted from Lorraine's shoulders in an instant. "Thank you, Adelaide. I can't tell you how much this means to me."

"Don't mention it," Harris said with a wave of her hand. "After David died, I wasn't sure I'd ever find my footing again. Cassie made sure I was always on solid ground. I owe her a lot, and I know if she were here, she wouldn't hesitate to help you. I wouldn't be able to live with myself if I didn't do the same."

"She's a great investigator," Lorraine said. "And a good friend."

Eyebrows pinching together, Harris asked, "Why didn't you go to Jason about this?"

"Did he not mention anything to you?" When Harris shook her head in confusion, Lorraine explained. "He's in Nashville. We found a possible lead on our Apex problem. He decided to take matters into his own hands and head down there."

"And I'm sure the presence of one Agent Viotto had nothing to do with it either," Harris said, eyes sparkling with mischief.

"My thoughts exactly," Lorraine said with a laugh, feeling lighter now that they were no longer talking about her problems. "I'm not sure how Cassie took it. I haven't heard from either of them since he got there."

"If I know Cassie—and I do—she'll see right through him and any flimsy excuse he can come up with." With a sigh that sounded equal parts envious and adoring, Harris added, "But only death would drive those two apart, and even then, I'm not sure it would stick."

23

Cassie waited until Chris pulled the vehicle to the curb outside her hotel to unbuckle her seatbelt, but she didn't make a move to get out of the car. They had grabbed dinner and talked about her experience at Millie's apartment, and Cassie's thoughts were still back in that bedroom, replaying the way Maxine had revealed her identity and attacked.

Except, Cassie reminded herself, she hadn't attacked. Cassie was convinced Max had wanted her to see that photo of Millie and Governor Warren hiking in the Smoky Mountains, surrounded by violets. There was something important about that scent, something Max was trying to convey to her, but as much as Cassie and Chris had wracked their brains, they couldn't figure it out. And Max had been silent since their last encounter.

"Were you expecting a visitor?" Chris asked, nodding toward the front of the hotel where a man sat on a bench, staring at their car.

"This time, yes," Cassie said, allowing a ghost of a smile to appear on her face as she took in Jason's form, from the stiffness of his shoulders to the warmth of his eyes. They'd decided that even though it was smarter not to be seen together often while they were both in Nashville, they needed a night to get back on solid ground. "He texted me at dinner asking if we could talk."

"In my experience, those words never bode well."

Cassie patted Chris' arm at the same time she hooked her fingers into the latch to open the car door. "If anyone has a bone to pick, it's me. I think I'll be okay."

"I know," Chris said, sounding a touch contrite. "Let me know if you need anything. Otherwise, I'll see you tomorrow."

With a nod, Cassie stepped out onto the curb, waiting for Chris to pull away before turning to face Jason, who had stood from his spot on the bench but hadn't approached. She appreciated him leaving the ball in her court, but she hated this uncertainty between them. The beginning of their relationship had been awkward and slow and embarrassing, and now that they'd fallen into a more comfortable routine with each other, she didn't like the idea of going backwards.

Striding over, Cassie stepped in close and stood on her tiptoes to whisper a kiss over his lips. Startled, Jason hesitated for only a fraction of a moment before he wrapped his arms around her waist and pulled her to his chest, deepening the kiss until she no longer noticed the feel of the breeze against her skin or the sound of crickets singing from the nearby bushes.

When they finally broke apart, the tension in Jason's shoulders had eased and his warm eyes had turned molten. "Don't get any ideas," she chided. "I need to call Harris and you need a shower."

Jason winced. "Yeah, sorry about that. It was a long day."

"Tell me about it," Cassie said. "I've got a lot to fill you in on, too. But later."

Strolling through the front doors of the hotel hand in hand, Cassie led Jason up to her room, unlocking the door and throwing her purse down on the bed before heading into the bathroom to read the note housekeeping had placed there, stating they had replaced the blown lightbulb and broken hairdryer. Meanwhile, Jason searched all the obvious places Apex could've planted listening devices and came up with none.

"Guess that's a good sign," he said.

"Hope so. You should be good to go with the shower," she said. "She's been quiet since our last run-in, but if it starts acting up, I'd get out sooner rather than later. Trust me on that one."

Grinning, Jason planted a kiss on Cassie's cheek and patted her butt as she left the bathroom. She rolled her eyes, but her heart fluttered at his overt affection. Neither one of them was silly by nature, but their flirtation brought out a different side to them both. It was nice to return to some semblance of normalcy.

Cassie waited until the shower had been running for a minute or so before dialing Harris' cell phone number. It rang twice before the other woman picked up, a smile in her voice.

"Hey, you must be psychic or something. I was just talking about you."

"Very funny," Cassie said, but she couldn't stop the grin that spread over her face. "Good things, I hope?"

"Always." There was a brief pause. "Lorraine stopped by."

Cassie sat up straighter. "Is everything okay?"

Harris spoke over the sound of jangling keys. "Yes and no. She's fine, but she had a run-in with Richard Blackwood."

Cassie pursed her lips. "What does he want with her? And are you just getting home?"

"Don't you dare judge me. You work harder and longer than I do." There was the creak of a door hinge and the subsequent sliding of a deadbolt before Harris spoke again. "Apparently, Blackwood tried to recruit Lorraine to the dark side."

"To do what?"

"Enact a little revenge on Jason for taking those pictures of his affair. He wasn't subtle when he threatened her mom, either. But instead of giving in, she came to me. She wants to find a way to even the playing field—without getting anyone else in trouble. That includes you and Jason, as well as her mom. I don't know how you were lucky enough to get her on our side, but we better do our best to make sure she stays there."

"It was David," Cassie said. "He's the one who first reached out to her. First saw her potential."

The line went silent as they both were swept up in memories of David. "I love that he still finds a way to help us, even after he's gone."

"Me too," Cassie said, allowing the emotion to spread through her for a moment before clearing her throat and refocusing. "What are you and Lorraine going to do?"

"Go through all the information I have on Blackwood and Wickham to see if she can connect any dots. She's not too interested in rocking the boat and getting them arrested, not to mention how long it would take to build a case. But we're looking for something we can use as leverage."

"Mutually assured destruction," Cassie said.

"Exactly." Harris groaned like she had just flopped onto her couch. "Despite you *actually* being psychic, something tells me you were calling for another reason."

"We're making progress on the case. Turns out the entity is Millie's sister Maxine, and she's dropping clues left and right. I just can't figure out what they mean."

"You will," Harris said, with more confidence than Cassie felt.

"I'm more concerned about the lack of progress we're making on the Apex angle." Cassie pinched the bridge of her nose. "You heard about Jason showing up unannounced?"

"Oh yeah," Harris said, the hint of a chuckle in her voice. "How'd that go over?"

"Not well," Cassie said. "Partly because the entity is playing puppet master with my emotions. And partly because—"

"—it pissed you the hell off?"

"Something like that." Cassie stood from the bed and walked over to the window, parting the curtains to peer at Nashville's city lights peppering the night like twinkling stars. "But he wants to follow a lead on a disgruntled former employee. I just don't like the idea that he's here, so close to Anastasia and one of Apex's central hubs—especially now that Blackwood has threatened Lorraine."

"Don't worry about Lorraine," Harris said. "I'll keep an eye on her. She and her mother will be safe. You two focus on Apex and let me know if I can do anything from here."

"Appreciate that." When the shower cut off, Cassie returned to perch on the edge of the bed. "Jason's just getting out of the shower. I should go."

"Are you two going to kiss and make up?" Harris asked, and Cassie could hear the waggle in her eyebrows.

"That's none of your business," Cassie said, her tone playful. "You have any advice?"

Harris was silent for a moment. "You and Jason have a solid relationship. He's overbearing because he cares, but that's not an excuse to push your boundaries. You're allowed to stand your ground. Relationships are a lot of work, but when you find the right person, you realize you don't mind putting in the effort."

"Sound advice," Cassie said, impressed.

"You don't have to sound so shocked, Quinn."

"Just wondering why you never applied that same sentiment to your relationship with my sister."

"I take back everything nice I've ever said about you. Next time I talk to Laura, I'm getting all the dirt on you from when you were an awkward teenager."

"She might think you're cute, but she's my sister. You can't buy that kind of loyalty."

"I can be very persuasive," Harris said, and this time there was no doubt in Cassie's mind that she was waggling her eyebrows.

"Gross," Cassie said. "I'm telling her you're a perv."

"She already knows."

Cassie groaned. "Goodbye, Adelaide."

"Goodbye, Cassie."

Hanging up, Cassie tossed her phone onto the bed and flopped back, only to jolt up again a second later when Jason spoke.

"How's Harris doing?"

"You scared me to death," Cassie said, holding her chest and willing her beating heart to slow. "How long were you listening?"

Smiling, Jason stood there in fresh boxers and a new t-shirt. "Just the very end."

Cassie eyed his change of clothes. "You came prepared."

"Prepare for the best, expect the worst."

"I don't think that's how the saying goes."

"No?" He smiled, sauntering over. "It's worked out for me so far."

Cassie swallowed, uncomfortable with the charge in the air. It wasn't that she didn't want him to spend the night—she just knew they had to get a few things out of the way first. "Richard Blackwood tried to coerce Lorraine into helping him destroy your business and reputation. He threatened her mother."

The words had the same effect as an ice-cold shower. Jason's jaw dropped in surprise, and he backed up a step, taking a moment to digest her words. "Is she all right? Did anything happen? Does Harris know?"

"She's the one who told me," Cassie said. "Lorraine is fine. So is her mother. He approached her at work and gave her an ultimatum. She went to Harris for help. They'll figure something out together."

Dragging a hand down his face, Jason groaned. "Do you think it's coincidence that it happened the same day I flew out?"

"I don't know. If Apex hadn't dropped him, I would've been inclined to think they were behind this." Cassie chose her next words with extreme care. "As much as I appreciate you being here, I think Lorraine might need your help more than I do."

Jason dropped his hand and looked down at her, a mix of emotions she couldn't quite decipher on his face. "I thought you said Harris was keeping an eye on her."

"She is, but this is about *you*. Don't you think you should go back and help her take care of it?"

Pain lanced its way across Jason's face, and he stepped around Cassie to sit on the edge of the bed. He kept at least a foot of space between them. "Of course I don't want her to deal with that on her own, but Omega will only speak to us if we're both there."

She sat up straighter. "He agreed to meet?"

"Not yet. He wants to make sure we're willing to put our money where our mouth is. Apex has information on someone named Pearl Everly. Do you think you can find out who she is and what they have on her?"

Cassie sputtered. "I have limited access to Apex's records, and the second I go digging, alarms will go off. I can't risk looking into her without catching their attention."

"What about Viotto?"

"He might be able to, but I haven't told him why you're here."

"We should keep it that way. Tell him you had a vision or something, but make sure he's quiet about it." Jason's eyes were feverish with excitement. "Omega is the answer to all our problems. I know it. I just need more time."

"How much more?" Cassie tried to keep the frustration out of her voice, but given the frown on Jason's face, she hadn't succeeded. "Because Blackwood won't follow your timetable. And neither will Apex."

Jason remained silent for a while, and Cassie could tell he was thinking through all his options. When he finally looked up and met her gaze, his eyes were hard. "You asked me to trust you. Now I'm asking you to do me the same courtesy. Harris is helping Lorraine. You're working the case with Agent Viotto. This is how I can contribute."

After a moment, she said, "Okay. I know Lorraine is in good hands, but we created this mess by taking that job from Coretta Blackwood. It's only fair we do everything we can to get home as soon as possible to help clean it up."

"Agreed," Jason said, leaning forward and placing a quick kiss on her cheek. "What do you want to do now?"

Cassie didn't miss the hope in his voice and written across his face. But she only had one thing on her mind.

"All I want right now is a good night's sleep."

24

If Cassie had any delusion of feeling rested by the time the sun peeked over the horizon, it was cast away with the latest version of her recurring nightmare. The hallmarks of the dream were all there, from the swirling fog, the faint breeze, and the weight of an invisible hand on her throat to the goosebumps that raced along her skin. Dirt and rain mixed with smoke to ground her in the present, but this time, she also caught a faint whiff of violets.

Having conscious thoughts during a dream was a surreal experience. She at once knew this wasn't real yet could do nothing to stop it from unfolding in front of her. The ability to analyze the nightmare in real-time was useful, but she couldn't stop frustration from building in her chest like a can of Coke that had been shaken too many times. The release never came, and all she could do was sit back and watch.

Footsteps indicated it was time for the figure to approach, lit from the back until it was just a silhouette amidst the haze surrounding her. From behind, a trickle of sensation announced the second figure. An unseen force turned her on the spot, and for the first time in over thirty days, something changed.

Instead of seeing the figure retreat into the fog, she came face to face with Chris, frozen as if he were a mere snapshot. Around his shoulders was a black cloud, distinct from the fog that filled her dreamscape. This had a weight to it, viscous and ethereal, like a being who could manipulate their cells to become incorporeal. Somewhere in the back of her mind, Cassie dredged up the name Maxine Abrahms.

As shocked as she was at the deviation in her nightmare, Cassie's attention was drawn to the red blossoming across Chris' chest. His eyes were wide with shock and pain and regret, his mouth open in a silent scream. It held for one second, two, three—and then the cloud disappeared in the blink of an eye. Like hitting the fast-forward button on a movie, Chris was pulled backward in double time, his hand reaching out for her like it had so many times before.

Jerked around to face forward again, Cassie's gaze locked on the raised gun and the finger that lay against the trigger. Head swirling with the visual of Chris' death, she didn't have time to think about looking up to the person's face to see if she could identify them before the sound of a gunshot woke her from her nightmare.

Cold dread invaded every cell of her body, but just like last time, she was unable to move. Unable to shiver against the ice that formed in her veins. She willed her arms and legs to stir, but it was like they belonged to someone else, not bothering to heed her commands. Tears formed in her eyes, but she couldn't blink them away. A soft whimper escaped her mouth—the only rebellion she could muster against the weight that kept her body in place.

Movement next to her caused a shock of panic and dread to surge through her body, and though she thrashed against her restraints, all she could do was lie there and wait. If only she could open her eyes and see what monster stalked her in the night. Instead, she was forced to live in the darkness, alone and—

"Cassie?" a voice said, gentle and concerned. "Cassie, are you okay?"

Her name sent a surge of familiarity through her body that chased away the panic. Another whimper escaped her mouth, a little louder this time, and filled with fear and sorrow.

"Cassie," the person said. "Wake up."

Another weight landed on her shoulder, but this one was warm. It chased away the ice in her veins. As though she were experiencing a time lapse video, Cassie could feel her body thawing, and sensation returned first to her arms and chest, then to her legs and feet. Finally, she could move her head, and she turned to find Jason's large, expressive eyes staring down at her in concern.

"Hey," he said, voice gentle as he brushed a strand of hair out of her eyes. His own were still puffy with sleep. "You okay?"

Cassie's tongue was heavy in her mouth, dry and stuck in place, so all she could do was nod.

"Same nightmare?"

This time, Cassie shook her head.

As she got her bearings, Cassie's attention was drawn to the end of the bed. A woman stood there as though she'd been studying Cassie while she slept, her face no longer hidden by the curtain of greasy hair. Cassie could see Maxine now. Sallow skin and milk-white eyes greeted her, but there was no look of animosity—only curiosity and, perhaps, hope.

"Cassie?" Jason asked again.

Cassie turned to him, trying to unstick her tongue from the roof of her mouth. When it finally came free, she sucked in a deep breath and said, "I'm okay."

"What happened?"

Cassie looked back to the end of the bed, but Maxine was gone. The only indication she'd been there to begin with was the faint tendrils of black smoke fading into the darkness.

Sitting up, Cassie had to swallow a few times before she could speak. "Same nightmare, but different stuff happened this time. Chris—" Her voice caught as she remembered the wound to his chest. "I think Maxine froze the dream so I could see him. See that he was hurt."

Jason's brows furrowed. "Why would she help you?"

"I have no idea," Cassie said, staring at the end of the bed and willing the woman to reappear and give her some answers. "But it was so strange. I always thought the dream was about the day Piper attacked me. But Chris didn't get hurt then. She did. And it wasn't in the chest."

"It was the shoulder, wasn't—" The sharp ring of Jason's phone cut him off, and he rolled over to pick it off the nightstand. "It's Harris." He hit the answer button and putting it on speaker. "Hey, what's up? You're calling early."

Harris' voice was all business. "Is Cassie there? She wasn't answering her phone."

"Sorry," Cassie said, leaning closer to make sure Harris could hear her well enough. "I put it on silent last night."

"We have a problem."

Jason and Cassie stiffened and exchanged a look before he said, "What kind of problem?"

"Someone leaked Cassie's name to the press. They know she was the one Piper attacked. That she works for us and at the museum, and that the two of you work together as private investigators. It's a good thing you're both in Nashville right now because this just turned into a bigger shitshow than it already was."

Jason blew out a heavy breath. "What do we do?"

"Nothing right now," Harris said. "At the moment, people are trying to figure out why a random podcaster decided to fly across the country and attack a woman in Savannah. But soon—"

"They'll realize I've been working with you as a psychic consultant." Cassie's heart thumped so loud in her chest, it was all she could hear for a moment. "They'll have questions."

"We've managed to keep your name out of the papers and away from local and national interest for years," Harris reassured her. "This won't be any different. I just need time to think of a strategy."

"Who do you think leaked it?" Jason asked.

"Your guess is as good as mine," Harris said. "But it's between Blackwood and Apex. Neither of them are happy with you, and stirring the pot like this has the benefit of serving as a distraction and making it easier to get you guys to do what they want." A phone rang in the background, but Harris didn't acknowledge it. "And there's something else."

Cassie wasn't sure she could take more. "What is it?"

The phone stopped ringing, and Cassie could hear the relief in Harris' voice, even as she delivered their next blow. "Agatha Webster died last night."

Jason's eyes grew wide. "Douglas Hughes' mother?"

Before Harris could answer, the ringing started up again. "Yeah. Doesn't look suspicious from what I can tell, but I thought you should know. Look, I have to go. Keep an ear to the ground at Apex, all right? I want to know if they were behind this and what they're hoping to get out of it. I'm meeting with Lorraine tonight, and we'll see if we can figure out if Blackwood was involved, too."

Jason hung up after their goodbyes, and he and Cassie slumped back onto the bed, their fingers gravitating toward each other until they were entwined. Cassie felt as heavy as a tree, but Jason's hand in hers was enough to give her the strength she needed to attack the day—whatever else it decided to throw her way.

Rolling over, Cassie threw an arm and leg across Jason's body and clung to him like he was the only flotation device in a raging sea. "I'm sorry about last night."

Jason wrapped his free arm around her and squeezed. "I'm sorry too. Considering the amount of stress we're both under, we really shouldn't be surprised if tensions get high. We just have to remember we're both trying to accomplish the same thing."

She nodded into his chest. "Apex is our number one priority."

Just then, the television on the dresser across from the bed flicked on, the volume rising until it was loud enough to make Cassie wince. Just when she thought she couldn't take it anymore, it cut off with a loud pop and the faint smell of smoke.

Groaning, Cassie sat up and glared at the TV. "Maxine, you need to stop breaking things. They're going to charge me for that!"

In answer, the air conditioning kicked on and sent an icy blast of air careening toward the bed.

"Maxine is doing that?" Jason asked, pulling the covers up to his chin as he shivered against the chill. "Why?"

"My guess is that she doesn't want to play second fiddle to our case against Apex." When the machine switched over to a gentle heat, balancing out the temperature of the room, Cassie rolled her eyes. "I haven't forgotten about you or Millie. I promise I'll figure out what happened to her—to both of you."

"I'm not sure whether to be scared or grateful," Jason said. "But at least she's trying to be helpful."

"For now," Cassie grumbled. Then, turning to him, "Hey, do I seem different to you?"

Jason searched her face. "Different how?"

"I don't know. Tainted, somehow? Like I've got a cloud hanging over my head?"

Jason shook his head. "You look the same to me." Leaning close, he ghosted a kiss over her lips. "Feel the same too."

Smiling against his touch, Cassie leaned in to deepen the kiss, mentally calculating how long they had before Robert picked her up in the company car. But just as she rolled on top of Jason with a mischievous smile on her face, she heard the shower turn on at the same time the lights in the bathroom flickered to life.

Groaning, Cassie glared at the empty air in the middle of the hotel room. She couldn't see Maxine, but she knew she was there, watching them with a mixture of annoyance and impatience.

Cassie pushed off of Jason as he groaned in protest. "I'm going, I'm going."

Sitting up, Jason crossed his arms over his chest. "Please tell Maxine that I'm not happy with her right now."

Another icy blast of air conditioning hit the bed, causing Jason to burrow under the blankets again.

"She knows," Cassie called over her shoulder as she tossed her hair up in a bun and prayed Max was willing to give her at least ten minutes of hot water to kickstart her day. "And she doesn't care."

25

Cassie had, indeed, gotten ten glorious, uninterrupted minutes of warm water to take a shower, and despite all the electric shocks she got on her way out the door, she couldn't complain. While Jason went off to find out more about the former Apex employee, Omega, she headed back to headquarters to meet up with Chris. Armed with yesterday's revelations, and sporting a bright yellow sundress like armor, she was ready to get to the bottom of this case.

Chris had met her at his car with a pair of coffees in hand, one of which he handed her without preamble. And then he handed her a folded piece of paper, which she opened to reveal a scrawl of notes.

"What's this?"

Chris waited until they were inside the car before he spoke. "The information you asked for last night."

"On Pearl Everly?" Cassie looked at his speedy handwriting more closely. "All ready?"

"You said it was important."

"And you're sure no one will be able to tell you accessed this information?"

"As sure as I can be." Chris navigated the car out of the garage and onto the road. "You want to tell me what this is all about?"

"I do," she said, drawing the word out and filling it with regret.

"But you won't?"

"I can't. Not yet anyway. Once I find out more concrete information, I'll let you know what's going on. Until then, it's better if you're out of the loop. Plausible deniability and all that."

Cassie skimmed the piece of paper out of curiosity. Pearl Everly was a young girl who had gone missing years ago. Case still unsolved. There were a few other details, but information was sparse and without more context, Cassie couldn't figure out why Omega would be interested in her disappearance. But right now, that was Jason's problem.

Got it, she texted him.

Jason's answer was immediate. *I'll let him know.*

Before Cassie knew it, Chris had pulled into a parking spot in front of the building Maxine used to live in. Peering out of the windshield, Cassie blinked against the morning sun reflecting off the apartment complex's windows and took in the crumbling brick façade. A few people smoked cigarettes and clutched coffees to their chests as they stared down at cracked sidewalks and half-barren shrubs out front.

"This is a far cry from the place Millie lived in," she said, leaning back and blinking the spots from her eyes.

"Used to be an old factory, I think. The owners were hoping once it became a residential area, the rest of the neighborhood would follow, but it never did."

"Interesting that Millie dated the governor of Kentucky and lived in a nice apartment while her sister lived here and died of a drug overdose."

Chris hunched his shoulders and looked like he was waiting for a bomb to drop on them. After a few seconds without witnessing the end of the world, he relaxed and blew out a breath.

Cassie's laugh was strangled with curiosity and confusion. "What was that for?"

"Wasn't sure if Maxine would be mad about what you'd said. She's a little bit"—he lowered his voice to just above a whisper—"volatile."

Cassie lowered her voice, too, but it was more of a stage whisper.

"Max isn't here right now. But if you'd like to leave a message, she'll get back to you as soon as she can."

"I thought she was with you all the time?"

"Kind of. Spirits come and go. They fade from our realm and back into theirs depending on how much energy they have. After yesterday and this morning, she might be weak. Or she could be building up her energy to give us another show later on. Who knows?"

"I was kind of hoping you would," Chris said, pushing open his door and stepping out of the vehicle.

Cassie followed suit, shrugging again when she met him around the front of the car. "Max is an interesting spirit. She's haunting people rather than places, though it seems like she's capable of manifesting stronger in locations that mean something to her."

"Like her sister's apartment." When Cassie nodded, he continued. "That's what I meant. Why isn't she here at her own apartment? This is where she died, after all."

"Good question. But I don't have the answer to that."

They were quiet as they made their way up the front sidewalk, dodging loose concrete and weeds large enough to make Cassie concerned they may have sentience. No one paid them any mind when they entered the building, either because it was too early to show any interest, or they just weren't interesting enough to begin with.

Inside, Cassie stopped in the foyer and took it in. Despite the outside of the building having seen better days, the inside was clean, if a little worn, and smelled of lemon-scented disinfectant. The aroma made her nose twitch, and she had to rub away the sensation to stop herself from sneezing.

What caught her attention, however, was the spiritual activity. Like little pinpricks on a map, she could feel specters floating from apartment to apartment, meandering down hallways, and haunting dark corners of the basement. Most of them were faded—more whispers of light and shadow than anything else—and stuck in the rituals they'd occupied in life. None of them paid her any mind. All the better to focus on Max's case.

"Anything?" Chris asked, breaking her concentration.

"Nothing out of the ordinary," she said. "Come on, let's go meet Enrique."

Enrique Rivera was the site manager for this building and half a dozen others within a five-block radius. Chris had spoken to him on the phone the day before and set up an appointment. Unlike their meeting with Governor Warren, FBI credentials were more than enough to get them through the door here. He was willing to escort them up to Max's old apartment, where someone new was living, but had emphasized that he couldn't force the occupant to let them in to look around.

Enrique led them to a tiny elevator that chugged upward until it landed on the fifth floor. The three of them filed out and stopped in front of apartment 512. Without hesitation, Enrique knocked, and a few seconds later, a young woman answered the door in her nightgown, looking confused and a little worried. Her blonde hair was tied back in a braid, and the circles under her eyes were so deep they looked like bruises. Cassie's heart pounded against her ribcage as she thought the worst, but settled once she heard two young kids screaming and running around the apartment.

"Morning, Sylvia. Sorry to disturb you so early."

"It's not a problem," the woman responded, but she couldn't gather much energy to make her words sound genuine. "Everything okay? Did I miss another notice for maintenance?"

"No, no, you didn't miss anything," Enrique said, a kind smile gracing his face when the woman sagged in relief. "This is something else. I'm here with Agent Chris Viotto from the FBI and his colleague Cassie Quinn." When the woman's eyes went wide, Enrique rushed on. "Nothing to worry about. They just wanted to know if they could look at your apartment and take a couple pictures. They're investigating Maxine Abrahms' case."

"Oh," Sylvia said, moving a little to the side to block more of the apartment beyond. Whether she did it on purpose, Cassie couldn't tell. "I'm getting the twins ready for school. Is it possible—"

"It won't take more than five minutes," Chris said, stepping forward and reaching out his hand. "We're so sorry to disturb you this early, but it's vital that we just do a quick walkthrough."

Sylvia shook Chris' hand, dropping it after a single pump. When she spoke again, her voice was so low, Cassie had to lean forward to hear. "That woman died two years ago. What are you hoping to find?"

"We're not sure," Chris said. "But we'll know it when we see it. And I promise not to disturb any of your belongings. We'll be in and out, and you'll never see us again."

Glancing between Chris and Enrique, Sylvia looked like she was wrestling between her desire to refuse their request and just get it over with. Cassie saw the moment she relented, resisting the urge to pump her fist in victory.

"Five minutes," Sylvia said, not budging from the doorway. "And please don't mention anything about what happened here in front of my kids. I'd rather they not know."

"Of course," Chris said, putting on his best choir boy face. "Thank you so much for your time."

With another studious look at both Chris and Cassie, Sylvia stepped to the side and allowed the three of them to enter. The apartment carried with it the faint aroma of maple syrup and coffee, and Cassie spotted two plates on the kitchen table with a half-eaten breakfast and a coffee cup that appeared untouched.

A boy and a girl around five years old chased each other around the table so fast they were nothing more than blurs of curly brown hair and red and blue pajamas. They screamed and giggled with joy, their little feet pounding into the floor so loudly that Cassie winced in sympathy for their downstairs neighbors.

"Kids," Sylvia said, more exasperated than angry. "Sit down and finish your breakfast or we're going to be late."

"Who are they?" the boy said, coming to a halt and eyeing Cassie and Chris with interest.

"Friends of Mommy's. You remember Mr. Rivera?"

"Buenos días, Señor Rivera," the kids chorused.

"Buenos días," he replied, his face going soft at their greeting. "What's for breakfast?"

"Pancakes!" The girl slid into her seat and cut off a chunk before spearing it with her fork and shoving it in her mouth, maple syrup running down her chin.

With Enrique distracting the kids, Sylvia turned to Cassie and Chris, motioning for them to follow her. "This way."

She led them through the kitchen and into the living room, where she switched off the cartoons blaring from the small television sitting on a peeling entertainment stand. Toys were strewn about the floor, and a fine layer of dust sat on every surface.

"This is where she was found," Sylvia said, a tiny shiver passing through her body.

Chris looked at Cassie, but she didn't get so much as a cold breeze or a whiff of violets. Still, she took out her phone and snapped a couple pictures, just in case. But even at a quick glance, she could tell the camera hadn't picked up anything they couldn't see with their own eyes.

"Would it be okay if we looked at her bedroom?" she asked. "Do you know which one it was?"

With a wave, Sylvia led them deeper into the apartment. "It's a mess," she said, "so I'm not sure what you'll be able to see, but you can look."

The woman stepped into what appeared to be the master bedroom. A queen size bed, a pair of dressers, a small desk, and a full-length mirror left little space to squeeze over to the other side to get to the closets. The bed was unmade, and clothes were piled around the room, along with a few toys. Jewelry and makeup littered the surface of one of the dressers. Cassie tried not to look too closely, but she couldn't help noticing a few overdue bills on the desk.

Chris looked to Cassie again, but this time, she waited a moment before delivering the disappointing news. Stepping farther into the room, she turned her back to the others so she could better concentrate on her other senses. But try as she might, Cassie couldn't pick up even the faintest trace of Maxine's spirit or any clue as to the cause of her overdose. She held up her phone and took a few pictures, fighting off the wave of disappointment when once again, nothing appeared out of the ordinary.

Turning back to Sylvia, Cassie plastered on her biggest smile. "Thank you so much for your time."

Sylvia cocked her head to the side, as though surprised they were done already. "Did you find what you were looking for?"

With a pointed glance at Chris, Cassie said, "Just like no news is good news, sometimes it's better when what you're hoping for isn't there."

"And what were you hoping for?" Sylvia asked.

"Anything the other officers weren't able to see."

That was, after all, her specialty.

26

IN UNDER TEN MINUTES, CHRIS AND CASSIE STOOD INSIDE A DIFFERENT apartment building and knocked on a different door. Though the previous complex wasn't luxurious by any stretch of the imagination, this one was one strong breeze away from being condemned. The smell of bleach didn't cover up the stench of urine in the entryway, and they'd had to take the stairs up to the third floor because the elevator was out of service.

Whoever had cleaned up the entryway hadn't bothered with the staircase, and the smell was so rancid, it made Cassie's eyes water. Bolting up the steps, the pair of them burst out onto the third floor, gulping breaths of air tainted with weed and popcorn, but it was a far cry from what they'd just come from.

Two years ago, Nashville's Chief of Police Darryl Lowe followed up on an anonymous call for a wellness check at Maxine's address. She lived there with her boyfriend, Parker Gibson, who had been out of town at the time. From what Cassie and Chris read about the guy in the police reports, he'd been detained a few times prior to Max's death for drug-related crimes. After her body was discovered, Parker couldn't afford rent anymore and moved out. Not long after that, he did a year of jailtime and now lived only a few blocks away from his former address. They hoped Parker would provide some more insight into Max's life and subsequent death.

Stopping in front of the door to Parker Gibson's apartment, Chris knocked sharply. They only waited a few seconds before the deadbolt scraped open and the door swung wide enough for the chain lock to pull taut. A pale man peered out at them from the crack, his eyes scrutinizing them for a moment before he spoke.

"Can I help you?"

"My name is Agent Chris Viotto, and this is my colleague, Cassie Quinn. We were hoping to ask you a few questions about Maxine Abrahms?"

The man furrowed his eyebrows, his gaze darting between the two of them before he licked his lips and stammered, "W-why? She's been dead for over a year."

"We're investigating her sister's disappearance," Cassie said, keeping her tone pleasant and even. They couldn't risk being turned away without answers, not after striking out at Max's old apartment. "We know the two of them were close, and that Max died two years to the day after Millie disappeared. We're just hoping to connect some dots. Figure out what happened to them."

Cassie saw the man's Adam's apple bob in his throat as he swallowed. There was a jitteriness to his movements that made her wonder if he was high or just paranoid. Maybe both. Disappointment hit her like a Mack truck. Even if he agreed to talk to them, how reliable would his story be?

Cassie jumped when the door shut with a click, the man disappearing behind it. But a second later, the slide of the chain lock ground out from the other side, and hope blossomed in her chest stronger than anything she'd experienced so far. That hope doubled when the door opened to reveal Parker Gibson standing there in a button-down shirt and slacks.

Cassie had to crane her neck to look up at him, taking in his long face and thin frame. He was built like a long-distance runner, and the cut of his shirt revealed taut muscles. His black hair was messy, but the shine of gel told her that it had been done on purpose, and his smooth jaw made him look younger than he was, despite the world-weariness in his darting green eyes. The tapping of his slender fingers against the doorframe was the only indication he was nervous to speak with them.

"Come in," he said, stepping to the side and allowing them to enter.

Chris gestured to the man's outfit. "Are you on your way out?"

"Interview today," he said. "Second one for this company. I've got about a half hour before I need to leave." He licked his lips again, though his gaze had settled on Cassie's. "Will that be enough time?"

"Should be," Chris answered. "Can we sit down somewhere?"

Parker startled a little, as though realizing he'd been rude not to offer. "Of course. The couch is comfortable."

He led them back through the hallway and into a tiny living room, which housed a battered love seat and recliner, plus a small television on an end table. Morning sunlight poured in through the curtainless windows, forcing Cassie to blink away the brightness until her eyes adjusted. The white paint only further illuminated the room, and despite various nails sticking out of the walls, there were no pictures hanging anywhere.

"Did you just move in?" Chris asked, picking one side of the sofa.

"Nah," Parker said, choosing the recliner. "Just not much of a decorator."

Cassie settled in next to Chris and was surprised to find it comfortable, despite its weathered look. "Thank you again for taking the time to talk to us. You must be surprised we're asking about Max after all this time."

Parker chewed on his lip. "If I'm being honest, it's kind of nice to talk about her. No one else does. Not with me, at least."

"No?" Chris asked. "Not even her parents?"

Parker huffed out a laugh. "They didn't like me very much when she was alive. Even less now that she's—" He broke off with a shrug, swallowing the word like it tasted bitter on his tongue. "I haven't talked to them at all."

"Why didn't they like you?"

"Because I'm an addict," Parker said, as though he were talking about something as simple as his height or eye color. "I've been sober since I got out of jail. Been working hard to get my feet back under me. Hasn't been easy, but I finally feel like things are looking up. I called the Abrahms once, but Max's father told me never to contact them again. Can't say I blame him for feeling that way."

"How come?"

Parker looked down at his hands in his lap, picking at the skin along one of his thumbs. "They think if it wasn't for my habit, Max never would've overdosed. Hard to argue with that logic," he said with a sigh. "If I could go back and do everything differently, I would."

Guilt stabbed at Cassie's chest, and she felt her heart break for Parker. When she'd first seen him at the door, she thought they'd run into another brick wall. But here he was, struggling to recover from everything that had happened to him.

"I'm sure I don't need to explain this to you," Chris said, his voice gentle, "but Max would've found another way to get her hands on that stuff if she really wanted to. You shouldn't blame yourself."

Parker's hands stilled, and when he looked up at the pair of them, his eyebrows were knit in confusion. "Max wouldn't have known where to get them. I know she could be kind of impulsive, but she never did the hard stuff. Not until that day."

Cassie sat up straight. "Wait, what?"

Parker looked at them like they'd each grown two heads. "Max wasn't an addict. Drank when we went out. Smoked weed once in a while. But that's it. I hid my drug use from her for most of our relationship. I knew she'd worry about losing me like she lost her sister, and I didn't want to scare her. But I also couldn't kick the habit. Not on my own, at least."

Chris turned to Cassie. "It was an opioid overdose. The police found injection marks on her forearm and all the paraphernalia around her. If she wasn't an addict—"

"You don't exactly start by shooting up," Cassie said. Tingles spread from the top of her head down to her toes as realization dawned on her.

Turning back to Parker, she asked, "A lot of people start with pills. Are you sure she'd never done any before?"

"Positive," Parker said, his words like steel. "We'd go to parties where they'd pass them around like candy and she always said no. That's when I first tried it. We got into a few arguments, so I stopped doing it when we were together. Eventually, I stopped telling her outright."

Cassie knew her next question would be difficult to say out loud and even more difficult for Parker to hear, but she had to know the answer. "Was Maxine suicidal?"

Parker chewed on the inside of his cheek and looked away. "Yes. She talked about it sometimes. Had some scars on her wrist from when she was younger. She'd gone to therapy in the past, but it hadn't helped. She wanted to go back, try again, but she didn't have health insurance."

"Makes sense why she did it on the anniversary of her sister's disappearance," Chris said.

A whisper of breath on the back of Cassie's neck sent a shiver down her spine, but instead of a blast of cold air, warmth enveloped her like a heavy blanket draped across her shoulders. A surge of compassion, gratitude, and love filled her chest until it felt like she'd burst. When tears pricked at her eyes, she tipped her head back to look at the ceiling, willing them not to spill over down her cheeks.

"I don't think she killed herself," Parker said, his voice low but steady. "On accident or on purpose."

That forced Cassie's gaze back to the man sitting across from them, but Chris spoke first. "Then what do you think happened?"

Parker blew out a breath, ruffling the hair along his forehead. "Don't know. I've had a lot of time to think about it since it happened, and it just doesn't make sense. But no one will listen to me."

"We will," Cassie said, her voice warbling. She swallowed, trying to steady the beating of her heart. "Tell us what you think, and we'll do everything we can to find out what happened to both Maxine and Millie."

Parker studied them for a moment before his shoulders sagged. At first, Cassie thought it was in defeat, but then she realized it was in relief. She could only imagine the number of people who had dismissed him and what he had to say because he was an addict—like his thoughts and feelings were tainted because of his drug habit. In reality, Parker Gibson seemed to be the only person still alive who gave a damn about Maxine and what had happened to her.

"Millie and Maxine were polar opposites," Parker said, leaning forward and bracing his arms on his legs like he was awaiting impact. "But they were close. I've got two brothers, and we were never like them. They fought and disagreed, but it never drove them apart. No matter what they were going through in their own lives, they'd drop everything to help the other one. I'd seen it more than once." One side of Parker's mouth tipped up in a wry smile. "Pissed me off a few times, too, when we had plans and Max ditched me for Millie. But looking back, I realized it's because I envied them. That closeness and trust."

The pain in Cassie's chest swelled, and she rubbed a hand over her heart to relieve some of the pressure. "It must've broken Maxine when Millie went missing."

"Max went out of her mind. She was relentless, calling people and posting things on social media. She never stopped looking for her. Never stopped hoping she'd come back. But after a while, everyone gave up. Even their parents."

"That must've been difficult for Max."

Parker shrugged. "She'd never been close to her parents. They played favorites, you know? Millie was the perfect one, and Max was the screwup. She never held it against her sister, but it was the basis for every argument she'd ever had with her parents. When they gave up, she wrote them off. She hadn't talked to them in months. If I hadn't called them to tell them what had happened, they might never have known."

"But you have to admit the timing is strange," Chris said. "Two years after Millie disappeared? I can understand why the authorities thought it was suicide."

Parker was already shaking his head before Chris had even finished his sentence. "I'm telling you, she wouldn't have done that. Max never gave up hope. There were nights where she'd cry herself to sleep, where she'd finally admit she thought Millie was dead, but she'd never stop looking for her, even if all she found was a body."

"If you don't think it was suicide," Cassie said, "and you don't think it was an accidental overdose. That means—"

"She was murdered," Chris finished. "Do you have any evidence to support that?"

"If I did, I would've handed it in already." The bitterness in Parker's voice was tangible. "All I know is that she kept meticulous notes about her sister's disappearance. She was doing her own investigation into what really happened that night. And when I was packing up to move out of our old place, I couldn't find any of it."

"Could she have thrown it away?" Chris asked.

"That was my first thought, but she had a lot of notes. I would've noticed if she'd just tossed them all in the garbage can."

"You think someone murdered her and took her notes."

"Yeah. But they didn't take everything. She had something on her when she died."

Cassie's heart pounded, and the warmth that had been enveloping her squeezed tighter. The scent of violets came and went like a spring breeze carrying the aroma from miles away. "What was it?"

Parker stood and walked into the only bedroom in the apartment. Chris and Cassie hardly had time to exchange a startled look before he was back, handing Cassie a piece of paper with black ink scrawled across it. It took her a few seconds to decipher Max's rushed handwriting.

"What does it say?" Chris asked, leaning closer.

"It just says *where did the money go?*"

Chris looked up at Parker. "Do you know what this means?"

Parker shook his head. "I've been wracking my brain, but I have no idea. It's not like anyone told me much about Millie's case." He looked down at his feet. "And I wasn't exactly in the right state of mind to pay attention when Max tried to talk to me about it."

A buzz from Cassie's purse had her pulling her phone out and checking the caller ID. It was Jason.

"Hey, what's—"

"We did it." Jason was breathless with excitement. "He agreed to meet us."

Cassie's head was so wrapped up in Max's story, she couldn't remember what Jason had been doing that morning. "Who?"

"Omega," he said, impatient. "The former employee."

"When?" she asked, pulse thundering. "Where?"

"Right now. Can you come meet me?"

27

Chris wasn't happy when Cassie dipped out on the rest of their day, even though she'd told him Jason had an emergency with his case. Not exactly a lie, but Chris looked like he suspected something more was going on. The idea that he might think she was ditching him to hang out with her boyfriend didn't sit well with her, but she hoped Chris knew her better than that. It would've been ten times easier to just tell him what was really going on, but she couldn't bring herself to do it. Guilt would consume her if she told him, all for this to turn out to be a dead end.

Jason met them around the corner from the Apex building in his rental, barely waiting until Cassie buckled her seatbelt before hitting the gas and merging back into traffic. As they passed Chris, she gave him a small wave, causing the frown on his face to deepen.

If Jason felt the tension and guilt radiating off her body, he didn't show it. He drummed his fingers along the top of the steering wheel even though the radio was off, and despite the heavy mid-morning traffic, he was vibrating with energy.

"How'd it go this morning?" he asked, checking his side mirror as he switched lanes.

"About as well as expected," Cassie replied. "Max's old apartment didn't give us anything. Then we met up with the guy she was seeing at the time. He doesn't think it was suicide or an accident."

"Oh?" Jason asked, pulling out his phone and altering between checking the road and scrolling for something on the screen.

"Yeah." Cassie let the car fall silent for a moment. Then she added, "Found a message Max had written. Something about missing money."

"That's weird."

"Yeah."

"Speaking of messages," Jason said, handing over his phone. "This is what Omega sent me after I gave him the information on that girl."

Cassie took the phone, biting down on her annoyance. She couldn't blame Jason for being distracted. He'd been struggling to set up a meeting with this former Apex employee, and he was doing this for her as much as he was doing it for himself. This was the biggest break they'd had against Apex since they decided they couldn't just sit back and do nothing.

Centennial Park. Parthenon. Eleven a.m., sharp.

She blinked down at the message. "Well, that's both incredibly specific and infuriatingly vague."

"Welcome to dealing with Omega."

"Apex could be behind this."

Jason let out a startled laugh. "Maybe, but it's an awfully elaborate way to get to us, especially with you walking through the front door of their building with a badge on your chest every single day."

Cassie flinched at the sting of his words. "It's not like I had a choice. If I didn't have to be there, I wouldn't."

"I know that." Jason sighed, then moved one of his hands from the steering wheel to her leg and gave it a squeeze. His touch didn't linger. "But the sooner we can get you out of there, the better."

"What do you think he wants with that information?"

"No idea, but pretty soon it'll be the perfect time to ask him."

"All right, catch me up to speed. What do you know so far?"

"Not much." Jason tapped his brakes when someone cut him off. He didn't react beyond that as he bit his lip in thought. She could see him rewinding back to the beginning. "You know how we had trouble finding anything on Apex in the beginning?"

Cassie nodded. "All the information on their site is surface level. There are thousands of positive reviews and testimonials, with a few mediocre ones I'm sure were thrown in to make it look realistic."

"Exactly." Jason went back to drumming his fingers on the steering wheel. "Not a lot of complaints about the company, and the ones that existed were either ridiculous or just personal preference. People who weren't happy with their publicity services because they didn't become famous overnight, that sort of thing."

"Yeah, sure." The energy inside the car escalated until Cassie had the urge to drum her own fingers on her leg. "Then Lorraine stumbled onto some forums, right? Conspiracy theories."

"First she tried working backwards, looking at Apex's clients and seeing if there were any controversies tied to them. That was a bust, though."

"Because they buried them all?"

Jason laughed. "Apex is good, but not that good. There were just too many. And a lot of them were petty things, like cheating spouses or drug problems. Nothing like what we were looking for."

"Murder," Cassie said. The word hung in the air for a moment, and Cassie felt the bitter taste of copper on her tongue, like she'd bitten the inside of her cheek without realizing it. "They covered up Douglas Hughes' murders for years, and then killed him so they didn't have to risk him talking to us and giving anything away. I doubt that was the first time that had happened, and it probably won't be the last."

"Unless we do something about it." Jason drew in a deep breath. "But it's not just about murder. In North Carolina, they wanted that senator to win the presidency. That failed, so they picked a new candidate. There's a reason they want someone in the White House, and I doubt it's to make this country a better place. At least not for the average American."

"What did Lorraine find?"

Jason sighed, and she knew he didn't like how little they had to go on. "She started looking in the dark corners of the internet. Not the most reliable of places, but some posts deserve a closer look."

Cassie sat up straighter. "Someone mentioned Apex?"

"Well, no." Jason winced when he saw the frown on Cassie's face. "A lot of times, they use code words so they don't draw attention to themselves. Once Lorraine realized this, she started looking for Apex in other ways, without using their name."

"How?"

"Companies involved in political coverups. Certain politicians we know worked with Apex. It wasn't easy, but there was a trail to follow."

"If Lorraine found it, that means Apex could find it. Why haven't they done anything about it?"

"There are very few credible people on that site," Jason said. "And even fewer willing to stick their necks out. It's not worth their time, especially since so many members are uber secretive. They probably monitor the posts, but unless something comes out of it, there's no point in investing resources into shutting it down."

"How did you find Omega?" Cassie asked.

Jason stopped at a light and watched as a group of people crossed in front of him. "Lorraine figured out they were referring to Apex with the codename Alpha, which made it a bit easier to find the posts talking about what they might be involved in. Some of it was nonsense, but a few pieces of information lined up with what we already knew. And Omega had authored every single one."

"Alpha and Omega," Cassie said. "That's not a coincidence."

"The beginning and the end. I assume Omega is hoping to be the one to take down Apex."

"Lorraine said she'd sent him a direct message?"

"She tried reaching out a few times, but he didn't answer right away. He's notorious for being unavailable most of the time, only showing up once in a blue moon to make a post people go crazy over. My guess is that he was looking into who we were and what we've been up to."

That sent a shiver of dread down Cassie's spine. "How much does this guy know about us?"

"Not sure."

"That's not exactly comforting. For someone who's been hypervigilant about not rocking the boat, you sure are diving in headfirst."

"You didn't see this guy's posts," Jason said, pulling into the lot on the side of the Parthenon. "He's been following Apex for longer than we have. He has the kind of information that can help us take them down. I just know it."

Cassie wanted to believe him, but something held her back.

Jason put the car into park. "If you've got a bad feeling about this, let's talk it out." He pointed to the clock on the dash. "We've only got two minutes to change our minds."

Cassie rolled her eyes. "Come on," she said, pushing open her door. "We don't want to keep the Almighty waiting."

28

The Parthenon in Centennial Park was on the list of attractions Cassie had wanted to see while in Nashville. Not only was it a full-scale replica of its Greek counterpart, but its lower levels housed some nineteenth-century paintings she'd wanted to view.

But now, walking alongside the columns toward the front of the building, the view beside her was bittersweet. The Parthenon would always remind her of her time in this city and why she was here. It would be forever cast in Apex's long-reaching shadow.

Jason stopped at the bottom of the steps leading up into the building and checked his watch. "It's eleven."

"Should we go inside?"

"Let's wait here for a minute. See what happens."

Cassie looked up at the front of the building, then peered through the columns to see how many people were inside. It was another beautiful day in the South, warm in the sun and cool in the shade, with a nice spring breeze that did nothing more than ruffle the hair around her shoulders and cool some of the sweat on the nape of her neck.

Tourists were out in droves. She and Jason had stepped away from the crowd, yet she was still being jostled from all angles. Children laughed and screamed, while couples held hands and tried to take pictures as though they were the only ones there.

Cassie felt a sharp pang of envy, wishing she could be amongst the care-free sightseers, when someone knocked into her, causing her to stumble into Jason and almost send them sprawling. A few snappy words sat on the tip of her tongue, but she swallowed them down when she felt the man press a slip of paper into her palm.

It featured a crude rendition of the uppercase Greek letter Omega.

Grabbing the front of Jason's shirt, she shoved the paper into his line of sight and then angled him toward the stranger until she felt his body tense with realization. Without pulling his eyes away from the man, Jason gave a sharp nod and pushed his way through the throng of people, not bothering to apologize when he stepped on someone's foot or elbowed them in the arm.

Cassie stayed locked on the man too, despite his simple navy coat and blue jeans. His shoulders were hunched, and she could just make out some gray under a baseball cap. Even with a slight limp, the man pulled away from them, hobbling around to the opposite side of the Parthenon and disappearing.

A crowd of children on a school field trip clogged the sidewalk, forcing Jason and Cassie to wait until they passed. When the coast was clear, they turned the corner at a near sprint, and Cassie was relieved to see the man sitting down in the middle of an empty bench, his arms spread along the back as though he were relaxing in the late morning sun.

When Cassie and Jason were within earshot, the man held up a hand. "That's close enough."

They came to an immediate halt. Now that they faced him, Cassie could see his cap was pulled down low over his eyes and he wore a big pair of reflective aviators. A neat gray beard obscured the lower half of his face, hiding the shape of his jaw. Everything about the man was put together except for his hair, which was long enough to touch his neck. Could it be a wig?

"Are you Omega?" Jason asked.

"I am." The man's voice was gruff, like he had gravel in his throat, and there was no discernable accent, not even a southern one.

"I'm—"

"Jason Broussard," the man finished. "And Cassandra Quinn."

"Cassie," she said, although she wasn't sure why.

He chuckled. "It's nice to meet you, Cassie. You've been causing all sorts of trouble for Alpha. I'm impressed. Keep it up."

"That's the idea," she said. "I hear you might be able to help us with that?"

"Depends."

"On?"

"You have what I asked for?"

Cassie stepped forward until she was within arm's length of the man and then slipped the piece of paper from her pocket. When she held it out, Omega stayed still for a second or two before grabbing the note. Unfolding it, he skimmed over the information and then slid it inside the pocket of his jacket.

Cassie retreated to Jason's side. "I don't suppose you want to tell us what that was all about?"

"Not really, no."

"We did what you asked," Jason said. "Now it's your turn. We want to know everything."

Omega brought one foot up until it rested on the knee of his other leg. Still leaning back against the bench with his arms across the top, he looked like he was having a casual conversation with a couple of friends. But his tone turned weary. "I've been around the block a few times. Had a couple of people over the years come close to exposing what Alpha is really up to behind the scenes. All of them are dead now. Not a single one got close enough to the truth. You sure you're ready for this?"

Cassie and Jason answered in unison. "Yes."

Pursing his lips, Omega drew in a deep breath before he spoke. "The company has been around since the eighties, under different names. It wasn't until the new millennium that they became who they are now. People have come and gone over the years, but their purpose has remained the same."

"You make them sound like some shadowy Bond villain," Jason said, shaking his head.

"Even Bond would have trouble digging out the roots Apex has cultivated over the years."

"But for what purpose?" Cassie asked. "That's what we can't figure out."

"It boils down to three things—money, power, and influence."

"Apex already has plenty of that," Cassie replied.

"Alpha," Omega said, looking left and right before returning his mirrored gaze to her. "Sure, they've got dozens of politicians in their pockets. Along with movie stars and tech giants. If they pooled their resources, they'd have plenty of money and power. But it's *influence* they want. With enough money, you have the power to make anyone do what you want them to do. But with influence, you make them *choose* to do what you want them to do."

Jason pinched the bridge of his nose. "Why does that matter?"

Cassie could sense Omega's assessing gaze behind his reflective glasses. "You tell me."

"Culpability," Cassie said, the answer coming to her like a lightning strike. "If, uh, *Alpha* handed a wad of cash to someone and told them to commit a crime, the authorities could follow the money trail right back to their doorstep. But if they could convince the person that they *want* to commit the crime, the company can't be held responsible. Not without plenty of evidence to prove they manipulated the person into doing it."

Omega smiled, his teeth bright and white in the late morning sun. "Now you're getting it."

Jason let out a sigh of frustration. "We've investigated their clients. Their board members. There's no telling what they're trying to accomplish. There are no connections there."

"Maybe to the amateur's eye."

"I'm no amateur."

"You are compared to these guys. And you better get used to feeling this way—like you don't know jack shit. Like there's a red dot in the middle of your forehead, but you can't spot the sniper hiding in the trees. Alpha is out of your league. They're out of my league. They're operating on a whole other plane of existence."

"You've managed to duck them for this long," Cassie said.

Omega shrugged. "Part of that's luck and part of that's brains. I know when to keep my head down. Besides, if I had any real evidence, they would've taken me out a long time ago. I'm a thorn in their side, sure, but it's not worth calling an extraction team over."

"If you don't have any evidence, then why are we here?" Jason asked.

"Because I can't go out and do the dirty work," Omega said. "But you can. And once you get what we need—*and* promise me protection—I'll testify as your star witness."

"This is a joke," Jason said, turning to Cassie and tugging on her elbow, though she could tell it was just a ruse. "And a waste of time. He doesn't know anything, and we're just chasing our tails."

"Wait." Cassie pulled free from his grasp. "They're desperate to get someone into the White House. It's a powerful position to be in, but there are checks and balances for a reason. That won't grant them unlimited power. They can't just do whatever they want."

"You're under the presumption that what they're doing is illegal."

Cassie shook her head. "The American public is too divided for the president to make any sweeping changes. It would have to—" Realization hit her all at once. "It would have to be something commonplace. Mundane. Ordinary."

Omega sat back with a smirk on his face. "You got it much faster than the others."

Jason looked between the old man and Cassie. "I don't understand."

"If you wanted to destroy a country and take away its power, how would you do it?"

With a shrug, Jason said, "Bomb them?"

"What would that accomplish?" the man asked, shaking his head. "You'd be the villain in everyone's book. What's worse, they'd be the heroes. The underdogs. The *survivors*. The entire world would turn against you. No, there's a better way to do it."

"From the inside," Cassie said. "It's better to undermine them. Subtler, at least. At the end of the day, you might still be the bad guy, but everyone else would look at them and say they did it to themselves. They should've known better. That's what they're doing with the presidency. But what you're talking about is bigger than that. Bigger than Americans fighting amongst themselves. What you're talking about is global."

"Now you're starting to get it," Omega said, his voice turning serious.

"Who would want to take the U.S. down from the inside?" Jason asked.

Omega laughed. "Who wouldn't?"

"There are frontrunners," Jason said, as though he hadn't heard the man's retort. "Russia, for one. North Korea, but they don't really have the resources." His head snapped up as he stared down the man sitting before them. "China?"

"You tell me."

"China is an emerging global superpower. Their government wouldn't be heartbroken if the United States got taken down a peg or two. Even just distracting our administration could allow them to gain more footing in the global market, finally take over Taiwan, and who knows what else. But how would they do it?"

"It'd have to be indirect," Cassie said, trying to follow his line of thinking. "Like lifting certain sanctions. Or allowing the use of certain technologies."

Jason nodded along. "But what kind of sanctions?"

Omega waved his hand. "Take your pick. There are sanctions against Chinese companies for providing support to militaries working against American interests. Others have been sanctioned for sending equipment to cartels in Mexico in order to aid in the production of drugs, which would eventually find their way onto American soil. The big one, though, is related to semiconductor chips used for creating microprocessors found in just about every electronic device you can imagine. Computers, phones, cars, you name it. They're also used to train artificial intelligence, and guess where those get made?"

Jason didn't hesitate. "Taiwan."

"Bingo."

"Allowing American companies to use Chinese technology could be a security concern. Even if the Chinese government had no interest in using that information for themselves, they could sell it to the highest bidder."

"There you have it," Omega said, standing up. "Now you know where to start looking."

Jason bristled. "Wait, that's it? You're leaving? You've hardly told us anything."

"You're further along now than you were this morning," Omega said with a shrug. "Be grateful I gave you that much. It's your turn to do some digging. Put the puzzle pieces together. I'll be in touch when I think it's safe. When I'm sure I can trust you with more."

Jason sputtered as Cassie watched Omega slip back into the crowd, disappearing as quickly as he'd come.

"Ridiculous," Jason muttered, dragging a hand down his face. "This is unbelievable."

"Unfortunately," Cassie said, digging out her phone and searching her contacts. "It's not."

The phone rang twice before the woman on the other end picked up.

"Hey, Lorraine. We have some news. You got a minute?"

29

Lorraine had just pulled into her driveway when Cassie called. Her first thought when she saw the name on her screen was that Cassie had lucky timing, or that maybe it was something more. Even after working with Cassie for the last month, Lorraine still wasn't sure how her abilities worked and if they applied to something as trivial as a phone call.

On a typical day, Lorraine would've still been at work and unable to answer her phone while at her desk. But today, she'd left early for a doctor's appointment amidst the warden's current silent treatment. She was relieved to be home now. Even more relieved when she saw she'd be getting an update from Cassie.

But whatever luck Cassie had didn't feel like it transferred to Lorraine when she answered the phone. On the contrary, the tale Cassie spun made the pit of dread in Lorraine's stomach deepen until it felt like a bottomless abyss. All her hope slid over the edge and disappeared into the darkness until she was left clutching her chest like that would be enough to keep her from falling apart.

The conversation had only lasted a few minutes, and Lorraine was silent for most of it. She hoped Cassie hadn't heard the trepidation in her voice when she agreed to look into the information Omega had provided before hanging up.

Unbuckling her seatbelt, she closed her eyes and tipped her head back, taking measured breaths until her heartrate slowed to a pace less concerning than the drumbeat that had increased in volume and tempo the longer Cassie spoke. Lorraine needed to get herself together before she walked inside and greeted her mom.

Lorraine would never admit it out loud, but she felt in over her head. Apex was already the monster that went bump in the night when they thought the company was only interested in playing puppet master with American politics. But now that they were talking about ties to the Chinese government? Taking them down seemed impossible.

After all, she was just a normal girl who had spent her entire life in Georgia. The most she'd ventured outside the confines of her childhood home had been when she went off to college, and that had only lasted a handful of years. Then she came straight home to take care of her ailing mother. Forget going on dates or hanging out with friends. Not that she could complain. Eating ice cream and giggling at cheesy romcoms was all she needed.

Or so she thought.

When Cassie stepped in and promised mystery and adventure, she hadn't hesitated to work with her and Jason. But some days, she wished she had. At first, it had been fun looking into Apex, like solving a ten-thousand-piece puzzle without any idea what the final picture would turn out to be. She had convinced herself she was too small to show up on their radar, that all she'd done was gather information. In the grand scheme of things, that was hardly a punishable offense.

But that had been when she thought Apex was just another group of power-hungry people, not agents for a foreign government looking to—what? Funnel money back to the home country? Invade another nation? Light the United States on fire and watch it burn? This fight was much too big for her. Every move Apex had made up until this point had been subtle and clever. She shuddered to think what it would look like when they began to make bolder strokes.

And still, she'd told Cassie she'd investigate it. A few more puzzle pieces were in place now, and the picture was becoming clearer. The edges were filled in, and as they worked their way toward the center, it would become easier to discern the final image. But that begged the question—what would they do about it?

"That's not your job," Lorraine said to herself. "They just need you to do the leg work."

After what seemed like her hundredth deep breath, she gathered her purse and empty coffee mug, then stepped out of her vehicle with a wry smile. How in the world had she ended up in the middle of a conspiracy theory straight out of some spy movie from the eighties?

Using her hip to shut the car door, Lorraine kept an eye on her feet so as not to trip over the uneven sidewalk leading up to the front door. It had been in desperate need of repair for the last few years, and with the extra income from Jason, she'd saved up enough to tackle it this year.

She listened for the tell-tale creak of the porch floorboards, which had once felt homey and now felt dangerous. She'd been debating whether it'd be worth it to replace a few pieces of wood and stain the whole porch to match, or if she should just tear the whole thing up and start from scratch.

Lorraine sorted through her wad of keys until she found the one for the front door. But when she held it up to the keyhole, she saw that the door wasn't locked. It wasn't even closed all the way.

Cold dread slipped down her spine, and she shivered against the warm afternoon. Jacqueline never left the house unless it was with Lorraine.

Pushing through the door, Lorraine's mind sped through her worst fears. Had her mother fallen and called an ambulance, and they'd forgotten to close the door? Had there been an intruder who'd ransacked the house? Or had someone come in with the express purpose of hurting a woman who spent all her time at home alone while her daughter went off to her job?

"Mom?" Lorraine called, not even considering that someone could still be in the house.

The front door opened into the living room, which was as neat and orderly as it had been that morning. The house smelled of coffee and leftover lasagna, and the faint whisper of a television came from the back room. The sheer normalcy of the house should've put Lorraine at ease, but she wouldn't relax until she set eyes on her mother.

Dumping her stuff by the front door, Lorraine made her way toward the only sign of life in the house. "Mom?" she called again. "Are you here?"

"Where else would I be?" came Jacqueline's answer, a chuckle in her voice.

Lorraine's laugh sounded more like a sob. When she rounded the corner and found her mother in her usual spot in bed, propped up and watching the news, she felt dizzy with relief. There wasn't a hair out of place as her mother smiled up at her, a shawl wrapped around her shoulders.

"Honey," she said, reaching out for Lorraine to take her hand. "Are you okay? You look like you've seen a ghost. And you're as cold as ice."

"The front door was open," Lorraine said. "I got scared. I thought something might've happened."

"Oh, dear." Jacqueline patted Lorraine's hand in sympathy. "Richard must not have closed it all the way when he left. I was too tired to walk him to the door."

"Richard?" Lorraine asked, forcing her voice to remain steady. Her mother never got visitors.

Jacqueline nodded, letting go of her daughter's hand and adjusting the shawl around her shoulders. "Mayor Blackwood—well, I suppose he's not the mayor anymore. I was surprised when he knocked on our door! He's even more handsome in person. Of course, I don't like what he did to his wife. I know it's not very traditional of me, but some people really should get divorced instead of trying to stick it out for the sake of the relationship. A lot of people would be much happier that way."

Lorraine's ears were buzzing in time with her heartbeat, making it difficult to comprehend everything her mother was saying. "Blackwood was here? Why?"

"He said he's a friend of Warden Wickham's, and he's been hearing such wonderful things about you." Jacqueline beamed. "He wants to run for mayor again, and when he does, he'd love for you to join his team. Said he'd double your pay. Can you believe that?" Her mother clicked her tongue. "A lot of people are saying bad things about him right now, and I'm not saying what he did was right—his poor wife—but he was so genuine and humble while he was here. I think he's truly sorry about what he's done. It's important to tell people when they've made a mistake, but we also have to give them a chance to apologize and do better next time, you know?"

"He offered me a job?" Lorraine couldn't keep up with everything her mother was saying. "He wants to run for mayor again?"

"That's what he said, and you should consider it. You deserve more than what the warden is paying you. And I never liked you going to that prison every day, either. It's too dangerous. Working for the mayor would be much safer, and you'd have better opportunities in the future after a job like that."

Lorraine swallowed the lump that had risen in her throat, knowing Blackwood hadn't really been here to offer her a job. "Is that all you talked about?"

Her mother gushed. "No. We talked about everything and anything. He's a very nice man, despite what the news would like us to believe." She grabbed the remote sitting on the nightstand and turned off her television with a decisive nod, as though it had personally offended her. "I even offered him a cup of tea, and he insisted on making it himself. Poured me one, too. But he must've used the chamomile by accident because I couldn't keep my eyes open after that. I hope I wasn't rude when I asked him if he could come back. I wasn't sure when you'd be home, and I was so tired, I knew I wouldn't get through the afternoon without a nap."

Lorraine fought to keep her mother from noticing the tremors that rocked her body. She'd never be able to prove it, but without a doubt in her mind, she knew Blackwood had put something in her mother's tea. This was a warning shot—a reminder of what was on the line.

"In fact," her mother said through a yawn. "I'm going to doze again for a little while. I must not have slept well enough last night."

"All right," Lorraine said, leaning down to kiss her mom on top of her head before backing out of the room. "Sweet dreams. I'll make some soup for dinner, just in case you're coming down with something."

"Sounds good," her mother said, eyes already drooping.

Lorraine switched off the overhead light and closed the door. Walking down the hall and into the bathroom, she managed to shut herself inside before the first sob escaped her throat. She switched on the faucet to drown out her crying before she leaned against the wall and slid down until her butt hit the floor. The tile was cold, but she barely felt it. Her thoughts were too consumed with the message she'd received loud and clear from Richard Blackwood.

30

Cassie stepped out of the little Prius and watched as her rideshare driver took off down the street. A stab of guilt hit her for not calling Robert to drive her this evening, but he worked for Anastasia. The less that woman knew about what Cassie was up to, the better—which is why she'd also taken the hit for the car on her own credit card and not the one Apex had provided.

Not that it mattered. Senator Hughes had likely already told her he'd invited Cassie to dinner. It'd be just her luck that she'd have to dine with Anastasia by her side, too. Then there'd be no hope of getting anything useful out of the presidential hopeful.

Squaring her shoulders, Cassie walked up the winding sidewalk, taking in a lawn uniform in color and height. Not a single blade of grass dared to hang over the edge of the path and cause guests any sort of discomfort. All the flowers were bright and perky, and the solar lights illuminating her way were soft and cozy, never shining too brightly into her eyes.

The house itself was magnificent. She hadn't had time to look up its history, but it didn't take someone like her to know it had stood on this land for quite some time. Made of red bricks as bright as a barn door, the house should've looked garish, but was both robust and elegant. A large wraparound porch sat along the right side, the white bannisters gleaming against the colorful façade of the house. All three floors sported black shutters that finished off the senator's home with a stately appearance. It was at once opulent and tasteful, and Cassie couldn't help but think that was the perfect way to describe Senator Hughes himself.

It didn't escape her attention that there was a significant amount of spiritual activity on the grounds, but the ghosts were old and faded, like a photograph that had been left in the sun too long. Most of them kept to the outskirts of the property, but the attic held an interloper that she imagined had lived in the house even longer than Senator Hughes. None of them felt like they would give her trouble tonight, and she was relieved to have one less concern weighing her down.

Before she could ascend the concrete steps, the front door opened, and the man of the hour stepped onto the porch with a wide grin. He wore tan chinos and a white button-down shirt with the sleeves rolled up to his elbows. Once again, he looked immaculate, even when he was dressed more casually than the last time she'd seen him. She'd swapped her yellow sundress for a simple navy skirt and white silk blouse.

"Ms. Quinn," he said, beaming as she stepped onto the porch. "I'm so glad you made it."

"Thank you for inviting me," she said, and found that her response was genuine. She didn't know what would come of this evening, but she was looking forward to it all the same. "You have a lovely home."

"Thank you so much." Hughes gestured for her to follow him through the door and down the hall. "It took some time to restore it to our liking, especially because we wanted to keep as much of it original as possible, but in the end, it was worth it. If I'm lucky, this will be the house I die in."

A woman looked up as they emerged from the hall and into a sitting room adorned in red and white. "Dear, that's entirely too morbid a thought to kick off our evening."

Hughes chuckled. "This is my wife, Patricia. Patty, this is Cassie Quinn."

The woman glided across the room to shake Cassie's hand. "It's a pleasure to meet you, Cassie."

"Likewise," she said, stunned by the woman's classic beauty. Her chestnut hair was pinned up with pearls, and her smile was soft amidst heart-shaped lips. Not a wrinkle could be seen on her ivory skin, and what little makeup she wore enhanced her big brown eyes and rosy cheeks. Tall and slender, she wore an olive-green dress that hugged her curves but didn't restrain her movements.

All of a sudden, Cassie felt disheveled in her simple skirt and flats.

"Did Ross already warn you?" Patricia asked, offering up a theatrical wince.

Cassie's thoughts flew back to her fear that Anastasia was hiding somewhere in the back. "Warn me?"

"Not yet," Hughes said, mirroring his wife's expression. "Cassie, unlike a lot of my colleagues, we live in this house. And by that, I mean—"

"There was mail strewn all over the dining room table about half an hour ago and you may spot a stray LEGO underneath one of the chairs."

Cassie grinned. "Don't worry, I'm not here to write an exposé."

"Good because that wasn't the real warning," Patricia said, looking to her husband.

This time, Hughes' wince was less theatrical. "We have two beautiful children, Patrick and Rosa. They're twelve and ten, and while Rosa still thinks I hang the moon in the sky, Patrick is learning to resent the name I'm making for myself. We had a long talk about what it might mean if I became president, and Patrick didn't like the idea as much as Rosa did."

"In other words," Patricia said, stepping up to her husband and putting a comforting arm around his waist, "he might be a brat at dinner, and I hope you won't think we're terrible parents for the way he acts."

That startled a laugh out of Cassie. "I promise I won't."

Beaming, Patricia went to grab the kids while her husband showed Cassie to the dining room table and sat her down in one of the seats.

Someone had already set out shiny white plates and gleaming silverware, along with water and wine glasses. The senator poured them each a glass of cabernet and then kept her company while his wife and kids brought out platter after platter of delicious food. Salad, collard greens with bacon, oven-roasted carrots, and mashed potatoes preceded the meatloaf Hughes had promised her at lunch the day before. It all smelled incredible. Within minutes, everyone's plates were piled high.

Despite Patricia and Ross' warnings, dinner was uneventful. In fact, Cassie felt like an old friend who'd dropped in to say hello and be a fly on the wall for a normal family dinner. Rosa talked a mile a minute about school and all the fun things she'd learned, barely touching the meal in front of her as a result. Patrick, on the other hand, shoveled two plates' worth of the homecooked food into his mouth, only speaking when his father asked him a direct question. When he was done, he gathered up his dirty dishes, took them to the kitchen, and then raced back upstairs. Cassie caught Patricia and Ross exchanging a look of surprise and, if she was reading their expressions correctly, relief.

When the adults were finished, Patricia stayed behind to make sure Rosa finished off at least half of her food, waving off Cassie's offer to help clean up the table. Senator Hughes kissed his wife on the cheek, poured Cassie another glass of wine, and invited her to join him in his study for a more private conversation.

Hughes' home office had been designed in shades of charcoal and cream, balancing dark masculinity with bright natural lighting. A built-in bookshelf took up one wall, while a panel of floor-to-ceiling windows covered the other. A leather couch and matching recliner sat opposite a sturdy desk atop a sprawling area rug. Little pops of color in the form of potted plants or his children's drawings stood out, and overall, the tone matched the rest of the senator's home—clean and tidy, but practical and well-loved.

"I have to admit," the senator said, gesturing for Cassie to take the sofa before sitting down in the recliner, "that dinner went better than expected. Usually, the kids argue through most of dinner until Rosa ends up in tears and Patrick gets sent to his room."

"Patrick's almost a teenager," Cassie said, settling into the couch and cradling her glass of wine. "He and Rosa are at different stages in their lives. They'll grow apart for a while, but I'm sure they'll come back together at some point."

"Are you speaking from experience?"

"Yes." Cassie took a luxurious sip of wine before she continued. "I have a sister. We were close growing up. It wasn't until later that we grew apart. My fault, really. But we've reconnected, and I didn't realize how much I'd missed her. Even if she still drives me a little crazy."

"I always wanted a brother growing up," Hughes said. "Of course, when I found out I had one—well, it wasn't exactly the dream I wanted to come true."

Cassie studied the senator's face, surprised that he was so open about his father's biological son and the fact that he'd been the Ash Wednesday Killer. "We don't get to pick our family, and we aren't obligated to stand by their side when we disagree with their words or actions."

"Are you talking about my brother?" Senator Hughes asked. "Or my father?"

Cassie hid her grin with another sip of wine. "Maybe a little bit of both."

"I can't imagine what you must think of me and my family. Douglas was a very sick individual, yet I have some sympathy for him. My father abandoned him, and he didn't know how to handle that. I'm not excusing his actions, but if he'd gotten help, maybe some of those kids would still be alive. Maybe all of them would be."

"When we last spoke, you were surprised to hear Apex may have been involved in covering up your brother's misdeeds. Have you spoken to your father about it?"

Hughes looked away from her then. "No. You must think I'm a coward." When Cassie remained silent, he chuckled and met her gaze again, the humor dropping from his face. "When my father adopted me, he became my hero. The life he gave me surpassed all my wildest dreams. I had always felt like my biological parents had abandoned me.

And when you're a kid, you take that personally. I thought—what was so wrong with me that even my own parents didn't want me?"

"Those are some big feelings for a kid to have."

"They are. And then along came Jack Hughes, who seemed larger than life and so full of energy and personality. I felt like Annie getting adopted by Daddy Warbucks." He laughed. "But with fewer musical interludes."

Cassie smiled, but she didn't want to waste any time while Hughes was being so open. "Have you ever seen a different side to your father?"

Taking a sip of wine, Hughes pondered his response. "As you grow older, your relationship with your parents changes. With both of us in politics, we were bound to clash. We try not to bring that home with us at the end of the day."

Cassie itched to push further, but she forced herself to take another sip of wine, relishing the pleasant burn of it cascading down her throat. As much as she was enjoying her conversation with the senator, she felt like a predator stalking its prey, waiting for the perfect time to strike.

"My father changed when he began working with Apex. Not negatively, mind you, but enough for me to notice. Some have said he's become more ruthless, but I always saw it as more determined. I admire the way he sets his eyes on a goal and accomplishes it."

"Is that why you decided to work with Apex as well?"

"For sure." Hughes drummed the fingers of his empty hand along the armrest of the recliner. "My father raised me to be decisive, to never give up until I crossed the finish line. Preferably in first place."

"Did that ever feel like too much pressure?"

"Maybe. But I knew my father loved me and wanted what was best for me. Working with Apex seemed like an easy choice at the time."

"And now?"

Hughes sighed. "Apex Publicity is a fantastic company. They're at the top of their game for a reason, and I owe my entire platform to them. They took the best parts of me and emphasized them across social media, speaking engagements, everything. Not many state senators run for office with a real chance at winning, and I can say with certainty that I wouldn't have been able to do that without Apex."

"Should I write this down?" Cassie asked, grinning and pretending to go for a pen in her purse. "Hand it over to Anastasia so she can put your testimonial on the website?"

Hughes chuckled. "Trust me, it's already there." He eyed her for a moment, searching her face for something. "You don't like Anastasia very much, do you? Or Apex in general."

"No, I don't," Cassie said, not sure how much to reveal about her distaste for the company. "I'm not a fan of their recruitment tactics, for one."

"They are determined, that's for sure. Especially Anastasia."

"In this case, I have no problem using the word ruthless."

Hughes hummed. "I'll admit they have some unorthodox strategies, but you can't deny that they work."

"Unorthodox? In what way?"

"They put a lot of emphasis on investment opportunities. At first, I wasn't sure how I felt about that, but they've found companies that align with my platform. It looks good to be seen putting money where my mouth is."

Cassie swallowed against an unexpected dry throat and mouth. "What kind of investment opportunities?"

"I'm not sure what everyone else is doing, but I'm excited about a company called Five Winds."

"I've never heard of them. What do they do?"

"They're building some of the best renewable energy tech out there. It's a Chinese company, and I know that raises a lot of eyebrows. But they've got more than a dozen factories right here in the United States, where they're hiring American workers to produce solar panels that will be used on American soil. I'm hoping they'll be a practical example of how we can stop relying on fossil fuels and start improving our relationship with a tech giant like China, all for our own benefit."

And just like that, another puzzle piece locked into place as Hughes confirmed everything Omega had told them was true.

31

Cassie stayed for a third glass of wine, her conversation with the senator moving naturally onto other subjects, even as her thoughts strayed back to the investments Apex wanted him to make.

But she wouldn't follow up on that tonight. From the senator's house, she'd called another rideshare, and this time her driver showed up in a Lexus. Her eyelids grew heavy as she sank back into the leather seat, exhausted from the potent mixture of wine and a full day of activities. She nearly fell asleep to the soft lull of the engine, despite being in a stranger's car. It was only when the vehicle stopped and the driver cleared his throat that she sat up straight and gave him an apologetic smile.

"Thank you," she croaked, her mouth dry from too much wine and not enough water. "Have a good night."

The man gave her a nod and pulled away from the curb as soon as she shut the door behind her. It was only when she blinked up at the building in front of her that she realized he'd dropped her off on the opposite side of the hotel from the front entrance.

Grumbling and wishing she'd thought to bring a cardigan, she made her way down the sidewalk much more awake than she had been moments earlier. It was after nine o'clock at night, and though there were plenty of streetlights to illuminate her way, the darkness felt deeper than usual. She could hear the roar of life from a block away, and she picked up her pace to escape the feeling of being watched which trailed after her like a shadow.

Her steps faltered as she passed an alleyway, but she forced herself to keep moving in the direction that promised brighter lights and the nighttime energy of a city that didn't go quiet until the early morning hours.

She'd made it two or three steps past the entrance to the alley before a hand clamped over her mouth and an arm wrapped around her waist like a steel trap. She was thrown off balance as someone dragged her back into the shadows, her cry of surprise muffled behind the attacker's palm.

It wasn't until she was halfway down the alley that Cassie's brain came back online and her instincts kicked in. She dragged her heels to slow their pace, sinking down and then pushing up and back with all her weight to make her attacker stumble. Cassie grabbed at the hand over her mouth, pulling back as hard as she could on the person's pinky finger to force them to let go.

Her attacker let out a curse and released Cassie. Spinning around to face them, it took a few blinks of surprise to realize that her would-be kidnapper was a stocky woman at least four inches shorter than her. She was dressed in head-to-toe black, including a beanie that was much too warm for this weather.

When the woman lunged again, Cassie knocked her arms away and took off down the alley, back toward the side street. But a few steps from the entrance, the woman's hand locked around Cassie's wrist like a vice grip and tugged her to a halt. But this time, her hand wasn't covering Cassie's mouth.

With a blood-curdling scream, Cassie fought against the woman, using everything at her disposal, including her nails and her voice and her legs. For once, she wished she'd been wearing heels instead of flats so she could inflict more damage when she kicked out against her attacker.

"Stop fighting me," the woman growled, her voice deeper than Cassie had expected. "I don't want to hurt you."

Cassie didn't believe a word she said, her instincts screaming at her to get as far away as fast as possible. Memories of that long-ago night came rushing back, and her body filled with the kind of adrenaline that gave a person super strength. Using every bit of torque and momentum she had, Cassie threw her elbow back until it connected with the woman's face.

"Goddammit," the woman said, letting go of Cassie again. "Stop fighting—"

But Cassie refused, instead using her newfound freedom to sprint toward the side street again. This time, she rounded the corner before she heard pounding footsteps behind her.

"Come back here!" the woman shouted. "Listen to me!"

But all Cassie heard was the roar of her blood pumping and the whip of the wind through her hair. All she could see was a group of people standing at the other end of the street, looking toward her, first in confusion, and then in alarm.

The pounding of footsteps behind her faltered and then stopped altogether when the small crowd started running toward her.

"Cassie," the woman called out.

The familiarity of her name startled Cassie into stopping and turning toward her pursuer.

"Listen to me," the woman said, her cheeks red and her eyes wide. "Piper—"

But Cassie never found out what the woman had to say about Piper. The group of strangers made it to Cassie's side, and the kidnapper turned on her heel and ran. One of the men chased after her, but stopped when he reached the end of the street, shouting after her before coming back.

Two women placed gentle hands on either one of Cassie's shoulders.

"Oh my god," the one said.

"Are you okay?" the other asked.

"Are you hurt?"

"Do you know who that was?"

"Do you need anything?"

"Should we call the cops?"

"I'm okay," Cassie said, still staring in the direction the woman had gone. "I'm not hurt. Please don't call the cops."

"Are you sure?" one of the women asked. "Where are you headed? We'll walk you to wherever you need to go."

"I'm okay now," Cassie said, backing away from them and retreating toward her hotel. "But thank you."

Spinning on her heel, Cassie all but ran back to her room, heart pounding in her chest and tears stinging her eyes. She hadn't connected the dots until now, but that feeling of being watched she'd felt just moments ago was the same one she'd felt the other day in the hotel's courtyard. And again outside the museum.

Her stalker wasn't a lost spirit, but very real and very much alive.

32

Swirling fog.

A faint breeze.

The weight of an invisible hand.

Dirt and rain and smoke and just a hint of violets.

Cassie's impatience felt like an electric buzz in her veins. Any fear of her recurring nightmare had all but disappeared after experiencing this moment so many times. She needed to know what her subconscious wanted to tell her, then get through the paralysis, and go about her life. There weren't enough hours in the day to deal with everything going on, even without the ambiguous dreams.

Like last time, everything played out the same until the second figure approached from behind. When she came face to face with Chris, he was once again frozen in place, the black cloud hanging around his shoulders, vibrating as if it were exerting itself to hold this moment in place for her.

Knowing she only had seconds, Cassie looked closer at the red blooming across Chris' chest. A single bullet had pierced his skin, digging deeper into muscle and sinew. It burrowed toward his heart, perfectly placed to end his life.

Cassie avoided his face, knowing she would see pain and shock and regret there, and instead searched the rest of his body. He held a gun in one hand, aiming at the person behind her. A shudder coursed through Cassie's body as she looked down the barrel.

With a final jerk of release, the black cloud disappeared, and the dream continued. This time, however, Cassie was better prepared for what came next. As she spun to face the first figure, she took in the hand that held the other gun. Female, without a doubt. No adornments like rings or nail polish. She forced her gaze upward, along the cuff of a sweatshirt, but amidst the fog, the color looked muted.

As though she were moving through molasses, Cassie urged her head upward to take in the woman's face, wondering why the entity had chosen to focus on Chris' death rather than the person who'd committed the crime.

The figure raised the gun another half inch just as Cassie's gaze found the woman's shoulder. But then the sound of the gunshot startled her awake, and she was met with the familiar sense of cold dread invading every cell of her body. Unable to move, Cassie stared up into the face of Maxine Abrahms, powerless to ask the questions on the tip of her tongue—why was she helping her? What was she trying to say? Who was the woman who had shot and killed Chris Viotto? And, most importantly, *when* would it happen?

A sharp knock on the door and a muffled voice startled Maxine, causing her to fade as though a cold breeze had dissipated a cloud of smoke. Cassie forced her panic away, focusing on her muscles and willing them to obey her commands. As a second knock on the door sounded, she wiggled her toes and fingers. When the door opened, she sat up in bed to meet Jason's worried eyes.

He crossed the room with two coffees in hand and set them on the bedside table before sitting next to her. "You okay? I was worried when you didn't answer. Glad you gave me a key to your room."

"Same old, same old," Cassie replied, rubbing the bleariness from her eyes.

"The dream again?" Jason tucked a strand of hair behind Cassie's ear. "Anything new this time?"

"Nothing helpful yet." Cassie grabbed a coffee and pulled off the lid so it could cool faster. "But I'm getting closer. Maxine's helping, even though I don't know why."

"That's nice of her," Jason said, quirking a smile. "Maybe it's her way of thanking you."

Cassie's heart warmed at the thought. "Maybe."

Jason studied Cassie's face for a moment. "You sleep okay? Other than this morning, I mean. You look a little—"

"If you say rough, I'm sending Max after you."

Jason held up his hands, amusement warring with trepidation in his eyes. "Tired. I was going to say tired."

Cassie gave him a disbelieving look while she blew air over the top of her coffee. "Kept waking up. Every sound set me on edge. Couldn't get—" She broke off, glancing at Jason and then away again. Taking a sip of her coffee, she winced as the hot liquid burned the roof of her mouth but willed the caffeine to work quickly so she didn't say anything she regretted. "Just couldn't get out of my own head."

Jason pursed his lips, waiting for her to meet his gaze again. "What happened?"

Rolling her eyes, Cassie set her coffee down and pulled her legs up to her chest. "Last night," she said, "I guess I was kind of attacked?"

Jason blanched. "What do you mean you were *kind of* attacked?"

"Please don't freak out."

"It's a little late for that."

"My driver dropped me off on the wrong side of the hotel, and when I passed by an alley, a woman grabbed me."

"Did you call the police?"

"No, nothing happened." Cassie let go of her legs and swung them off the bed, forcing Jason to shuffle out of her way while she stood and stretched. She needed to move forward, to be productive. "I got away. A group of people saw me and chased her off. It was fine."

"It wasn't fine," Jason said. "You were *attacked*. Why didn't you call me?"

"It was late," she said, though it was a lame excuse, even to her ears. "I didn't want to bother you."

Jason pinched the bridge of his nose. "Cassie—" He sighed. When he looked up again, his eyes were softer. "Are you okay? Are you hurt?"

"I'm fine, honestly. Nothing happened. She grabbed me, and I got away. I was a little shaken up, but I don't think she wanted to hurt me."

"What makes you think that?" Jason asked, as though forcing himself to give her the benefit of the doubt.

"She said as much. And then she mentioned Piper's name."

Jason drew his eyebrows together. "How does Piper even know where you are?"

"I have no idea. But we have bigger issues." When the AC clicked on, causing Jason to duck out from under the vent, she opened her drawers to find an outfit for the day. "Yes, Maxine. That includes solving Millie's case. As well as yours. I'm not going to forget about you."

The air conditioner shut off.

"Do all your ghosts have this much, uh, personality?" Jason asked.

"No," Cassie said, unable to hold back her smile. "Maxine's one of a kind."

"Right." Jason sighed, then stared her down in challenge. "You need to call Harris."

"Why?"

"Because someone leaked your name to the press. Then someone attacked you and mentioned Piper. Could've been to warn you, or it could've been to deliver a message. If you're not going to deal with this yourself, at least bring Harris in on it. Maybe she can pay Piper a visit."

"Fine."

Jason narrowed his eyes. "What? Just like that?"

"You don't have to sound so surprised."

"Not surprised." Jason crossed the room and swept her into a hug. "Just relieved." He stepped back but kept his hands on her arms. "You think Piper was trying to deliver a message?"

"Possibly. She's pissed at Apex right now, so maybe she wants to exchange information for her freedom. Or maybe this is just another one of her games."

"Harris will figure it out."

"Like she doesn't already have enough on her plate," Cassie grumbled. "What are you up to today?"

"Research. Following up on some of Omega's leads. Seeing if there's anyone out there who can confirm what he had to say or has anything else we can use."

"Last night, Hughes mentioned the company Five Winds. I think it's connected somehow."

"I'll add it to the list."

The knot that had been growing in her stomach since she saw Chris' pained face in her dreams grew tighter. "Be careful."

"I will," Jason said. "But I'm more concerned about you. Don't leave Chris' side today, okay? Call me if you need a ride or someone to walk with you. Let's not give anyone another chance to grab you."

"All right," Cassie said, knowing there was a good chance she wouldn't keep that promise.

"What are you and Viotto up to today?"

"Paying another visit to Governor Warren now that we've talked to a few other people. Then visiting the place where they found Millie's car."

"Hope you can sense something," Jason said, retreating to the bed and grabbing his coffee off the table.

"After three years, it's unlikely we'll find something the authorities missed." Then, forcing a smile, she said, "But it's not impossible."

Picking up Cassie's phone, Jason handed it over. "But first, call Harris."

Cassie rolled her eyes and took her phone, ignoring the impatient flicker of the bathroom lights as Maxine urged her to get her day started already.

33

Cassie had gotten a text from Chris the night before, telling her they'd make another trip north to Kentucky to meet with Governor Warren. As genuine as he'd appeared while telling them the story of Millie's disappearance, neither Cassie nor Chris could get the conversation with the Abrahms out of their heads. They'd painted a much more tumultuous picture than Arnold had.

The trip to Frankfort dragged, and the car stayed quiet most of the way. Cassie's head spun with errant thoughts, wondering if Chris was still mad at her for ditching him yesterday and whether she should tell him about Harris' phone call. She hadn't shared anything about her and Jason's meeting with Omega either.

The itch to ask Chris whether he'd witnessed any of the connections Omega had mentioned was so strong, she had to bite down on her tongue to keep from speaking about it. If Chris let something slip by accident, the whole operation would be put in jeopardy. For now, it was best to limit the number of people who knew what they were doing.

On top of the whirlwind of worries, she couldn't get the image of Chris' bloody chest out of her head. Informing him about Omega would place him in greater danger and increase the odds of it all going sideways.

But if Chris noticed the turmoil inside Cassie's mind that morning, he didn't say anything, choosing instead to turn up the radio and hum along to the songs he recognized. Three hours passed this way, with Cassie nodding off and jerking awake when the fog from her dream infiltrated her mind.

When Chris pulled into an expansive parking lot, Cassie leaned forward in her seat and blinked up at a huge warehouse in front of her. As they circled the building, she noted dozens of cars and several news vans. A crowd gathered at the entrance, and she caught sight of a red ribbon and a pair of giant scissors before people shifted, blocking her view.

A police officer stopped them before they could get too close, but Chris flashed his badge, and the man waved them along. A second officer met them as they parked, leading them toward the corner of the building and out of sight of the cameras. A man waited for them, but it wasn't the governor. It was the one who'd arrived as they had been leaving. His brother.

He cut an impressive silhouette in his dark suit and tie, though the scowl on his face did most of the heavy lifting. Cassie could see him sizing them up as well, his gaze lingering on Chris' hips and chest. With a start, Cassie realized he was searching for a concealed weapon. Did he think they were here to hurt the governor? Or was he assessing how dangerous they were if he made the first move?

"Agent Viotto, I presume," the man said. "And Miss Quinn."

"Yes," Chris said, holding out his hand. "And you are?"

"Aaron Warren." The man hesitated for a fraction of a second before shaking Chris' hand, then turning to shake Cassie's as well. "Governor Warren's brother. I understand you wish to speak with him?"

"That was the plan," Chris said, keeping his tone as breezy as the crisp morning air. "We can wait until he's finished, of course."

Aaron's calculated smile spread across his face, devoid of any warmth. "This is the second time you've arrived unannounced to speak with my brother. You got away with it the first time because I wasn't in the office. But that tactic won't work twice in a row. I'll have to ask you to leave."

Cassie's jaw dropped at the man's open hostility toward them, but Chris played it cooler than she did. "Since you knew my name, I assume you also know I'm a federal agent."

"Without a warrant."

"I'm not looking to search the man's house," Chris said. Then, as though the idea came to him in that moment, he tapped his chin. "Although I'm not against the idea." He glanced over his shoulder at the news vans behind them. "Might cause a media circus. That would be unfortunate. And at such an important juncture of your brother's career."

Cassie expected Aaron to ball up his fists or let a curse fly, but he surprised her by remaining as still as a statue, assessing Chris from top to bottom. The only indication of his annoyance was a tick in his jaw. "What do you want, Agent Viotto?"

"I'd love to speak with—"

"No," Aaron said, slashing his hand through the air to silence Chris. "I mean, what are you looking to get out of a conversation with my brother? From my understanding, he already told you everything about the day Millicent disappeared. He endured your questions without hesitation. Is there a reason you're back here to interrogate him? The man lost his fiancée. It's been three years, and he's still not over it. Dredging up the past is akin to opening the wound again and again—which, I might add, he's more than capable of doing on his own."

Cassie's heart squeezed. The governor's love for Millie and the pain at her disappearance had been easy to see when they'd spoken with him, but hearing it from his brother's mouth was like a slap across the face. "Our intention was never to open old wounds," Cassie said. "When we spoke to the governor, he was interested in helping us in any way possible. He wants to know what happened to Millie as badly as her parents do."

Aaron's scowl was laced with derision. "Don't you think I know that? I'm his brother. I've been by his side every day over the last three years. I've held him together when he didn't have the strength to do it himself." The man took a deep, measured breath. When he spoke again, his voice was level, though she could tell it took everything inside him to remain that way. "My brother has been through hell and back. This job"—he gestured to the crowd behind him—"is his calling, but it takes a lot out of him. You'll forgive me if I'm a bit protective."

"It's understandable," Cassie said. "I have a sister. There's nothing I wouldn't do for her."

"I apologize for what I said earlier," Chris said, looking the man in his eyes. "I don't want to cause trouble. Not for him and not for us. We just want to find out what happened to Millie and how it might relate to her sister's death."

Aaron snorted. "I can't tell you how many times I've wished my brother never met that woman."

Cassie reared back. "You didn't like her?"

"Millie wasn't who she said she was," Aaron said, rubbing a hand over his jaw and dragging his nails along the skin hard enough to leave red marks. "At least her sister was more honest about that."

The wind kicked up then, colder than it had been all morning, and Cassie knew Maxine was close by. Tendrils of dark fog crept along the ground at her feet, inching toward the man in front of them. She couldn't stop herself from stepping forward, as if to block them from view.

"What do you mean Millie wasn't who she said she was?"

Aaron glanced toward the crowd, as though checking to see if his brother could hear him. When he turned back to Cassie, his eyes were hard. "She was a gold digger. She loved his money and his job, but she never loved him. From the moment I met her, I saw right through her façade."

Tendrils of black smoke wound their way up Cassie's legs to root her in place while others reached forward, growing ever closer to Aaron's feet. She had no idea what would happen if Maxine touched him, in all her torment and fury. Would she haunt him like she haunted Cassie? Or would he collapse there on the spot, joining Max in the afterlife for all of eternity?

"So, you had a reason to want her out of his life," Chris said.

"Please." Aaron rolled his eyes. "I tried to talk sense into my brother, and he wouldn't listen. He was too in love. And despite how much I disliked her, I wouldn't have taken that from him. She proved me right in the end, anyway."

"How so?"

"The night she left, she made off with a considerable amount of my brother's money. For all I know, she's still alive, drinking margaritas on a beach in Mexico or something."

Max's note made much more sense now. "Your brother never told us that," Cassie said.

"He's come up with a hundred excuses as to why it wasn't her," Aaron said, his voice weary. "He's still in denial."

"What about Maxine?" Chris asked, even as Cassie willed him not to. There was no telling what Max would do if Aaron continued to speak about her and her sister like this. "What did you mean Max was more honest about who she was?"

"She knew she was trash. Didn't try to hide it behind fancy clothes and designer handbags like her sister. Died of an overdose, didn't she?"

The blood in Cassie's veins turned to ice, and she felt frozen in place just like when she woke up from her nightmare. Unable to move a single muscle, all she could do was look on as a spear of black smoke whispered against the toe of Aaron's shoe. A sense of victory that didn't belong to her surged throughout her body, building until it felt as though it might explode from her. Just a few more inches and—

"Agent Viotto," a voice from Cassie's right said. "Miss Quinn. What a surprise to see you again."

As Governor Warren approached, Max's hold on Cassie relinquished in a sudden gust of chilly air, and she swayed on her feet. Chris' hand came to her elbow to steady her, and she became all too aware of the number of eyes on her.

"Sorry," Cassie said, forcing a little embarrassed laugh even as she fought against the terror screaming inside of her. "Forgot to eat breakfast this morning. Got a little dizzy there for a minute."

"We've got some doughnuts and pastries inside," the governor said.

"Arnold," Aaron chastised. "We can't invite a federal agent inside for breakfast with this many reporters around."

"Aaron," Governor Warren replied, "don't be an ass."

"We're fine, really," Cassie said. "We're sorry to drop in on you again like this—"

"Are you?" Aaron asked.

"—but we had a few more questions."

"Of course," the governor said, shooting his brother a warning glance. "I've only got a couple minutes, but I'll answer what I can." Before his brother could protest, he said, "Aaron, they need you inside. I'll catch up."

Looking like he'd just been forced to suck on a lemon, Aaron spun on his heel and stalked off without a backwards glance. Governor Warren watched him go, and when his brother was out of sight, he let out a long sigh.

"I'm sorry if he was rude to you. Aaron's very protective. Always has been, but it's gotten worse since I've taken office. Can't say I blame him. There are a lot of people out there who would like to take advantage of me and my title as governor. I've always been the trusting one. He's the discerning one. We're a good balance."

"Was Millie one of those people who tried to take advantage of you?" Chris asked.

The governor's gaze snapped to Chris', his eyes flashing with anger before simmering into disappointment. "My brother seems to think so."

"Why didn't you tell us about the money she stole from you the night she disappeared?"

"Because I don't think she did," Arnold said, his mouth turning down in a frown. "She knew I would buy her whatever she needed." His voice grew more clipped as he spoke. "Look, I have to get back to the event. If you have more questions, please just give my office a call. I'd hate for you to drive all the way out here again."

And before Chris or Cassie could argue otherwise, Governor Warren turned on his heel and strode back to the building, where his brother waited for him with sharp eyes and a concerned frown.

34

ALL THE DOWNTIME THEY HAD IN THEIR CAR RIDE BACK LEFT PLENTY OF room for them to toss out theories, each more ludicrous than the last. Once they crossed back over into Tennessee, Chris pointed the car in the direction of the last known location of Millie Abrahms' car. It had been abandoned on the side of the road a few miles from the Great Smoky Mountains National Park. Not altogether strange, considering how much Millie enjoyed hiking, but why would the car be that far from the park's entrance?

Just finding the right spot proved tricky enough, considering it had been three years since the car had been hauled away. But with coordinates Chris had obtained from Apex and a few pictures from the crime scene, he managed to pull off the side of the road about a hundred feet from where the vehicle had been abandoned.

"You're sure this is it?" Cassie asked, peering out into the dense trees surrounding them.

"As sure as I can be," Chris replied, tucking his phone away into his suit pocket. "The car was left in the grass just after that curve in the road." He pointed a finger ahead. "I figured we can start here and walk our way up. See if you get any, you know, tingles."

Cassie rolled her eyes. "It's not always a tingle. Sometimes it's a chill. Or a shudder. Or a gut feeling. Or a—"

"Okay, okay," Chris said, laughing as he pushed open his door. "Just let me know if you get any *sensations*. I'll hang back. Let you work."

Cassie nodded, grateful he understood her need for space. Sometimes the feelings she experienced hit her like a wrecking ball, but given this crime scene was several years old, it was likely she'd have to pay closer attention to pick up the faint traces of whatever had happened here.

If anything had happened here, she reminded herself. Just because this was the place where the car had been abandoned didn't mean Millie had been killed here. If she had, that would leave a mark Cassie could tune into. But if she hadn't, it'd be even more difficult to pick something up.

"How long did they search the woods for?" she asked, stepping out of the car and closing the door with her hip.

"The police searched for two weeks." Chris walked around the hood to stand by her side. "Volunteers searched for another month after that."

"Six weeks," Cassie whispered. "Six weeks of searching, and they didn't find a thing."

"If there's something here, you'll find it."

"No pressure or anything."

He grinned. "Yeah, no pressure."

Cassie tried to smile and failed, instead turning to look at the road ahead of her. It was faded and rough, like it hadn't been repaired in some time. The trees on either side of the road were tall and thick, blocking out the sun and causing the temperature to dip a few degrees. She'd been smart enough to grab a cardigan on her way out the door to go with her plum pants and salmon top, and she pulled it closer around her chest to stave off the chill she felt creeping into her skin. For now, it seemed to be caused by the late morning breeze and nothing more.

Walking down the shoulder of the road, Cassie kept both her eyes and other senses open to the world around her. Birds chattered from the boughs above her head while squirrels skittered along the dried leaves deeper in the forest. The bubbling of a nearby creek was faint but added to the ambiance. If she'd been out in the woods for any other reason, she would've enjoyed the pleasant atmosphere. As it was, she couldn't get the thought of Millie's final moments out of her head.

Were those final moments here, alongside this road? Had she driven the same route they had, and then pulled over and abandoned her car, wandering off into the forest, never to be seen again? Or had someone stolen her vehicle and left it here to avoid being caught with it, leaving Millie to suffer somewhere else, far away from here? For years, these questions had been left unanswered. Would today be the day they were put to rest?

Cassie took three more steps and stopped, hearing the crunch of Chris' shoes halt behind her. Closing her eyes, she let her hand drift out until it stopped, as though she were resting it atop the trunk of the abandoned car that had been towed away long ago.

"Here?" she asked Chris.

"I think so," he said, his voice a whisper on the wind.

Cassie walked forward, dragging her hand through the air as though she were tracing the outline of the car. Up over the rear window, along the roof, and down the side of the windshield. She thought of Millie, of the pictures she'd studied and the stories she'd heard, but the woman's memory had long since faded, if it had been here at all.

Taking a single step backward, she imagined herself standing next to the vehicle. With her eyes still closed, she bent down and peered into the car, imagining what she'd see there. A purse on the seat? Keys in the ignition? A bottle of water in the cup holder?

The sound of a trunk slamming shut echoed through the air, causing Cassie to jump and spin around. She expected Chris to be standing at the back of his car, apologetic as he pulled something from their vehicle. But he was just a few feet behind her, eyes wide as his hand rested on his hip, close to his gun.

"Did you hear that too?"

He shook his head. "Hear what?"

Footsteps crunched along the gravel until they faded to whispers against the grass.

"Cassie, what—"

She ignored him as she followed the sound toward the woods. A branch snapped to her left, and she adjusted her trajectory until it felt like she was following the memory of someone pushing their way through the trees. They weren't concerned about the amount of noise they caused, making it easier to track them as they wound their way toward the creek. Every once in a while, they'd stop and remain silent for a few seconds, and each time, Cassie held her breath as though afraid they'd hear her ragged inhalations. But then they'd start up again, and she'd let out a sigh of relief before picking up the trail once more.

It wasn't until she stood along the bank of the creek that the sound faded. She strained to hear a hint of what came next, but she couldn't pick out any more footsteps. Chris joined her, looking from her to the water, and then to the trees around them. His hand hadn't left his gun, but he hadn't pulled it from the holster.

"It's gone," she whispered.

"What did you hear?"

"A trunk closing. Then footsteps. They stopped here."

"Maybe they crossed to the other side?"

She shook her head. "The creek is too wide to cross without stepping through the water. I would've heard it."

"Maybe it was smaller a few years ago? Or dryer, without as much water?"

"Maybe." But that didn't feel right either.

Chris' sharp inhale caught Cassie's attention, and she looked up to see him studying the water. The creek was about a foot deep and crystal clear, with a bottom covered in rocks of all sizes and shapes and colors. It was picturesque, yet unsettling, like she was standing on a steep incline and the gentlest breeze would toss her down the slope.

"They searched these woods for weeks," Chris said slowly, as though still trying to string his discordant thoughts into cohesive words. "Used dogs and everything. They couldn't pick up Millie's scent, but that didn't make any sense. If she hadn't been buried out here, then why had the car been left here? If she'd walked away, down the road, the dogs could've followed that. But they didn't."

"Because Millie was never here. Someone else was."

"Her killer?" Chris asked.

As a gentle breeze ruffled her hair, Cassie picked up on the scent of violets, fainter than she'd ever smelled them before. "I think so. But what was the killer doing out here?"

"Burying something," Chris said. "Not Millie. Something else."

"But the dogs—"

"Couldn't smell it. The killer buried it here, in the creek. Underwater, where they couldn't pick up the trail."

Cassie stared down at the water now, imagining a figure, identity unknown and blurry around the edges, standing in the creek up to their ankles, shifting rocks aside until they dug a hole deep enough to place something inside. Then they replaced the rocks, knowing it wouldn't look like the bed of the creek had been disturbed.

"It must be here," she said, pointing to the spot in front of her. "This is where the footsteps ended."

With wide eyes, Chris held her gaze before stepping into the water, not caring that his socks and shoes would be soaked. Cassie followed him in until they stood a foot apart. They both bent over and shifted the rocks in front of them. At first, their movements were steady and meticulous. But as bright yellow fabric poked out from the soil underneath, they became frantic with anticipation.

Their movements had disturbed the mud on the bottom of the creek, turning the water murky. With an impatient growl, Chris plunged his arm down into the hole they'd uncovered and pulled on whatever was buried there. With a splash of water and a few stumbling footsteps, Chris revealed their buried treasure to be nothing more than a simple backpack with yellow straps against olive-green canvas.

Wasting no time, Chris unzipped the main pouch and peered inside. After a few seconds, he met Cassie's gaze, his own wide with excitement as a smile tugged at the corners of his lips.

She had to stop herself from yanking the bag out of his hands. "What is it?"

"Hiking gear," he declared. "Including a men's size thirteen shoe."

35

I̶T FELT LIKE SOMEONE HIT THE FAST-FORWARD BUTTON ON CASSIE'S LIFE after they discovered the backpack. She and Chris had searched through every zipper and pocket only to discover generic hiking gear. In addition to the shoes, there was a shirt, a pair of shorts, and some socks.

It wasn't direct proof, but they could conclude that Millie had been with someone on the day she disappeared. Cassie's head swam with dozens of unanswered questions. She just had to pick a place to start.

"Now what?" Chris had asked, echoing her thoughts.

Cassie had waited for Max to provide another clue, but when none came, she grimaced up at her companion. "I'm not sure yet. Let's just drive around until something jumps out at me."

Chris had blanched at her. "Cassie, the park itself is over half a million acres. And we don't even know if she made it through the entrance."

"I know," she'd said, backpedaling toward the car. "Let's just have a little faith."

Chris had relented, driving into the park and traveling along the smooth roads through dense forest for nearly an hour before Cassie felt a tug in the pit of her stomach, warning her that they were about to drive past their turn. When she'd shouted at Chris to stop, he'd slammed on his brakes and pulled off the side of the road in a cloud of dust and crunching gravel.

They both sat there for a moment, panting. When Chris regained his breath, he looked around, peering through the trees into the distance beyond. "Cassie, there's nothing here. It's not a trail."

"I know," she said, chest still heaving. "But this is it. I know it is."

"Not to question your abilities, but how?"

"A gut feeling." She placed a hand over her stomach where the sensation she'd felt seconds ago was already fading. "And those," she finished, pointing out the window.

Chris leaned closer, peering down at the purple flowers blooming at the edge of the forest. "Violets?"

"Violets."

Climbing out of the car, Chris circled around to his trunk and pulled out a pair of running shoes and a wad of gym clothes. He stripped out of his suit with great efficiency as Cassie knelt to get a closer look at the flowers. Their scent was overwhelming, and not just from the blooms in front of her.

Maxine was telling her she was on the right track.

A moment later, Cassie stood and slipped on the pair of hiking boots they'd stopped to grab on the way into the park while Chris slung a brand-new backpack over his shoulder. The nearest town had had everything they'd needed—a couple bottles of water, some sandwiches, a first aid kit, and a few extra snacks. There was no telling how long it would take to find what they were looking for.

Before they entered the woods, Chris tapped his smart watch a few times. "My sister gave me this for my birthday a couple years ago. Records longitude and latitude, plus has a built-in compass. There's no chance we'll get lost or lose our way back to the car as long as I have this."

"As long as you don't lose *me*," Cassie teased.

"I won't leave your side," Chris said, suddenly serious. "I promise."

Cassie looked away and peered through the trees, taking her first tentative step into the shade of the forest. "Do you hike often?" she asked, wanting to return to a topic that didn't feel as heavy as his previous words.

"Not as much as I used to." Chris boosted the backpack farther up his shoulder, having insisted on taking the first shift with it. "My sister and I used to hit the trails a lot. Had some of our best conversations in the middle of the forest. She hasn't had as much time these days because of the kids. Especially since her husband died." A beat of silence followed before he turned a forced smile in her direction. "What about you?"

"Not really." Sidestepping a protruding root, she knew it was only a matter of time before her toe caught on one and she embarrassed herself in front of Chris. "I like walking through the woods when I get a chance, but I don't have a lot of time to take in the scenery back home."

He took a deep breath of air and let it out in a whoosh. "You should make time when you go back to Savannah. There's no better feeling than this."

Laughter bubbled up in her chest. "No better feeling, huh?"

He cut her a sly glance. "Okay, I can think of one or two. But this makes the top three."

They were silent for a few moments as they navigated through the dense trees, stepping around roots and ducking under branches. Cassie had no idea where she was going, but Chris seemed content to let her lead. The tug in her gut had disappeared, but once in a while, a cool breeze—separate from the one that flowed through the woods the rest of the time—would buffet her in one direction or another. Between that and the occasional patch of violets, she knew they were on the right track, even if she didn't know why Millie had made this same walk through the woods without following one of the trails.

Chris cleared his throat, and Cassie glanced behind her to see a hesitant look on his face. "Everything okay?" she asked.

"Yeah," he said, but his smile looked pained. "Just working my way up to saying something uncomfortable."

A prickle of dread tightened Cassie's throat and strangled any response she might have.

"I realize we haven't known each other for long," he said, looking everywhere but at her face. "But I just wanted to let you know that I care about you a lot, Cassie." He laughed. "God, that sounds awkward and a little creepy."

"Chris—"

"No, no, let me finish." Chris took a deep breath, and as they walked through a small clearing, he sped up to walk by her side. "I'm not trying to make this a thing, and I'm not trying to make you uncomfortable, but I need to get this off my chest." Waiting until she gave him permission with a quick nod, he continued. "Meeting you back in North Carolina was a freak circumstance, and again here in Tennessee. Talking to you and being around you is so easy, despite how crazy both our lives are."

"Thanks, Apex," Cassie joked, trying to lighten the mood and relieve some of the pressure building in her chest.

He laughed. "Being an agent isn't easy. It's taken a toll on all my relationships. There aren't a lot of people who understand the pressure we're under, the drive we feel. This isn't just a job, it's—"

"—a calling."

"That's what I'm talking about. You get it. More than anyone else I've met."

"There are other agents," she said.

"Of course. And I've dated a few, but it never works out. One agent in a relationship is bad enough. Two is impossible."

Cassie spoke her next words with deliberate slowness. "What are you trying to say?"

"I'm trying to say that in a different world, under different circumstances, I think I would've liked to get to know you better. I hope I'm not out of line if I say I don't think I'm the only one who's noticed our chemistry?"

Cassie stepped around the left side of a tree while Chris took a path to the right, and she used the few seconds away from his side to think through her response. When they met again on the other side, she gave him a small nod. "I've noticed it too."

Chris laughed, but it was quiet enough to be swept away on the wind. "I feel a *but* coming along."

"But these are the circumstances we've been dealt. You're a great friend, and I care about you too. I hope we get a chance to know each other better." Cassie licked her lips, not wanting to hurt Chris' feelings but needing to draw a line in the sand. "But as friends."

Chris was silent for a moment as they picked their way through the trees. "Jason's a good man. He's lucky to have you."

"I'm lucky to have him, too," she said. "You'll find someone, Chris. I know you will."

"Is that a premonition?" he asked, nudging her with his shoulder.

"Maybe." She nudged him back. "We'll just have to wait and see."

"How convenient." His sigh was long and drawn out as he wrapped a hand around the back of his neck and let his arm hang there for a moment. "I'm sorry if I seem, I don't know, a little melodramatic? Anastasia is up my ass about this case, and she's not afraid to remind me how easy it would be to upend my sister's whole life. I can't stop worrying about them. It's got me thinking a lot about the future."

"Hey, I understand," Cassie said, a cool breeze ruffling her hair until she turned them a little to the left. Sure enough, she spotted another patch of violets growing in a beam of sunlight. "We've both got a lot at stake." After a brief hesitation, she divulged what she'd been dying to tell him. "It's actually why Jason is here in Tennessee."

Chris knit his eyebrows together. "I thought he was working on a case?"

"He is," she said. "And that case is Apex."

Chris stumbled a little and had to grab onto a tree for balance. "He found something?"

Cassie waited until they reached the patch of violets and spotted the next one before she spoke again. "He found someone who used to work for Apex. They only go by the name Omega. Have you heard of him at all?" Chris shook his head in response, and she continued. "We met with him for the first time yesterday."

Chris blanched, coming to a full stop. "Cassie, that could've been a setup. That could've been dangerous. Deadly, even. What were you—"

Cassie tugged on his elbow to get him moving again. "Jason was with me the whole time. We met in public. With the amount of runaround this guy gave us just trying to get in touch with him, there was no chance he was working for Apex instead."

"That's why you asked me to look up Pearl Everly."

"I have no idea why he wanted that information, but it was enough to convince him to talk to us."

"What did he tell you?" Chris whispered, his tone reverent, as though he couldn't bring himself to hope for the best possible outcome.

"Does the company Five Winds ring any bells?"

"It does, actually. I think they deal in green tech? But I don't know much else about them."

"Omega said this is bigger than putting someone in the White House. Bigger than what you or I can handle. Bigger than what the FBI can handle."

"Global," Chris said, picking up her train of thought. "CIA? But who can we trust?"

"No idea. Jason's working on digging up more information as we speak. When we find something, I'll let you know."

Chris studied her for a moment, waiting until she met his eyes. "You weren't going to tell me yet, were you?"

Cassie winced. "Not because I didn't want to. I just didn't want to get your hopes up before we had any solid leads."

Chris nodded. "I appreciate that. But maybe I can help. I'll reach out to a few people, see if I can pick up anything through my usual channels. They're safe, I promise."

Cassie nodded, but her response was cut off as another ice-cold breeze buffeted her face. But this time it wasn't coming from the right or left. It blew her hair back off her neck, cooling the sweat that had gathered there. In front of her, the trees had cleared enough to reveal a rockface with an opening about halfway up.

But that's not what caught her attention.

Along the ground and climbing up through the crevasses of the outcropping were thousands upon thousands of violets. As the wind rippled across the indigo blooms, they leaned forward, as though fighting to pick up their roots and walk up the incline toward their journey's end.

Following the trajectory of the velvet pathway, Cassie's gaze rose until it landed on the end of the trail, where the flowers fanned out to create a lush bed of varying shades of purple. Even as a warm breeze jostled the other flora around them, the violets still all pointed in a single direction.

Toward the cave's entrance.

36

Lorraine's hands trembled as she walked into work.

She hadn't clued her mother into how strange it was that the former mayor had paid them a personal visit under the guise of recruiting Lorraine for a job. Maybe Blackwood would've stood a chance if Apex was still interested in working with him, but considering they'd suggested the mayor's wife hire Jason to take the incriminating photos, it was unlikely he'd ever hold office again. Not to mention they hadn't lifted a finger to throw him a bone since then.

While Jacqueline Krasinski was out of the loop, Lorraine was not. She only got a few hours of sleep on a good day, and last night had been one of her worst, having stayed awake all night to think over her options.

Her initial idea to take her problem to Harris had backfired. That was the only reason Lorraine could think of as to why Blackwood had paid her mom a visit. Did he have someone tailing Lorraine? Had he somehow planted a tracker on her or her car? Just a few months ago, the thought wouldn't have occurred to her, but she'd been so embroiled in Cassie's world that it seemed laughable she hadn't checked before heading over to the police station.

Armed with a flashlight, she'd snuck out of the house in the middle of the night and searched her car from top to bottom and front to back but hadn't found anything. She'd even come up empty-handed when she searched her clothes, not knowing what she was looking for but sure she'd spot it if it was there.

That left one option: Someone was watching her. And probably the house, too.

The thought had occurred to her after she'd gone back inside, and she'd been too afraid to peek through the curtains on her bedroom window to see if anyone sat across the street with binoculars or a large camera. Would Blackwood do the deed himself, or would he hire a private investigator? Unbidden, she'd thought of various other options—police officers and criminals and hitmen.

"Lorraine, are you okay?" someone asked behind her.

She jumped, only to realize she'd never hit the button for the coffeemaker to dispense its liquid gold. Glancing over her shoulder, she spotted one of her co-workers looking at her in confusion.

"Sorry, Joe." She laughed, hoping it sounded natural, before pressing the button for the biggest, strongest cup the machine could make. "Didn't sleep well last night."

"I feel you," Joe said, rubbing a hand down his face.

"At least you have an excuse," Lorraine said, tapping her fingers against the counter in an erratic rhythm. The last thing she needed was more caffeine in her system, not with her anxiety so high already, but she risked losing her job if Wickham caught her napping at her desk. "How is little Jimmy?"

Joe's smile crinkled his eyes at the corners, and if she wasn't so exhausted, Lorraine would find his reaction adorable. "He's doing amazing. Doesn't love to sleep, but he loves to laugh. I swear I've never heard anything so sweet in my life."

Lorraine opened her mouth to give some generic response, but Warden Wickham appeared in the doorway to the kitchen. His eyes sparkled in a way that set her teeth on edge. "Miss Krasinski, could you join me in my office, please?"

"Of course," Lorraine said, grabbing her steaming cup of coffee and clutching it to her chest as she crossed the room. "Have a good day, Joe. Say hi to Mary for me."

"Of course," Joe replied, his tone apologetic as she scurried after the warden.

Lorraine dropped her mug off at her desk and grabbed her phone, shoving it in her pocket before following Wickham into his office. He stepped through the door first, and she was so intent on not treading on his heels that she didn't look up until he had already closed the door behind her. That's when she noticed the other person in the room.

Richard Blackwood.

The man smiled from ear to ear, like he'd just received news he'd been reelected mayor. "Lorraine. So good to see you again."

Lorraine sucked in a breath, looking to Wickham for an explanation. She didn't know why she expected to see guilt or sympathy on his face at the way he'd ambushed her, but it was nowhere to be found.

"Please," he said, gesturing to the chair next to Blackwood. "Have a seat."

"What's this about?" she asked, angry that her voice shook just a bit.

"Have a seat," Wickham said, his tone leaving no room for argument.

Lorraine wanted to hold her chin high and refuse to do what he'd asked, but she was already at a disadvantage here in so many ways. Deciding to comply for the time-being, she slid into the chair and leaned back into its plush cushions, hoping she looked more comfortable than she felt.

"Thank you," Wickham said. His smile was more of a smirk, as if he knew he'd just won the first round. "I trust you had a good night?"

If Lorraine had any doubts Wickham was in the dark about what Blackwood had been up to the night before, they were dashed away. He'd never asked her that question before. Grinding her teeth together, she managed to say, "I've had better."

"Oh no," Blackwood said, feigning alarm. "I hope everything's okay at home? With your mother?"

Lorraine's head snapped in his direction, and if she'd had the ability to light him on fire with her gaze alone, the entire building would've gone up in flames with him.

Hating that she'd given her surprise and anger away, Lorraine ignored Blackwood's insincere question and turned back to Wickham. "What's this about?"

"Come now, Lorraine. You have better manners than that," Wickham said, and the lack of warmth in his voice made her feel like she was nothing more than a mouse caught between his claws. He remained standing, leaning against the edge of his desk and lording himself over her. "Mayor Blackwood has a proposition for you, and I'd like you to give it some serious thought. It could be excellent for your career."

Lorraine held back a snort of derision. What career? But then his words sunk in, and she turned to Blackwood. "You were serious about wanting me to come work with you?"

"Of course." Blackwood held a hand to his chest as though she'd wounded his pride. "The warden has done nothing but speak highly of you and your work ethic. I could use someone as dependable as you around the office." Dropping his hand, he looked to his friend. "That is, as long as you're okay with lending her out?"

Wickham twisted his lips down into a frown, but his eyes twinkled. "It'll be a shame to lose such a pretty face around the office, but we all have to make sacrifices for the cause, don't we?"

Lorraine barely kept the look of disgust from taking over her entire face. These men were pigs, but to talk about her like a piece of equipment while she was in the room with them? Her stomach twisted into such a knot, she felt bile rise into her throat.

"And I'm sure we could move some money around to make sure you're duly compensated," Blackwood continued, not noticing the inner war raging within her.

"Move some money around?" she asked, repeating his words like they came from the other end of a tunnel.

"I have much more to play with than the warden here, and I daresay I have a bit more practice using government funds to my advantage." He chuckled, and the warden joined him, but he couldn't hide the way his gaze sharpened on the other man. "And with the significant raise you'll be receiving, you'll have no problem making sure your mother stays safe and sound."

All the anger left Lorraine's body in a single whoosh of air. Thinking about how her mother had dodged a bullet last night without even knowing it made Lorraine's stomach churn like she was out in the middle of the ocean during a storm with no more than a rubber raft between her and the elements. And these two were like a pair of sharks circling her, waiting for the perfect moment to strike.

Deflating, Lorraine had to swallow twice before she could speak. "That's all I care about," she whispered. Clearing her throat, she spoke a little louder, not wanting them to miss a single word she said. "My mother. She's the only person I care about. I'll do whatever you want."

Blackwood's smile stretched so wide, she thought his jaw would come unhinged. "That's exactly what I wanted to hear." He turned to the warden. "You were right about her. Pretty, poised, and pliable."

"What more could you ask for in a woman?" Wickham said, giving her an appraising once-over.

Lorraine ignored the disgust that rippled through her. "And what is it you want me to do, Mayor Blackwood?"

Blackwood closed his eyes, as though he could taste what it would be like to have his title back. When he met her eyes again, he looked hungry. "I already told you what I want."

"You want me to ruin Jason's reputation. But how? He's a good man who's doing good work. I'm nobody."

"Don't be so hard on yourself," Wickham said. "You're a beautiful woman, Lorraine. It wouldn't be hard to believe that your boss had trouble keeping his hands to himself."

"He would never—"

"That's beside the point," Blackwood said with a wave of his hand. "It's your word against his. Everyone knows that's all it takes these days."

Lorraine swallowed down her retort. In a small voice, she said, "Ruining Jason won't restore *your* reputation."

"But it *would* make me feel better," Blackwood said, his chuckle like ice and velvet all at once. "Besides, there's another thing you'll need to testify to."

She was afraid to ask. "What's that?"

"That the pictures he took of me were staged."

"Altered," Wickham said. "Much more believable. You can work miracles with Photoshop." He turned to gaze down his nose at Lorraine. "You're handy with a computer. You could say he forced you to do it."

Blackwood clapped his hands together, making Lorraine jump. "Even better!"

Trying not to show the way she was gulping down air, Lorraine asked, "Anything else?"

"One more tiny little favor," Blackwood said, not even trying to look apologetic. "You'll have Cassie tell Apex to give me a call. I want to be back on the payroll, and I'm willing to keep Cassie's name out of this if they comply. I know how fond they are of her."

It all clicked into place for her then. "So you're the one who leaked her name to the press."

He held up a hand in mock solidarity. "I will neither confirm nor deny, but I can ensure it won't happen again. As long as they're willing to work with me on this."

Lorraine barked out an unamused laugh. "You're blackmailing Apex? Is there any version of this that doesn't end up with you at the bottom of a ditch?"

Blackwood went stock-still, any trace of humor gone from his face. "I do not threaten easily, Ms. Krasinski."

"But this is Apex we're talking about," Lorraine said, barely breathing enough to force the words out of her mouth. "This goes way beyond a publicity company. They're—"

"I know who they are. I know who lines their pockets. You think I'm afraid of some big shot Chinese tycoon who never had to work for anything a day in his life?"

"No," Lorraine said, shaking her head violently. "But you do want to get back into bed with them. There has to be a reason—"

"The reason is that it's mutually beneficial. When Hughes fails to land himself a seat in the Oval Office because his father didn't put his biological son out of his misery when he realized the kid was a psychopath, then they'll need someone to take his place. I've got a proven track record and big enough balls to take on the White House. And that's not even mentioning the fact that one of my college buddies works for the NSA. They'd be idiots not to bring me back on board."

Lorraine thought it was laughable that Blackwood felt he was that indispensable to a company that had a reach as wide and greedy as Apex's, but she didn't let it show on her face. If he wanted to risk the kinds of consequences that came with this level of arrogance, she wouldn't stand in his way.

"So, what do you say, Lorraine?" Wickham asked, leaning back in his chair and clasping his hands behind his head. "Does that sound like the deal of a lifetime, or what?"

Nodding, she swallowed down the bile that still sat in her throat. "I guess there's only one thing left to say."

"Oh?" Wickham asked, his grin growing ever wider.

Lorraine stood. "I quit."

37

Cassie wasn't sure how long she stood there, her gaze transfixed on the violets that scaled the rocky incline before her. The scent of their blooms was overwhelming, but not oppressive, especially in the open air and amidst the gentle breeze. With the sun warming her shoulders and the burn of their hike lingering in her muscles, Cassie never felt more alive than in this moment.

Is that how Millie felt as she made this same trek three years ago?

"You're seeing this, right?" Chris asked.

Forgetting he had been there by her side, Cassie startled and glanced in his direction, seeing that he couldn't take his eyes away from the purple sea in front of them. "Yeah," she replied. "I think this is it."

"As in?" Chris hedged.

"Millie's final resting place."

Chris blew out a breath. "After all this time, I figured she wasn't alive."

All Cassie could do was nod, knowing it was better to uncover the truth than to let the mystery sit for several more years to come. As if Max agreed with her, she felt a gentle pressure in the middle of her back, like she'd placed a palm there to nudge Cassie forward.

"Okay," she said to Max, her voice gentle and apologetic. "It's time."

Taking the first step was the most difficult part. Cassie didn't want to step on the tiny flowers leading up to the cave, but it was impossible not to crush them underfoot. She had spent so long associating the smell of violets with Millie and Max that it was hard not to feel as though a part of them lived in those flowers. Max had been the only one to reach out and interact with Cassie, but was Millie here too, in each amethyst petal and emerald leaf?

"Max led us here," Chris said, following in Cassie's footsteps and wincing when he crushed a dense group of flowers. Maybe he felt it too. "But she didn't know where Millie was, or else she would've told someone."

"She is telling someone," Cassie said. "She might not have known when she was alive, but she must've discovered what happened after she died. That's why I've been smelling violets everywhere I go. It's why she knocked over that picture in Millie's bedroom."

"But how?" Chris said, sounding equal parts fascinated and frustrated. "I mean, how does that work?"

Cassie couldn't help but laugh a little. "Beats me." When Chris shot her a confused look, she shrugged. "I realize I know more than most about the afterlife, but there are so many things I'm not privy to."

"Would you want to know if you could?"

Cassie thought about that for a moment. "I don't think so. Some mysteries are better left unsolved. And some images you can't get out of your head once they're in there. I've already seen so much. I'm not sure how much more I can handle."

"Fair enough."

"What about you?"

"I'd want to know. I think it would make it easier to prepare for what came next, you know? I don't like walking into situations unarmed. At least I'd know what I was up against."

"Sounds about right," Cassie said, throwing a grin over her shoulder at him.

"How do you think Max found out about this place?"

"Not sure." Cassie chewed on the inside of her cheek while she leaned into their climb up the side of the hill. It was getting steeper with each step they took. Soon, they'd be practically scaling the side of the outcropping to get up to the cave. "Maybe she saw Millie on the other side. Or if Max was killed, maybe it was by the same person who kidnapped or killed Millie. They could've told her as she was dying. Might've been the reason she wasn't able to move on."

"God, that's tragic."

Cassie hummed in response, but she was breathing too hard now to continue the conversation. Looking up, she followed the obvious path up to the cave. They wouldn't have to climb the rock with any kind of gear, but it was steep enough that they'd have to slow their pace and make sure the footholds were solid before moving on. She was never more grateful to have stopped for boots than she was in that moment.

"We can go slow," Chris said. "I'm right behind you in case you slip."

"Thanks," she said, but her mind was already ahead of them, inside that cave.

Taking a steadying breath, Cassie continued, instinct driving her to lean forward to keep her center of gravity as close to the rock wall as possible. Dirt coated her hands as she found notches to grasp, but she didn't care. All that mattered was the next step. Getting closer to the cave. Closer to Millie.

The violets acted as a trail guide, growing close to the best places to grip with her hands or steady herself with her feet. After a few minutes, she stopped looking ahead to gauge the next few steps and trusted the blooms would lead her in the right direction.

It wasn't until she reached a ledge and took a moment to rest that she realized they were just outside the cave now. A cool breeze flowed from the entrance, wrapping her in a gentle embrace that encouraged her to keep moving forward.

Chris clamored up behind her, standing with his hands on his hips while he peered into the dark entrance. "We didn't think to bring flashlights."

"Think our phones are strong enough?" Cassie asked, already stepping forward.

"Guess we're about to find out," he said, following her.

They both retrieved their phones and turned on the flashlight feature before holding them up and taking that first tentative step inside. There were no more violets, but the chilly cavern air was like an ocean current dragging Cassie forward, pulling her in the right direction.

Chris mentioned something about not wanting to run into a bear or a mountain lion, but Cassie could barely hear him. In a daze, she put one foot in front of another until she'd walked the length of a football field in what felt like a matter of seconds. Surrounded by darkness, their feeble lights only illuminated the area directly in front of them. Even so, Cassie knew when she was close to what they were looking for.

As though someone had dragged a shadowed blanket off her, Millie's body was revealed one inch at a time. First, a shoe standing upright on its own. Then its match, still attached to a foot and connected to a leg bone. A single femur, dark with discoloration and hosting leathery fragments of what used to be muscle tissue. The hip bone, sitting in the center, detached from the spinal column. The rib cage broken into pieces and scattered across the floor like long-forgotten toys. Skeletal arms thrown to either side, one missing an entire hand. And finally, a skull, devoid of any human emotion and yet Cassie felt the echo of fear and confusion, of hurt and regret and anger, hanging in the air like a heavy shroud.

"Jesus," Chris said. "Animals got to her."

Cassie didn't say anything. The light from her phone caught on a swirl of smoke around the skull, which coalesced into the shape of a woman. Max leaned over the fragments of her sister's body and shook with despair. Cassie wanted to reach forward and place a hand on the woman's shoulder to comfort her.

Max looked up, ghostly tears tracking down her gray face. Seeing the destruction of Millie's body made Cassie's stomach churn. She wanted to look away, to save herself from future nightmares, but Max's gaze demanded she memorize this moment.

Help me, Max seemed to say. *Help me avenge her.*

Max's life had been difficult, her death even more so, yet she was not here for herself. Her ending was part of the story, but Max had stayed behind to take care of her sister, to help Cassie discover the truth of what had happened to her. To make someone pay for the crime they had committed.

Cassie didn't look away. She took in every detail of the corpse, from the shredded clothing to the shattered bones. The way the animals' claws and teeth had left behind marks deeper than anything that had hurt her while she was still alive.

"We need a forensic team to tell us how she died," Chris said. "Won't be able to figure out what damage was from her death and what was from the animals unless we get a closer look. But we found her. That's a good first step."

It was, but Cassie couldn't bring herself to feel relief. Not when there was so much left to do.

Max stood, her hands balled at her sides, and turned away from Cassie, walking deeper into the cave. Cassie followed her, careful to give each piece of Millie's body a wide berth.

It was hard to see Max amidst the backdrop of darkness in the cave. Holding her phone aloft, Cassie caught glimpses of milk-white eyes and flickering movement. She was so focused on following Max that she hadn't realized she'd reached the back of the cave until she almost ran head-first into it. With a little gasp, she halted and pressed a hand to the wall, comforted in feeling something solid beneath her fingers.

"Cassie?" Chris called from a few dozen feet away. "You okay?"

"I'm okay," she said, hating how even a whisper echoed like thunder in the cave.

"Did you see something?"

"No, I was—"

Max appeared from her right, a violent torrent of pain and anger. She dislocated her jaw and let out a cruel scream, so loud that Cassie dropped her phone to cover her ears with her hands. She could feel the way Max pushed at her psychic barrier, looking for weak points to exploit. But with every ounce of her remaining concentration, Cassie shut out the other woman, looking up into her eyes to prove she wasn't afraid.

Howling, Max dove toward Cassie, moving past her to melt into the shadows, the echo of her pain ringing in the air. Gasping for breath,

Cassie held a hand to her chest, hating the way she'd had to distance herself from Max. They'd been together for only a few days, but Cassie felt like she knew her, like she could've been a friend in another lifetime. But now, Max was rage incarnate. Her only purpose in death was to solve her sister's murder, and yet here Cassie was, not moving fast enough for a timeless being.

"Hey," Chris said, approaching with his light held high above him. "What happened?"

"Max is furious."

"Is that why you went off in this direction?"

"I thought she wanted me to follow her. I thought maybe she had something to show me."

"What did she do?"

"Screamed a lot," Cassie said. "I don't think she knows what to do now. Ghosts are like raw nerves—more feelings than conscious thoughts. This must be rough for her."

"Can't say I blame her."

Cassie bent to pick her phone off the ground, relieved to see her screen hadn't shattered.

Chris turned back toward the cave entrance. "We should get going. We'll have to hike back to get enough service to call the authorities. Then, by the time they show up and we get back to the cave, it'll probably be close to dark. I know she's waited three years to be discovered, but I don't like the idea of leaving her for another night. Not when we finally know where she is."

"Yeah, I—"

Cassie's words caught in her throat as Chris turned back to her, his light sweeping across the ground at their feet. A flash of silver had caught Cassie's attention, and for a moment she thought it was the ethereal glow that usually accompanied Max's presence, having returned to take her anger out on them some more.

But when Cassie pointed her light in that direction, she saw it was a money clip, covered in mud and spots of rust. Leaning closer, she realized it was still bright enough to read the letters stamped along the front.

"What does it say?" Chris said, having followed her gaze and bending down to get a better look.

"A.W.," Cassie read.

Chris grunted. "For Arnold Warren or Aaron Warren?"

"Your guess is as good as mine."

38

When they got back to the car, Chris contacted the local authorities as well as the Metropolitan Nashville Police Department, which had handled Millie's missing case three years ago. Against every instinct, Cassie had called Anastasia to give her an update on the proceedings. The woman had answered the phone with sugar-coated words and purred into the receiver when Cassie had told her they'd found Millie's body. She had withheld their discovery of the money clip, not wanting to give Anastasia the information she so desperately wanted—something to use against Governor Warren. She didn't want to risk Apex twisting the story if his brother had been involved instead.

Head swirling with possibilities, Cassie sat in the passenger seat of Chris' car while he stayed on the phone. Even a two-minute conversation with Anastasia was enough to tip Cassie over the edge, so she reclined in her seat and closed her eyes, reveling in the sun hitting her leg and the warm breeze caressing her skin through the open window.

Since they'd left the cave, Cassie hadn't felt Max by her side. There was a profound sense of loss with that realization, despite all the headaches the spirit had caused. She wasn't sure if Max had moved on now that her sister's body had been discovered, or if she was resting in that place beyond, building her energy to come back and ensure justice was served.

If either of the Warren brothers were the culprit, then Millie's case would be solved, but Apex would get exactly what they were looking for—ammo against Senator Hughes' biggest competition in the presidential race. And they'd be one step closer to accomplishing their goal of putting their very own puppet in the White House.

"Hey," Chris said, jerking her out of her thoughts. "They're here. You ready?"

Cassie nodded and returned her seat to the upright position, stepping out of the car as soon as a pair of cruisers pulled up behind them. Chris greeted them first while Cassie hung back, but she didn't have long to stew in her thoughts. As soon as Chris introduced her to the deputies and handed over the backpack of evidence they'd found in the creek, two of them asked Chris and Cassie to take them through the hike back to the cave while the other two stayed behind to direct traffic and pass along instructions.

On the way through the forest, Chris and Cassie took turns describing how they'd ended up looking into this case, how they'd discovered the cave, and what they'd found inside. Chris let Cassie take the lead on most of the details, allowing her to choose how much to reveal about her abilities and the way they'd stumbled upon the location of the body of a woman who'd been missing for three years. For her part, Cassie kept her story to the important facts, skirting around any details that would've seemed too convenient or absurd to believe. Chris backed up her changes in the story, and the deputies didn't blink an eye.

When they reached the cave, the officers brought out four high-powered flashlights, and their small group stepped into the cavern with less trepidation than Chris and Cassie had the first time. Knowing what was there made the rediscovery of the body less shocking, but no less disturbing. Cassie's heart broke from the clinical way the deputies assessed Millie's remains and took turns guessing what might've happened to her.

Not long after that, Nashville's Chief of Police arrived on the scene with another pair of officers and some members of the forensics team. The chief was a tall man who constantly tugged his pants higher so his protruding stomach didn't hang down over his belt. There was no telling if his rosy cheeks were due to the exertion of the trip to get to the cave or eczema. His beady eyes were dark and small, and always seemed to be watering. He kept a wide berth from the body in the center of the cave.

While Chris and Cassie repeated their story to the man, the others set up floodlights and equipment, taking pictures and cataloguing every piece of evidence they could find. Cassie watched in a daze as they bagged up human body parts like they hadn't once belonged to a living person, someone Cassie had gotten to know over the last couple of days through her connection with Max.

Despite knowing they would find it eventually, Cassie led the chief over to the money clip and waited until someone bagged it up and handed it to him to study. His eyes traced the design but didn't give away his thoughts.

"It says A.W.," Cassie said.

The man glared in her direction. "I can see that."

Ignoring his tone, she said, "It could stand for Arnold Warren. Or his brother Aaron."

"Miss Quinn." The chief handed the bag to one of his officers. "If I thought you were so willing to do my job for me, I wouldn't have bothered walking all the way out here. Do you want my badge and gun while you're at it?"

Cassie tensed, unsure why the man was being hostile. Before she could find her words, Chris stepped in, using his considerable height to tower over the police chief. "This woman has been missing for three years. It took Cassie three days to find her body. Perhaps you would be better off turning your badge over to her, Chief Lowe. I think she'll be in town for a few more days. Maybe she can solve a couple more cases for you."

Chief Lowe turned his icy glare in Chris' direction. "You think you're being funny, son?"

"No, I think I'm being honest. She did you a favor by solving this case. It's not like she wants any credit for it."

"A favor?" Chief Lowe said, a chuckle in his voice. "You think you did me a favor by handing me evidence that suggests, at worst, the governor of Kentucky might've murdered his fiancée, and at best, his brother did it in his stead? We're about to have a circus on our hands, and you want me to thank her for bringing it to my town?"

"I didn't bring anything to Nashville," Cassie said, crossing her arms across her chest as though that would contain her anger. "Apex brought me in to solve this case, and that's what I did. I'm not looking for gratitude, Mr. Lowe. I just want Millie Abrahms to get the justice she deserves. And the same for her sister, Maxine."

Chief Lowe's glare only intensified. "Max Abrahms died of an overdose. That was an open and shut case. What justice does she need? She did it to herself."

"Are you sure about that?"

"I did the wellness check myself. Yes, I'm sure." Before either of them could say anything else, the Chief brushed by Cassie. "You two can pack up. You've done enough here."

But Cassie hardly heard his words. When his arm grazed hers, a powerful chill coursed through her body and made her stumble back into Chris, who wrapped his hands around her shoulders to steady her. The pressure of his fingers came to her as though through a dream, distant and vague. The cave disappeared only to be replaced by Max's wide eyes, no longer milk-white but clear and terrified. The skin around her face, pink and alive, was pulled tight across her features as her mouth fell open in shock. Confusion and betrayal rocked through her, replaced finally with understanding and then blissful unconsciousness.

"Cassie?" Chris whispered in her ear. "Are you okay? What happened?"

"I'm not sure," Cassie said, following Chief Lowe's back as he returned to the entrance of the cave. "But I don't think Max was dead when the Chief did the wellness check on her."

39

The last thing Cassie wanted to do was ask Anastasia Bolton for help.

Yet, here she was, sitting in her office trying to work up the nerve to ask for exactly that. Guilt and frustration pumped through Cassie's veins, making her lightheaded. She clenched her fists in her lap, knowing she was only delaying the inevitable by sitting here, merely watching Anastasia study her with a smug grin.

Her only solace was that Chris was still by her side, sitting in the chair next to hers. After they realized Chief Lowe wouldn't give them the time of day, they'd hiked back to the car, packed up their belongings, and made the return trip to Nashville. There wasn't much else to do other than wait for the team to process the crime scene and reach out with their conclusions.

"Do you realize how incredible you are?" Anastasia asked Cassie. Most people would've said those words with a touch of awe, but there was only hunger in Anastasia's voice. "We've had several other psychics tackle this case, only to be discouraged at every turn."

"Mediums," Chris said, tossing Cassie a playful grin. She couldn't bring herself to grin back.

Anastasia ignored him. "In three days, you found Millie's body. Solved the case."

"It's not solved yet," Cassie said. "We don't know who killed her."

"Don't we?" Anastasia asked, her head cocked to the side. "You found the money clip with Arnold Warren's initials on it."

Cassie couldn't bring herself to be surprised that Anastasia had learned that bit of information already. "Initials he shares with his brother."

"Besides, that's hardly proof," Chris said. "Just because his money clip was there, doesn't mean he was. And if he was there, that doesn't mean he killed her. We need motive and evidence to convict him."

"It's enough for the court of public opinion," Anastasia replied, shuffling some papers around on her desk before folding her hands over the top of them and leveling Chris with a smile. "And that's good enough for me."

"It's not enough for me," Cassie said, her tone firm. "I came here to solve this case. We haven't done that yet."

"Then why are you sitting here in my office paying me this lovely visit, and not out there doing what needs to be done?" Anastasia asked.

Cassie ground her teeth together, sure that Anastasia knew what she was about to ask. "Because we need your help."

Anastasia raised an eyebrow. "What could I possibly do for you?"

It took every ounce of willpower for Cassie to force the words out past her teeth. "Chief Lowe is hiding something."

"How do you know that?" Despite the dubious question, Anastasia's eyes sparkled.

"How I know most things other people don't?"

"Don't be coy, Cassie." Anastasia leaned forward and licked her lips. "If you want my help, I'll need to know everything you know."

Cassie chewed the inside of her lip. This felt like giving away trade secrets. Every detail she shared made her feel like she was loading another bullet into Apex's gun. But what other choice did she have?

"When the Chief brushed by me, I saw Max's final moments. She was surprised and confused, and then terrified and angry. Chief Lowe saw her right before she died."

Anastasia's voice was sober when she asked, "He killed her?"

"I'm not sure," Cassie said. "But he knows more than he's letting on."

Anastasia drummed her crimson nails against the surface of her desk. "Interesting. I didn't think he had it in him."

"Can you help us or not?" Chris asked.

Anastasia directed her words to Cassie, as though Chris hadn't even spoken. "I hired you to solve Millie's case, not Max's. This isn't our problem."

Cassie ground her teeth together so hard, her jaw ached. "Their cases are related. Everything we've discovered about Max's death tells me she didn't kill herself. She didn't even accidentally overdose. Someone did this to her, and I bet it's because she was getting close to the truth about her sister."

"Again, that's not my—"

"What do you want, Anastasia?" Cassie knew she was digging herself deeper into the hole Apex had placed her in, but she couldn't walk away from Max. "What will it take for you to do something about this?"

If Anastasia had looked hungry before, she was downright ravenous now. "Your talents should not go to waste. We'd love for you to stick around and solve another case for us."

"Cassie—" Chris warned.

"Fine." Cassie ignored the way Chris stared at her, mouth agape. "But only if we solve both Millie and Max's murders."

"And how, exactly, would you like me to help you?"

"How do you normally handle situations like this?"

"You won't like my answer to that."

Cassie huffed, looking anywhere but Anastasia's steady gaze. She and Chris had explored their options to confront the chief on their way back from the park, and they'd both come to the same conclusion.

Apex was the most efficient way to get what they needed.

"You have considerable resources," Cassie said. "I suggest you use them to convince the chief of police to be honest about what he knows."

Anastasia tipped her head back and laughed. "A bribe? Now you're thinking like an Apex employee."

"I never said—"

"You didn't have to," Anastasia said, picking up her desk phone and dialing a string of numbers in quick succession. "Hello, Robert." She paused, listening to what the driver had to say on the other end. "Yes, if you have a moment." Another pause. "As soon as you can." A gracious smile spread across her face. "Thank you."

"Where are we going?" Cassie asked.

Anastasia rose from her chair. "It's high time we laid all of this to rest, don't you think?"

40

Cassie watched as Anastasia applied a new coat of lipstick prior to leaving her office, as though she could improve upon perfection, and the two of them followed her out of the building and into Robert's waiting car. After Anastasia slipped into the front seat, Chris and Cassie slid into the back, and the man gave them each a polite nod before pulling away from the curb and out into traffic.

"Where are we going?" Chris asked for the third time since Anastasia had made her little proclamation.

"Indulge me," Anastasia said. "It'll be more fun if it's a surprise."

Cassie traded a glance with Chris, and she wondered if he felt the same amount of trepidation she did. Even on a good day, Cassie didn't like surprises. Especially when Anastasia was the one delivering the package.

The sun was just on the horizon by the time they hit the road, and Cassie watched through the tinted windows as it dipped out of view, turning the sky the exact shade of a day-old bruise. Anastasia scrolled through her tablet in silence, and Chris alternated between watching her with curiosity and keeping an eye on the road.

Less than an hour later, they crossed the state line into Kentucky. Cassie caught Chris' eye and pursed her lips. He nodded in response.

Having come to the same conclusion about their eventual destination, Cassie's stomach rolled in response. Where else would they be heading but to speak with the governor and his brother?

While Cassie was not surprised when the governor's mansion came into view, she was taken aback when a police cruiser led them through a security gate and down a winding drive to a private parking area in the back. It wasn't until both vehicles came to a stop that she noticed the sign for the Metropolitan Nashville Police Department on the side of the car.

When Anastasia stepped out onto the pavement, the officer behind the wheel revealed himself to be Chief Lowe, who joined her with a glower. It only faltered when Chris and Cassie stepped into view, causing the man to give a little jolt of surprise before he looked away. Anastasia responded with a predatory smile.

"Let's get this over with," he mumbled.

"Come now, Darryl," Anastasia purred. "There's no need to be rude." Then, as though a switch had been flipped, the next words out of her mouth lacked their usual sensuality. "Are they both here?"

"Yes."

"Then lead the way."

Lowe's sigh was resigned, but he followed Anastasia's command without hesitation. Cassie let her eyes drift from the back of the man's hunched shoulders and up to the governor's home. It reminded her of the White House, but less imposing. Still, it cut an impressive silhouette against the night sky.

The Chief led them along a manicured path and up to the door where a security guard ushered them inside. It had been shockingly easy to gain entrance to the mansion after hours, and Cassie wondered how much of that had been thanks to Chief Lowe and how much had been Apex.

The interior of the estate was a blur of lacquered floors and crisp wallpaper, plush couches and ornately framed paintings. Under different circumstances, Cassie would've loved to stop and study it all in detail, but her mind whirred with all the possible outcomes of this confrontation. Anastasia had a plan, but Cassie couldn't begin to guess what the other woman would do.

When the security guard knocked on an impressive door carved with intricate designs, a muffled voice from inside called, "Come in." The guard gestured for them to enter. Lowe did so without hesitation.

Governor Warren sat on an antique couch upholstered in crimson and accented with navy pillows. He wore his reading glasses on the tip of his nose as he studied a stack of papers in his hand. When he looked up and caught sight of Lowe, he smiled.

"Darryl," he said, placing the papers and his glasses on the cushion beside him. "This is a surprise."

"Where's Aaron?" Lowe asked, his voice gravely.

"He was just grabbing us some drinks. Do you want something?" Arnold's gaze slid from Lowe's when Cassie and Chris entered, then sharpened when Anastasia followed in their wake, shutting the door behind them. He rose from the couch, his jaw tensing as though grinding his teeth. "What's the meaning of this?"

"We need to talk," Lowe said.

Arnold studied him for a moment before his face went pale and slack. He stumbled back down onto the couch, his gaze bouncing from one person to another before settling on Cassie's face. "You found her?"

Never had she wanted to feel Max's presence more than in that very moment. Whether it was fury or despair, she would take that over having to feel all these emotions on her own. But something told her Max was well and truly gone, having finally revealed her sister's body, just like she'd tried to when she was alive.

With a soft nod, Cassie said, "Yes."

Arnold cradled his face in his hands just as the door opened. Aaron froze when he saw the group before him, but regained his composure in a matter of seconds. Crossing the room and handing his brother a glass filled halfway to the rim with amber liquid, his gaze settled on Chief Lowe's.

"What's this about, Darryl?"

"You know," Lowe said, not without a touch of sympathy and remorse.

Aaron's gaze also bounced around from one person to another, but he settled on Anastasia. "That's it, then? Years of friendship down the drain because this bitch told you to heel?"

Anastasia tipped her head back and laughed. "You give me far too much credit, Mr. Warren. I'm simply a cog in the machine. Your brother could've been, too. And then we might've avoided this whole mess."

"You didn't bring back-up. No spectacle. That means one of two things." Aaron's gaze never wavered, even as he brought his glass to his lips and drained half its contents in one go. "You either don't have evidence and credible testimony, or you're here to negotiate."

"The latter, of course." Anastasia pointed to the navy sofa across from where Arnold sat. "May I?" Without waiting for a response, she sauntered across the room and sat, crossing her legs at the ankles and adjusting her skirt with prim satisfaction. "Shall we?"

It took a few seconds for Cassie's mind to catch up with what Anastasia had said. "Two women have been murdered. We're not negotiating."

Arnold's head snapped up. "Two women?"

Anastasia flipped her hair over her shoulder, using the moment to toss a glare in Cassie's direction. "Let's hear the full story, and then we'll decide what's best—for all parties involved."

Cassie shook with unrestrained rage, but a warm hand on her shoulder stilled her. Looking up, she saw Chris wearing a frown on his face. He shook his head. Cassie's heart dropped at the same time her face fell. Anastasia was in control of the room and everyone in it. Now was not the time to create waves. Not before they knew the truth.

Aaron slugged back the rest of his drink and slammed the glass down on a table. "What's stopping me from calling in my brother's men and having them escort you all off the premises, and taking you somewhere no one will ever find you?"

Anastasia leaned back against the couch, looking like she not only owned the room, but the entire mansion and all the land it sat on. "For one, those aren't your brother's men. They haven't been for quite a while. You can try, of course, but you'd just be wasting everyone's time."

"What did you mean," Arnold said, "two women were murdered?"

"Let's not get ahead of ourselves," Anastasia said. "It's better to start at the beginning. The night Millie left your hotel and didn't return."

"What about it?" he asked. "I already told the authorities what happened."

"But you lied about staying in your hotel the next day, didn't you?"

"No," Arnold said, but there was no conviction in his voice.

Lowe's voice was rote and devoid of any emotion when he spoke. "Yes, you did. You called your brother to stay there and take your calls. You sound identical on the phone, and he knows your policies as well as you do. No one knew the difference."

"The perfect alibi," Anastasia said. "Everyone who spoke to you on the phone or left room service outside your door could testify to the fact that you were there the entire time."

"I never meant it as an *alibi*," Arnold said.

"Maybe not at first, but that's what ended up happening, isn't it?" When no one answered, Anastasia pressed forward. "I imagine you followed Millie home a few hours later. The neighbor who spotted her is elderly, so she would've been in bed by the time you pulled into the driveway. You spent the night together, and the next morning, she suggested you go for a hike. Get some fresh air. Talk things out. Really make sure you both wanted the marriage."

"We did want the marriage," Arnold said, his eyes begging for them to believe him. "We loved each other."

Anastasia continued as though he hadn't said anything. "You went for your hike. But something changed along the way, didn't it? I'm guessing it had something to do with some money that had gone missing? You can deny it if you want, but the police already have proof of the text messages between you and your brother. Just because Chief Lowe never let that particular detail slip doesn't mean there isn't a paper trail, you know."

"She never would've stolen from me—"

"I told you she was trash," Aaron said, cutting his brother off. "You didn't want to believe me."

Tears tracked down Arnold's face. "She wouldn't have—"

"Your brother told you there was a considerable sum missing from your bank account," Anastasia said. "He told you to ask Millie about it. You confronted her. I don't think it's too much to presume that led to an argument. From what I understand, your relationship was volatile."

"She said she didn't take it. I believed her."

"What changed, then?" Anastasia asked. And before either of the Warren brothers could answer, she held up one crimson-tipped finger. "Let me remind you that it won't be difficult to create a narrative that paints both of you in a terrible light. This is your chance to get ahead of the curve."

Arnold looked up at his brother, and Cassie noticed he was trembling. After a moment, Aaron nodded once, sharp and jerky, before crossing over to the nearby wall and leaning against it, arms crossed over his chest so tight, his muscles bulged.

"She said she didn't," Arnold repeated. "But then we found the cave. Decided to take a break. She wanted me to grab the food out of her backpack while she explored deeper. That's when I found—" He choked. "I found the—"

"The money clip," Anastasia said. "Yours or your brother's?"

"Mine," Arnold answered. "It went missing the week before. I was devastated. I didn't care about the money, but the clip was a gift from my late father."

"So you confronted her about that too," Anastasia said.

"I was so angry." Arnold's eyes were distant, as though he'd been transported back three years to that moment in the cave. "Our entire relationship felt like a lie. I threw the money clip at her. Surprised her, I think. First time I ever did something like that. She stumbled backwards. Tripped. Fell."

While Cassie couldn't tear her eyes away from the man in front of her, Anastasia scrolled through her tablet as though this were nothing more than a meeting she had no interest in attending. Without looking up, she said, "I received the coroner's report about ten minutes ago. Blunt force trauma to the back of the head, consistent with a fall that landed her on top of one of the sharp rocks inside the cave. Is that what happened?"

Instead of answering, Arnold just sobbed into his hands.

41

"What happened next, Governor?" Anastasia asked. "Did you try to help her, or did you leave her there to die?"

Arnold's head snapped up, his face distorted with anguish. "There was so much blood. And she wasn't responding. I knew I couldn't move her without causing further injuries. There was no service in the cave to call a rescue team, so I ran back toward the car. But we hadn't been following a trail. She loved just walking through the forest, making her own way."

"But you didn't call a rescue team, did you?"

Arnold shook his head. "Muscle memory. I dialed my brother's number. Told him everything that had happened. He said he'd take care of it."

"And then what?" Anastasia asked, looking at Aaron.

Aaron stared down at her, unflinching. "I took care of it."

"You left the hotel to meet your brother," Anastasia said, filling in the blanks. "But by the time you got there, Millie was dead. Even though it had been an accident, you knew it wouldn't be good for your brother or his prospects. Not if he wanted to become president. A kidnapped fiancée would make for better optics than one who'd died under mysterious circumstances."

"You moved the car," Chris said. "Made it look like either Millie or her kidnappers had abandoned it. Then you took your brother's clothes and gear and buried it in the creek a quarter mile from the side of the road. It was the only way to ensure no one would find it—not the cops, their dogs, or some random hiker."

"But Cassie found it," Anastasia said, beaming in her direction.

Cassie ignored her, keeping her eyes trained on Aaron. "You left her there to be eaten by animals. No one knew where she was or what had happened to her. All so you could save your brother's political career."

If she expected Aaron Warren to look remorseful, she was sorely disappointed. "Your point?"

"Max went crazy wondering what happened to her," Cassie said. "She knew her sister wouldn't just disappear without telling her where she was going. Kidnapping was always a possibility, so she started her own investigation. When she discovered the missing money, she knew something was rotten. Millie wouldn't have kept a windfall like that from Max, not when it would've helped her move into a better apartment in a better neighborhood."

"Chief Lowe knew Maxine was getting close to the truth," Anastasia said. "He told you as much, Aaron."

"Is that so?" Aaron asked, lobbing a glare at the chief.

"You sent the chief over to Max's apartment under the guise of an anonymous wellness check." The twinkle in Anastasia's eyes negated the pout on her lips. "Then he shot her up with enough heroin to kill her ten times over and destroyed her notes. Well, except the one she'd scribbled on a scrap of paper and stuck in her pocket. The one question that would lead her to the truth."

"*Where did the money go?*" Cassie asked, remembering the harried way the words had been written on that piece of paper. "Why would anyone kidnap her if she had that much money to trade for her life? It didn't make sense."

"Is that true?" Arnold asked, staring at Lowe. "You killed her?"

Lowe didn't meet anyone's eyes when he answered. "Yes."

"Why?"

"He promised me a job in the White House," Lowe answered, glancing at Aaron. "And a lot of money."

"Why are you admitting this now?"

"*They* promised me more," Lowe said, his gaze sliding to Anastasia's delighted face.

Arnold looked to his brother. "How could you do that?"

"Don't look at me like that," Aaron said, his face contorting in disgust. "Like a wounded puppy. This is your mess. I was just cleaning it up."

"I wonder," Anastasia said, "did you ever tell the governor how his money clip ended up in her backpack?"

Aaron glared at her while Arnold turned a quizzical expression in her direction. "What are you talking about?"

Anastasia grinned down at her tablet, tapping away until she found what she was looking for. "I found your missing money. It's safe and sound, in an account registered under your brother's name. Not only did he have your fiancée's sister murdered, but he's also been stealing from you. And he planted your money clip in Millie's backpack to make you believe she was the real culprit."

With shaking hands, Arnold took the tablet when Anastasia held it out to him, and Cassie could only imagine what was going through his mind as he looked down at the irrefutable proof that his brother had been the one taking advantage of him all along.

When he looked up at Aaron, his expression was detached, as though he couldn't quite wrap his head around all of this new information. "Why?"

"Because she would've held you back," Aaron said, almost growling. "You can do anything, Arnold. Governor, senator, president—it's all at your fingertips. And you were going to throw it all away over a piece of ass."

"I loved her," Arnold said, blinking as though he were fighting to stay conscious. "It would've only been worth it if I could share it with her."

"Didn't love her as much as you loved being in office, though, did you? Otherwise, you would've admitted to the truth three years ago."

Anastasia looked as though she was a lone fox who'd walked into a coop full of sleeping chickens. "Now that we've gotten all that out of the way, we can negotiate. Chief Lowe is willing to testify that your brother murdered both Millie and Maxine Abrahms. I'm willing to leave you out of it, given you pull out of the presidential race, endorse Ross Hughes, and come play for the home team."

"She was no one," Aaron said, stepping forward and looking murderous. "I'm your brother."

"You can rot for all I care." Arnold turned his back on Aaron. "You're no brother of mine."

Then he moved toward the door, leaving Cassie to wonder if the truth even mattered when no one but the people in that room would ever know what had really happened to Millie and Max.

42

"Breaking news. Aaron Warren, brother of Kentucky Governor Arnold Warren, has been arrested for the murder of a woman whose death a year ago was ruled an accidental overdose. The woman was none other than Maxine Abrahms, the sister of Governor Warren's fiancée, Millicent Abrahms, who disappeared three years ago. But if you thought the story couldn't get any stranger, think again. Earlier this evening, Millicent's body was discovered in the Great Smoky Mountains National Park after a pair of hikers came upon the body when they left the marked trail to investigate a nearby cave. Tennessee and Kentucky state authorities as well as federal investigators are working in tandem to solve the case as quickly as possible. While the MNPD has not confirmed the cause of Millicent's death, an anonymous source has stepped forward as a star witness, providing credible evidence Aaron Warren was involved in covering up her disappearance. There's no telling how much Governor Warren knew about his brother's actions or whether he was involved in either woman's untimely death. Rachel is on location outside the precinct, ready to bring us more information as soon as it becomes available."

"Thank you, Marlene. I'm here—"

Cassie exited out of the video on her phone and looked up at Jason, who sat behind the wheel of his car with a mixture of shock and trepidation on his face. Even though she'd had a few hours to come to terms with what was happening, Cassie figured her own expressions mirrored his.

Jason blew out a breath. "It's all happening so fast now."

Cassie nodded, swallowing a few times before she erased the dryness in her throat. "After Chief Lowe agreed to turn on them, Anastasia pulled every string she had to fast-track this. By tonight, the news will be reporting exactly what happened. Well, Apex's version at least." Bile rose in Cassie's throat, burning as hot as her anger. "I also imagine Senator Hughes will release a statement to keep his name in the headlines."

"That's risky," Jason replied.

"Why?"

"Seems to me a lot of people liked Governor Warren. Felt bad for him after Millie disappeared. Now the public will feel like the wool had been pulled over their eyes, even if the courts prove he wasn't involved. People will be more skeptical of everyone, more discerning about who might be capable of this sort of thing. I wouldn't be surprised if someone investigates Hughes' family, looking for similar skeletons in their closet. And they've got them."

"Ross Hughes is clean," Cassie argued, although she wasn't sure why.

"You can't know that for sure," Jason replied. "Arnold lied about his involvement in Millie's death. Who's to say Ross isn't doing the same? They're both politicians. Lying is what they do."

Cassie had no argument for that, so she remained silent.

"Hughes' father used Apex to cover up his biological son's murder spree for decades," Jason continued, his voice softer now. "Even if Ross had no idea, that will tarnish the family name, just like it tarnished Arnold Warren's."

"Apex would never allow that to happen," Cassie said. "They've covered it up for this long. The only reason we found that connection was because Douglas' mother told us. And now she's gone, too. The only people left who know are you, me, Chris, Adelaide, and Lorraine. And we don't have any proof."

"Yet," Jason said.

Cassie remained silent, not willing to get her hopes up. After Arnold threw his brother to the wolves, Cassie had slipped away with an apologetic glance to Chris. She'd needed to get out of there and find a place to come to terms with her guilt. Aaron deserved to be punished, but it didn't sit right with her that Arnold would avoid legal consequences for not reporting Millie's death, and that Chief Lowe would retain his position with the MNPD despite having been the one to murder Maxine.

As much as she wracked her brain for an alternative solution, she couldn't find one that had any chance of working. Not without crossing Anastasia and Apex Publicity. And she couldn't deny she had used their extensive power to make this all come to a head. Sure, she solved two murders and locked away the man who was ultimately responsible, but was that enough when she knew he hadn't been the only one involved?

"There's only so much we can do," Jason said, for what felt like the tenth time. She imagined he could read the emotions on her face like they were written in permanent marker. "You did a good thing today, solving Millie's case and helping Max move on. You couldn't have done that without Anastasia's help. Once we discredit Apex and reveal what they've been up to, I'm sure Chief Lowe will face the consequences he deserves for his part in all of this."

"I hope you're right," Cassie said.

Jason winked at her. "You know I am."

She rolled her eyes. "Let's not get ahead of ourselves. First, we need Omega to join the cause."

"No time like the present," Jason said, pushing his car door open and stepping out in the evening air.

Cassie hesitated, looking once more around the parking lot of the motel. It was a far cry from where they'd met the man in Centennial Park, but he'd been insistent on seeing them again, saying the information about Pearl Everly had led down some interesting rabbit holes. Refusing to share his findings anywhere but in person, he'd given them the address to a shitty motel that looked like it was known for hosting all sorts of clandestine meetings.

Cassie stepped out of the car and shut the door behind her,

smoothing her hair and her dress just to give her hands something to do while she took a few calming breaths. She couldn't get Anastasia's smug smile out of her head. Cassie still hadn't told Jason the deal she'd struck when she'd solicited the woman's help, and she was not looking forward to that conversation.

For now, they had more pressing matters at hand.

Jason waited until Cassie was by his side before holding out his hand. She took it, feeling more grounded with him there. As angry as she had been when he'd shown up unannounced, she was grateful he was here now. She couldn't have done this part without him.

Without exchanging a word, they walked around to the other side of the motel, stepping over broken bottles and cigarette butts every few feet. A pair of men leered at them from the open doorway to a room, but didn't say a word.

The motel was long, with at least a dozen rooms from one end to the other and two levels in total. Omega was on the far end of the second floor, which required them to climb a rusted staircase covered in mud and chewing gum, then navigate the narrow balcony to room 28.

They were still a couple of rooms away when Jason's body went rigid and he picked up his pace. Trying to keep up, Cassie watched her shoes to avoid tripping over her own feet. It was only when they skidded to a stop outside the room that Cassie noticed the door hanging ajar, splinters of wood littering the ground where someone had kicked it in and broken part of the frame.

Jason pushed Cassie behind him and used the toe of his shoe to open the door as wide as it would go. The protesting hinges relented after a few nudges. He held one arm out to keep Cassie back and stuck his head inside to check the room. Turning to her, he held a finger to his lips and motioned for her to wait. As he entered the room by himself, she felt the contents of her stomach threaten to come back up, but she swallowed back the feeling and resisted the urge to go in after him. She thrust her hand into her purse and pulled out her phone, ready to dial the police should something happen.

Less than a minute later, Jason reappeared in the doorway and motioned her inside. "It's clear. No one's here." He swallowed, looking pained. "No one alive, anyway."

Cassie gulped down several breaths of air before forcing her legs to move forward one step at a time. She didn't stop until she had crossed the threshold and stood at the end of the only bed in the room, unable to tear her eyes away from the body lying in its center.

Omega was on his stomach in the middle of the mattress, blood staining the comforter a deep crimson. He faced the window and his eyes were open, staring blankly at where the blinds had been drawn closed. Cassie noted they were a bright blue, having been unable to see them behind his mirrored sunglasses the last time they'd met. A mottled bruise across his right temple stood out against his pale and ashen skin. Three bullet wounds had torn through his back, piercing his heart. He had died instantly, but that was little comfort to Cassie.

"When's the last time you spoke with him?" Cassie whispered.

"A few hours ago," Jason replied, his voice ragged. "Something tells me everyone in this place looked the other way when it went down." Gulping, he turned wide eyes on Cassie. "Maybe it wasn't even him who contacted me. We should go."

The hair along the back of Cassie's neck stood on end, and she didn't resist the urge to look over her shoulder to make sure they weren't being watched. When she confirmed they were alone, she crossed the room and closed the door the best she could.

"What are you doing?" Jason asked.

"We need to search the place."

"For what?" Jason asked, looking around. "There's nothing here. I don't even see a suitcase. No way this is where he was staying."

"This is the only chance we'll get," Cassie said, using the hem of her shirt to open the dresser drawers. "If there's something here, we have to be the ones to find it."

Jason shook his head but headed over to the bathroom and grabbed a towel, using it to open the closet door. "He survived years without calling attention to himself. Then the minute I meet up with him, he's killed."

"He knew the risks," Cassie said, stepping around the puddle of blood on the floor so she could reach the nightstand. The only thing inside was a Bible, but she flipped through it anyway. "He wanted to meet up with us. He wanted to do something about Apex."

"How can you—" Jason shook his head, but then pushed through his emotions anyway. "How can you not feel like this is our fault?"

Cassie swallowed, looking away from his desperate eyes. "Because I can't handle another tragedy right now." Her voice came out quiet and raspy, like her dry throat was lined with shards of glass. "And we can't risk getting distracted. Not when we're this close to catching Apex."

Jason remained silent for a few seconds before disappearing into the bathroom and searching it. While he was out of the room, Cassie sent up a silent prayer before patting Omega's pockets to see if he'd been hiding anything. She'd just stepped back when Jason reentered the room.

"Nothing," he said, looking everywhere but at Cassie and the dead body.

"Same."

"He's not still—you know?"

"Hanging around?" she asked. "No."

"But he was murdered."

"Not everyone decides to stay behind, no matter how gruesome their death." She blew out a frustrated breath, thinking of David. For better or worse, she'd never gotten a chance to talk to him again after he died. "We should go."

"We need to call the police."

"Someone will find him," she said. "We can't risk being seen near the crime scene, not when Apex already has the altered tape with you on it."

Pain flashed across Jason's eyes, but he nodded and followed her out of the room, careful not to touch the door handle as he pulled it shut behind them. Checking that the coast was clear, Cassie led them back the way they'd come, noting that this time, Jason kept his hands deep in his pockets. Her heart ached for him and the man they barely knew—the man who could've been the answer to all of this.

When they got back to the car, Jason pulled onto the road and drove in silence for a few minutes before he turned into a half-full parking lot in front of a restaurant. He didn't say anything, just rested his forehead against the steering wheel.

"You okay?"

"No," he said, leaning back and rubbing a hand down his face. "How could someone have found him? It doesn't make any sense."

"Maybe Chris wasn't as careful as he thought." She was more terrified for Jason than she'd been since he'd shown up in Nashville. "I think you should go home."

Jason gaped at her. "What?"

She met his gaze. "The reason you were in Nashville is dead. It's too dangerous for you to be here, this close to Apex."

"What about you?"

"They won't hurt me. Not while I'm still useful."

"But the case is closed. You can come home too."

Cassie looked away. "I agreed to another one. That was the only way Anastasia would help us. I'm staying."

"Cassie—"

"I'm staying." She clenched her jaw. "But you should go home."

Jason remained silent as he put the car into drive and pulled back onto the street. Cassie knew he would do what she'd asked.

She also knew he might never forgive her for it.

43

Cassie's heart shattered when Jason dropped her off in front of her hotel without saying goodbye. He just sat there, hands gripping the wheel as though he were strangling it, his jaw clenched and ticking, his eyes hard and distant. He'd allowed her to lean in and kiss his cheek but didn't acknowledge the gesture. Didn't tell her to be safe. Didn't even look at her before he drove away.

She'd never felt more alone than she did in that moment. For days, she'd had a constant companion in Maxine, and there was now an emptiness where the other woman had taken up residence inside her. Cassie found that she missed Max's cool breezes, infused with the aroma of violets, and the way she communicated by flickering lights or an annoyed click of the AC unit. Even in downtown Nashville, everything seemed quieter without her.

And now, Cassie mourned Jason's absence. They were so adamant about protecting each other, they fought to be the one to throw themselves in front of the bullet. But at the end of the day, Apex wanted her too badly to do her any serious harm. The only way they could get to her was through the people she cared about.

Apex had won this round, finding a way to get her to take another case, but she'd be smarter next time. She saw what kind of game they were playing, and now she was more familiar with the rules. She'd figure out a way to beat them, one way or another.

Cassie's phone buzzed, and she pulled it out hoping to see Jason's name on her screen. Instead, it was Chris. Disappointment bloomed in her chest, angry and rancid even though he was the only person left in the city who was truly on her side.

Found some interesting info about Five Winds. I'm at the bar where we grabbed drinks that first day. You guys want to meet me?

Cassie should've felt excited about the news, but she just felt exhausted. Looking up at her hotel, she considered ignoring Chris' text and going inside to lie down. Maybe for a short nap, maybe for the rest of the night. Whatever he had to say could wait until morning, right?

But when Cassie turned back to the road, a familiar SUV pulled up to the curb, and when the passenger window rolled down, she spotted Robert behind the wheel. "Good evening, Miss Quinn. Do you need a ride?"

"No, thank you," she said, but the words would've been more convincing if they hadn't caught in her throat. "It's late, I'll call a car."

"I insist," Robert said, stepping out of the vehicle. When he rounded the hood and stopped next to the rear passenger door, he pulled it open and gestured for her to step inside. "It would be my pleasure."

Cassie gave the man a quick nod and slid inside, relieved when she saw she was alone. If Anastasia had been in the backseat, there would've been no chance she could wiggle free from her clutches to meet Chris. As much as Cassie didn't feel up for the bar scene, she knew he wouldn't have sent the text if it wasn't important.

Robert slid behind the wheel and looked at her from the rearview mirror. "Where to?"

"Let me find the address."

Cassie pulled up the location on her phone and relayed the information. With a sharp nod, Robert pulled out into traffic, and they were on their way. Cassie leaned back in her seat, wondering once again what Robert did during the hours he wasn't ferrying her back and forth.

"Looks like you're going to be stuck with me a bit longer," she said, wanting to chase away the silence that lived inside her now. "I extended my stay here in Nashville to work for Apex a little longer."

Robert glanced at her in the rearview mirror. "I'm glad to hear that. Hopefully, your time here will be productive."

"Yeah," Cassie said, her desire to have a conversation dying as quickly as it came.

Robert didn't seem driven to make small talk either, and they spent the rest of the ride listening to the sounds of Nashville's late-night traffic. Before she knew it, they were sitting outside the pub.

"Would you like me to wait for you, Miss Quinn?"

"No," she said, not sure how long she'd be out. Or if she'd even want to return to the hotel tonight, not when she knew there would be no one waiting for her there. "That's okay. I'll have my friend drop me off."

Robert frowned in disapproval but gave her a curt nod. "Let me know if you change your mind. I'm available all night. Have a good one, Miss Quinn."

"You too, Robert," she said. Out of everyone who worked for Apex, he was the calmest and least arrogant. A steady presence in her life since she'd landed in Nashville. Then again, she'd be spending more time inside his car soon enough. "Thank you."

"Any time."

Cassie slid out of the vehicle and walked down to the nearest crosswalk, waiting for the light to change before she was able to make it to the other side. By the time she looked back, Robert had already pulled out into traffic, his taillights indistinguishable from all the others out at this hour. She felt a strange sense of loss, like he was just another person who had left her behind.

Ignoring the way her chest ached, Cassie's hand landed on the door to the pub just as someone called out from behind her.

"Cassie, over here," Chris said.

Turning, she saw him standing a few paces away, leaning against the brick façade of the building at the corner where it disappeared into a dark alley way. "Hey," she said, hesitating for only a moment before joining him. "What's going on? Why aren't you inside?"

"Change of plans," he said. Then he looked over her shoulder as though searching for someone. "Where's Jason? Is he on his way?"

"No," she said, wringing the strap of her purse in her hands as though she could squeeze out all the pain she felt in her body and abandon it there on the sidewalk. "He went home."

"Why?"

"Long story. But it's for the best."

"Are you—"

"I don't want to talk about it." Cassie wasn't sure if Chris was about to ask if she was okay or if she and *Jason* were okay, but she didn't feel like answering either question. "You want to go inside?"

"We can't," he said. "Saw someone from Apex in there. Better we head somewhere else."

"Oh. Okay." She'd been looking forward to getting drunk on those cherry drinks he'd bought her the other day. But another bar would probably be able to make something similar. "Who was it?"

"Don Carver," he answered, motioning for her to follow him.

"Don's not so bad," she said, dodging the puddles that littered the ground between the two buildings. There was no telling whether they were full of water or something worse. "Lorraine investigated him and didn't find anything interesting, which I figure is just about the best-case scenario when you work for Apex Publicity. Plus, now he doesn't have to deal with Max."

"Yeah, Don's all right. Just about the only guy I can stand around there. But I still don't want him listening in on our conversation." Chris glanced over his shoulder. "You know, for someone who recently gave up the ghost—literally—you seem pretty down in the dumps." He held up a finger and then pointed toward a dumpster just ahead. "Pun not intended."

Cassie couldn't even bring herself to laugh, but she did force a small smile. "Didn't realize how much I'd miss having her around. She had a good sense of humor. But I don't think I'll ever enjoy the scent of violets again."

"You and me both."

They reached the end of the alley, and Chris pointed toward a parking garage. "I'm over here. We'll go somewhere a little farther outside the city. No use in taking unnecessary risks."

"I don't suppose you're going to tell me what this is all about?"

"Not yet." Chris crossed the street and headed up the sidewalk to the garage. "Want to make sure we won't be overheard."

Feeling a little less lonely and a lot more intrigued now, Cassie hurried to keep up with his long strides. "What was it like after I left the governor's mansion?"

"A shitshow. You saw the news?" Chris asked, and when Cassie nodded, he continued. "Anastasia was unbearable after that. Three hours in a car with her throwing me smug looks the entire time was just about all I could handle. Decided I needed a stiff drink. Or ten."

It made sense why Robert had been in the vicinity. He must've gotten back from Frankfort and driven by her hotel on his way home. Poor guy, she thought, wondering how many hours on average he spent in the car over the course of a day.

"Can't say I blame you," Cassie said. She'd paid a pretty penny to get back to Nashville in a rideshare, but it had been worth it not to deal with Anastasia for a couple of hours.

Chris walked over to the elevator and hit the button to go up. They waited in silence as it groaned to life somewhere above them and then made its way down as though it were on its last legs. She almost suggested they just take the stairs when the doors slid open with a *ding*, the empty car beckoning them inside.

"I'm on the top floor," Chris said, hitting the number seven on the panel.

"Great," Cassie replied with forced cheeriness, "it'll only take an hour to get there, then."

Chris laughed just as a woman called out for them to hold the doors. Still a couple dozen feet away, there was no way she'd make it in time. When it looked like Chris would ignore her call for help, Cassie reached out a hand and stopped the doors from closing.

"Thank you," the woman huffed, her face covered by a tangle of hair. "Seven, please."

"I've already pushed it," Chris said, in what Cassie thought was an inappropriately gruff tone. Then he stepped forward so he wouldn't have to make conversation.

Cassie stepped up next to him and turned her head to lob a glare in his direction, just as the old doors closed. He shrugged, unapologetic, and the atmosphere in the car turned awkward as they passed the second floor. Then the third. Then the fourth.

When they had just passed the sixth floor, Cassie couldn't stand it anymore and turned to apologize to the woman for Chris' behavior. This was the only reason she saw the stranger raise a gun and bring it down against Chris' temple.

As he crumpled to the ground, Cassie met the woman's wild eyes. It only took the span of two heartbeats to recognize the person standing before her, pointing a revolver at her heart.

Her would-be kidnapper, the woman from the alley.

44

Lorraine felt sick to her stomach as she opened the door of her home to see Blackwood smiling down from her front porch. Most of society would find him attractive, but she couldn't look at him without bile rising in her throat. He was a wolf in sheep's clothing.

"I have to admit your call came as quite a surprise," Blackwood said, not waiting for an invitation before gliding through the door. "Is your mother home?"

"No." Lorraine closed the door behind him. "She's out."

Blackwood walked to the middle of the living room before turning to face her. "It was my understanding she didn't get out much."

"Doctor's appointment," Lorraine said, glad it wasn't a lie. She couldn't risk making one misstep. "A friend took her."

"Right, right. Dr. Chopra, if I remember? I trust everything is okay?"

Unease slid down Lorraine's back like someone had dumped a bucket of ice-cold water over her head. "Everything's fine," she answered through clenched teeth. "Routine appointment."

"Last time I was here, I made Jackie some tea. She said it was to *die for*. Would you like me to make you a cup? You seem a little stressed."

"We're all out," Lorraine said, knowing full well the pantry was stocked. "That's not why I asked you here."

Blackwood waltzed over to the couch and made himself comfortable. "You put on quite a show this morning, Miss Krasinski. The warden was furious. But I knew you would come around."

"I'm not going back to work for him. I don't want anything to do with him anymore."

"That's fine." Blackwood waved away her concern with a flip of his hand. "Does this mean you've accepted my offer to come work for me?"

Lorraine wished the nausea in her stomach would go away. Only thinking of her mother's safety kept the contents of her stomach where they belonged. "I have some stipulations."

Blackwood raised his eyebrows and chuckled. "Let's hear them then."

"I don't want anything to do with the warden."

Blackwood rolled his eyes, but he still looked amused. "You said that already."

"You want me to destroy Jason's reputation, admit those photos of you were altered, and tell Cassie to have Apex bring you back on board. If I do all that, not only will I risk my own reputation, but I'll lose two of my friends in the process. Plus, there's the chance Apex doesn't like what I'm doing and takes matters into their own hands."

"All of this to say, what?"

"Cut ties with the warden. The man's a loose cannon and not nearly as cunning as you are." The compliment tasted sour on her tongue. "Whatever you're getting out of your relationship with him, we'll find someone else. Hire a new warden. One easier to control."

"I've known Wickham for more than half my life. You think I'm going to drop him for you?"

Lorraine shrugged, trying to look more nonchalant than she felt. "It's up to you. All I'm saying is that I've worked with him for years. I know how he talks about his friends behind their backs. I know what he's good at, and it's nothing you can't find elsewhere."

Blackwood stared at Lorraine for several heartbeats before his face cracked open into a wide smile. Then he threw his head back and laughed, clapping his hands together in sheer joy. "My God, I underestimated you. You've got yourself a deal."

"I'm not done."

Still laughing, Blackwood motioned for her to continue. "Go on."

"You leave my mother out of this. No visits. No chats over tea. No keeping tabs on her or the house. She's off limits."

"That's fine," Blackwood said. "Is that all?"

"Not quite."

The humor started to slip from Blackwood's face. "Don't push your luck, Lorraine."

"My last stipulation," she said, hoping this wouldn't be a dealbreaker, "is that you tell me everything you know about Apex."

When Blackwood laughed this time, it was in disbelief. "What makes you think I know anything?"

"Because I'm not stupid.," Summoning the courage to cross the room, she stood in front of where he sat on the couch. "You mentioned a few things in Wickham's office that caught my attention. If you're getting back into Apex's good graces, I want to come with you. Something tells me they can use my talents. And God knows I need the money. Like you said, those cancer treatments didn't come cheap."

Blackwood cocked his head to the side, and that one action made her want to step away from him. "And what talents," he said, dragging his gaze up and down her body, "do you have?"

"Computers," she said, unable to stop herself from clenching her fists by her side.

Blackwood stood, and Lorraine's instincts took over, causing her to take several steps back. But the former mayor never allowed too much distance between them. "An equal exchange then. You do me three favors, and I do you three favors."

She swallowed, not sure if puking in his face would be more mortifying or satisfying. "Yes."

He held out his hand. "Then you've got yourself a deal."

Fighting every instinct in her body to pull away, Lorraine slipped her hand into his, flinching when he pulled it to his lips and planted a wet kiss against her knuckles.

Giving her one more lingering look, Blackwood dropped her hand

and made his way toward the door. "Don't go getting cold feet, Miss Krasinski. Or the deal's off. I'll be in touch."

Lorraine didn't answer as he closed the door behind him. All she could do was stand stock-still and listen for the sound of him driving off down the street. Even then, she waited another minute before she sank to her knees and sucked in a gasping breath.

"He's gone," she called out.

"Thank God," Harris said, stepping out of the coat closet just around the corner. "Are you okay?"

"Yeah," Lorraine said, looking up at her from the floor. "You?"

Harris smoothed down a few hairs that had escaped her ponytail while she was in hiding. "Yeah. But I almost broke my cover half a dozen times. That guy is a sleaze."

"Do you think it's enough?" Lorraine asked, finally getting to her feet.

Harris stuck her hand in her pocket and pulled out a small device, hitting stop on the recording. "No," she said. But then a wide grin took over her face. "But it's a damn good start."

45

The elevator came to a halt on the seventh floor, and the doors slid open with a tired *ding*. Cassie wasn't sure whether she wanted someone to be waiting on the other side or not. They might be her abductor's accomplice, or perhaps just her next victim.

Cassie hadn't realized she'd pressed herself back against the wall of the elevator, giving the woman plenty of room to move to the doors and check the parking garage beyond. From the sliver Cassie could see, this level was almost empty. Less than a dozen cars sat spread throughout the area, and several of the lights were out, making it look altogether abandoned. Plenty of places for Cassie to escape into the shadows, but not many objects to hide behind that could shield her from a bullet.

As the woman was distracted, Cassie knew it was a prime opportunity to get the upper hand. Although Jason and Harris had taken turns teaching her some basic self-defense maneuvers, she was by no means as skilled as they were. Most of what they'd shown her involved taking someone by surprise in order to escape.

Before Cassie could decide whether she wanted to take the risk, Chris groaned from the ground and stole her attention. A trickle of blood ran down his temple, and she could already see the goose egg forming there, surrounded by a bloom of red that would soon turn purple.

The flash of blood made Cassie's throat constrict as she thought back to her dream. Was this it, then? Was this the moment her subconscious had been warning her about? Would this be where Chris' story ended? Tears gathered in her eyes as the thought slammed into her.

"Please." Cassie turned back to the woman. "Please don't hurt him."

The woman tossed something to Cassie. "Cuff him."

Out of instinct, Cassie caught the object, realizing a second later that they were a pair of metal handcuffs. They were warm in her hands, as though they'd been in the woman's pocket for hours and had absorbed her body heat. How long had she been stalking them? Worse, how long had she been planning on holding Cassie at gunpoint?

"Cuff him," the woman said again, moving the barrel of the gun over until it pointed at Chris' prone body. "Both hands. Around that bar. Make it tight."

Cassie knelt beside Chris and helped him sit up. His eyes were open now, but they looked out of focus. He lifted a hand to his temple and winced. Cassie shoved it away, taking a moment to see how bad the injury was. Red and swollen, it would leave a mark. But something told her Chris had been through worse.

"Cassie," Chris rasped, his eyes clearing. "Don't."

"I'm sorry," she whispered, hooking one cuff around a wrist and raising it to the handlebar that ran along the wall inside the elevator car.

"Please," Chris begged, but this time he was looking at the woman. "Don't hurt her."

"Shut up," the woman said. Then, to Cassie, "Hurry up."

Without another choice, Cassie slipped one side of the handcuffs through the bar and grabbed Chris' other arm, attaching the other side to his wrist until it clicked shut. There'd be no escaping that unless he could tear the bar from the wall of the elevator, and even then, he'd still be wearing handcuffs.

"Tighter," the woman ordered.

Wincing, Cassie squeezed first one side and then the other until the metal dug into his skin. Their eyes met, and she begged him to forgive her while he begged her not to go. Shifting to one side, he pressed his hip into her leg, and she looked down to see the gun strapped to his waist. Could she retrieve it without the woman noticing?

Something pressed into the back of Cassie's head. "Don't even think about it. Get up."

Cassie shook as she rose to her feet, backing out of the elevator slowly enough that she had time to press the button for the first floor, sending the car back down to ground level. Maybe someone would find Chris and use his own key to free him. She just needed to stall for a few more minutes.

"Turn around."

Cassie did so, using the minimal lighting to study the woman's features more closely than she had the other night. Once again, the woman was dressed all in black, having replaced her beanie with the hood of her coat, despite the warm weather. Mousy brown hair framed her round face, the ends dry and frizzy, sticking out every which way. Dark brown eyes stared back at Cassie in challenge and defiance. The gun was steady in her hand.

Using the weapon to motion Cassie deeper into the parking garage, the woman said, "Walk."

"Please," Cassie said, not moving. "Please don't hurt me."

"Weren't you listening?" the woman snarled. "I don't want to hurt you."

"Your actions say otherwise," Cassie replied, surprised her voice was steady.

"You didn't give me a choice. Now walk."

"Where are we going?" Cassie asked, knowing she was pushing her luck.

"Just walk."

With no other choice, Cassie placed one foot in front of the other, making sure her measured pace was slow enough to give Chris time to come up with a plan, but not too slow that it would piss off her captor.

"What's your name?" Cassie asked.

There was a beat of silence before she said, "Emma."

"My name is Cassie."

"I know."

"How?" Cassie asked, risking a glance over her shoulder. "How do you know who I am?"

"Piper."

"Are you friends with her?"

"Yes," Emma replied, and Cassie didn't miss the smile in that answer.

Cassie never stopped the sweep of her gaze around the parking garage, looking for anyone or anything that might help her. But with half the lights out and only a few cars on this level, her hopes diminished with each passing second. Unless Chris could get free, it was unlikely someone would arrive to aid in her escape. And Emma was smart enough to keep Cassie from walking too close to any of the cars in case she got any bright ideas.

"How did you two meet?" Cassie asked.

"I was one of her first listeners." The pride in Emma's voice was unmistakable. "Even before she started *Buried Deep*."

"Before she got big." Cassie hoped she sounded more impressed than terrified. "Wow, that's a long time. You two must be close."

"She trusts me," Emma said, not quite answering the unasked question. "Enough to do this."

"Emma." Cassie infused the woman's name with a sense of familiarity. "What does Piper want you to do?"

"Over there," Emma said, and Cassie had to glance over her shoulder again to see where the woman was pointing. Her heart dropped at the sight of how far they had walked from the elevator. Would she even hear when someone came up to this level? If she shouted, would they be able to pinpoint her location? "Go on." Emma shooed her with the gun.

Cassie followed the woman's orders. Now on the far side of the parking garage, Emma had Cassie stand near one of the main support pillars, in an area devoid of light. It cast the other woman in shadow. Cassie couldn't help but be reminded of her dream, despite the absence of fog. The first iterations of Cassie's nightmare had cast Piper in this role, and it startled Cassie to realize her subconscious hadn't been entirely wrong. Emma was an extension of Piper's will.

Cassie's heart soared even as her stomach dropped. She knew what came next—Chris would appear behind her, perhaps from the stairwell just a few feet away. He would pay the ultimate price, and Cassie couldn't stand for that to happen. Not to yet another person who had come into her life seeking friendship and getting more than they bargained for.

"Emma," Cassie said again, a slight waver in her voice this time. "What does Piper want you to do?"

"You won't run?" Emma asked, and the question seemed genuine. "I don't want to hurt you."

"I won't run," Cassie replied. "But I'm scared."

"I didn't mean to scare you." Emma dropped the gun to her side. "I just needed you to listen."

"To what?"

"Piper's message."

Cassie waited for the other woman to continue, but when there was only silence, she nodded her head in reassurance. "Okay. I'm listening."

Taking a deep breath, Emma screwed up her face as though she were recalling the words Piper had imparted to her. "She says she's sorry for what happened the last time you saw each other."

It took everything in Cassie not to snort in disgust. Piper had pointed a gun at her—twice now, if she counted Emma's actions as part of that ploy—and nearly pulled the trigger. Saying she scared her was a bit of an understatement.

"Okay," Cassie said, when she realized the woman was waiting for a response. "I accept her apology."

Emma beamed. "Piper's a good person. She's smart and funny and beautiful. And she cares about the victims more than she cares about all the attention she's gotten from doing the podcast. She cares about the people no one else does."

And then it clicked into place. If Piper was a cult leader, then Emma was her number one devotee. "But she was working for Apex—"

"No." Emma slashed the hand holding the gun, causing Cassie to flinch. "No, she would never do that. She was tricking them. Trying to find the real story."

Cassie didn't believe that for a minute, but she wasn't about to argue.

"That's what I've been trying to tell you." Frustration turned Emma's face red. "But you wouldn't listen to me."

Taking a slow, calming breath, Cassie said, "I'm listening now."

"You can't trust anyone at Apex." Emma stared her down, begging her to pay attention to what she was saying. "The second you're no longer useful, they cast you aside. That's what they did with Piper. It's not right."

"I agree," Cassie said, annoyed that after all this, Emma wasn't telling her anything she didn't already know. "Agent Viotto and I—"

Emma stepped closer. "Piper says—"

Several things happened in such quick succession, Cassie saw them like snapshots.

Emma's gaze shifted to a spot over Cassie's shoulder as the door to the stairwell banged open behind her.

The woman lifted the gun, its barrel not quite trained on Cassie's head.

A gunshot echoed off the concrete walls of the parking garage.

A wound materialized in the center of Emma's forehead before she crumpled to the ground.

Then Cassie whirled, heart pounding, and took in Chris' form, his chest heaving and his gun still trained in her direction.

Relief washed over her and all she could do was run to Chris and wrap her arms around him to assure herself he was real and here and still alive.

46

Cassie held on to Chris until she was sure this was not one of her dreams. When she pulled back, she caught his eye and beamed.

"We've got to stop meeting like this."

Chris didn't laugh. His eyes shifted to the ground behind her. "Cassie."

Cassie spun, terrified Emma would be on her feet again. But she wasn't. A pool of blood spread out around her head like a halo, and Cassie's relief turned to nausea. The adrenaline pumping in her veins proved she was alive, but it also served to remind her how close she'd come to meeting a different fate.

Taking a few steps toward Emma, Cassie kicked the gun out of the woman's hand, even though all signs indicated she wouldn't be getting up off the ground again. It would be just her luck if she found out zombies existed alongside ghosts.

"Cassie."

"Piper sent her," Cassie said, still staring down at the body. Why couldn't she tear her eyes away even when she wanted to?

"I heard," Chris replied.

There was something in Chris' voice that made her tense. Maybe it was the way the words sounded strangled coming out of his mouth. Or perhaps it was the fact that they were merely a whisper, and yet they surrounded her from all sides as they echoed off the walls as loudly as the gunshot had just a moment before.

Spinning back to face him, Cassie's breath caught in her throat when she finally locked eyes on Chris again. His stance was wide and solid, as though afraid a strong gust of wind might whip through the garage at any minute. Eyes that had always been clear and reassuring were clouded with tears, which rolled down his cheeks and soaked into lips that were turned down in a frown.

Frantic, she searched his chest for the red bloom she expected to see there, even as somewhere in the back of her mind she knew there had only been one gunshot.

Finally, his outstretched arm stole Cassie's full attention. The way it was stiff and unforgiving. How it shook but remained locked in her direction. Her mind rebelled against the image before her, refusing to believe Chris still had his gun in his hand. Pointing right at her.

"Chris?" Cassie asked, confused and terrified and heartbroken as her brain struggled to comprehend the situation. "What's going on?"

"Cassie," he croaked, and she wondered for a moment if this pained him even more than it pained her. "I'm so sorry."

"Chris." His name caught halfway between a plea and an admonishment. Was this some sort of joke?

"I didn't want it to happen this way," Chris said, not even trying to fight the tremors in his voice. "This is the last thing I wanted to do."

"Then don't do it." How had they gotten here? "Put the gun down. Let's talk."

"I can't," he said. "I can't, and I'm so sorry."

Then the truth dawned on her as though the sun had finally risen in the sky, burning away the fog that had consumed her dreams for so long. "Emma's message. Piper said not to trust anyone. She was talking about you."

Chris remained silent, as though allowing her this time to gain the closure she needed.

"When you shot her, you meant to kill her, didn't you?"

"Yes." His arm shook less now, but tears still ran down his face. "But I was afraid I'd hit you. I didn't want to hurt you. I still don't."

"I'm finding that hard to believe."

"Please, Cassie. You have to understand. My sister and her kids are all I have left. I haven't seen them in months. Anastasia won't tell me where they are. She said if you joined Apex, she'd let me visit them. But she lied. Then she said if we solved the Abrahms case, I'd get to see them again. But every time I do what I'm told, she changes her mind. Moves the finish line back a little farther."

"What'd she tell you to do this time?"

"You were getting too close to the truth." Anguish contorted his face. "I begged her to reconsider, that I could get you in line, but she said you were too righteous. Too determined. No longer useful to the cause."

"What did she tell you to do?" Cassie wanted him to say it out loud. To admit to what he was doing.

"Deliver your termination notice."

Cassie choked back a sob. A termination notice—like she was getting fired, and not being buried six feet under. Shaking her head, Cassie thought through what he'd said, wondering if there was an opening there, to get him to change his mind or keep him talking. But what would that do? No one was coming for her. "You killed Omega, didn't you?"

Chris shook his head. "I—"

"Actually," a new voice said, one that sounded strangely familiar to Cassie's ears. "That's not quite true."

Chris startled and shifted the gun to aim at someone behind Cassie. She craned her neck. It took several seconds to comprehend who she was seeing.

Brown hair parted at the side that matched the color of dark eyes set deep into a cleanshaven face. He still wore his trademark suit, tailored to fit his broad shoulders and wide chest. When Cassie had first met him, she thought he was in his early forties, but after getting to know him, she realized he was at least a decade older. Despite driving cars for a living, he was in incredible shape. And the way he held his gun in a steady hand told her that he was not unfamiliar with the weapon.

The man's name bubbled up her throat and slipped from her lips with a mixture of confusion and hope and trepidation. "Robert?"

"You're Omega?" Chris asked, and Cassie returned her gaze to his face, seeing that he was as surprised as she was.

"Drop the gun, son. This isn't going to end well for you."

"I can't," Chris said. "If I don't do this, she'll kill them."

"We'll find them," Robert reassured him. "We'll keep them safe."

Chris' gaze slid from Robert's face and back to Cassie's. "Promise me?"

Cassie nodded, knowing she would've given him the same answer whether he had a gun pointing at her chest or not. "I promise."

Chris' throat bobbed as he swallowed, and there was relief in his eyes even as the tears fell heavier down his face. "Thank you." His voice was strained, like it took every last bit of strength to utter that phrase. "Someday, I hope you can forgive me."

That was the only warning Cassie got.

A loud bang sounded just before white-hot pain exploded in her chest, forcing her back several steps. Her vision blurred and darkened along the edges. A roaring filled her ears, and her brain couldn't comprehend what was happening to her. The agony took over, drowning out her other senses.

As though someone had clamped their hands over her ears, she heard three muffled pops.

Even as her knees gave out and her vision tunneled, she saw red bloom across Chris' chest.

Cassie knew his face should be a mask of pain, but all she saw there was relief.

Then everything went black as she hit the ground.

47

There was nothing but the pain.

Every inch of her was covered in white-hot fire that burned brighter with each passing second.

She could taste it on her tongue, like copper and smoke. It scorched the inside of her nose, searing its way down her throat and into her lungs. The torment was a rush of disjointed noise in her ears, like waves crashing against the shore during a storm. Eventually, it gave way to silence, black and empty.

Cassie had no sense of time. Her eyes would flutter open, providing a glimpse of the chaos around her, only to close when they became too heavy to bear. The process would repeat, and she'd find herself at a new point in time, unable to make sense of the narrative, like a record skipping through a song.

Bright lights and wailing alarms.

Weightlessness and antiseptic.

The rush of oxygen and a pricking sensation.

And pain. Always the pain.

. . .

When Cassie did regain consciousness, it was one sensation at a time. The agony remained, but she could feel beyond it now. Even with her eyes closed, she could tell there were bright lights in her face. The rhythmic sound of beeping machines was reassuring. The biting scent of iodine fought against the sterility that clung to the air. Her tongue was dry and heavy, like she'd swallowed a handful of cotton balls.

She heard murmurs in the distance, but they were drowned out by the steady warmth of a nearby figure. Even with her eyes closed, she could picture his kind smile, his warm eyes, his steady hands. A silent whisper brushed against her temple, and while no words were spoken aloud, she heard his message loud and clear.

Be strong.

Be brave.

Live.

Cassie soaked in the figure's heat and breathed in his words, using them to strengthen her limbs, move her tongue, force open her eyes. As she blinked against the brightness hovering above her, only one word—one name—came to mind, and she uttered it like a desperate prayer.

"David."

Movement to her left caught Cassie's attention as her eyes grew accustomed to the world around her. Various machines were hooked up to her prone body, which lay in a bed far too small and stiff to be her own. As though she were capable of holding only one word at a time in her mind, she plucked the answer to her unasked question from the recesses of her memory.

Hospital.

The shadow at her periphery drew closer, growing in height and width. It chased away the warmth of David's memory, the strength of his words. A sob escaped her mouth at the loss, sure she had endured it once before and never thought she'd have to again.

"It's okay," a different voice told her. "You're going to be okay."

Looking up at the man that stood beside her, Cassie struggled to place a name to his face. Dark hair, dark eyes, tailored suit.

"Robert," she croaked.

He smiled down at her. "That's right. It's good that you remember."

Cassie tried to sit up, but a wave of dizziness forced her back down. It took a few moments to gather enough breath to speak again. "What happened?"

"You were shot," Robert said, his voice gentle even as his words slammed into her.

Cassie remembered that. Chris' apology and the red that had crawled across his chest like a living animal. Her confusion and horror. The promise she'd made him just before he apologized.

Just before he pulled the trigger.

"Is—" She couldn't get the full sentence out. "Is he?"

"Agent Viotto is dead," Robert said. "I'm sorry."

"He—" She wanted to say it out loud, like if she could just hear it, she'd believe it, and maybe some of this pain would go away. "He shot—"

"He shot you," Robert finished for her, and she detected a slight southern twang to his voice now. "In the chest. Either you're very lucky, or he never meant to kill you."

Cassie stared up at him, confusion written in the crease of her brow and the wobble of her chin.

"Where he hit you did minimal damage. I'm sure it hurt like a son of a bitch, but as far as chest wounds go, it was best case scenario. It'll take you a bit to get back on your feet, but the doctors say you'll make a full recovery. I'm just sorry you'll have another scar to add to your collection."

The events of the previous few days became sharper the longer Cassie remained conscious. "You're Omega," she stated. "Who was the man in the park? The man in the hotel?"

"A friend," Robert said, and Cassie could hear the sorrow in that admission.

It was all too much. There had been far too many deaths over the last few days, over the last few years. A normal person couldn't handle all of this, and Cassie was anything but normal. She wondered, without much feeling, if this was what she could expect out of life from this day forward—nothing but death.

"Did anyone call Jason?" she asked. All she wanted was his strong arms wrapped around her. "My family? Detective Harris?"

"Not yet," Robert replied. "I wanted to wait until you were awake, so you could decide if that's what you really want."

Furrowing her brows, Cassie looked up into the older man's face. "Why wouldn't I want that?"

With a patient sigh, Robert gazed down at her, the light from the window beyond casting him in a strange glow. "I called in a few favors when we were at the hospital." He dragged out his words, like he wasn't sure what she'd make of them. "I've been around for a while. Made some friends over the years. And what trust couldn't buy, money sure could."

Agitation flared in Cassie's chest, setting it ablaze again. "What are you talking about?"

"Apex has eyes and ears just about everywhere, which means we needed to go beyond where they could find us. Turns out, people stop looking for you when they think you're dead."

Cassie shook her head, refusing to believe what he was telling her.

"You died at the hospital, Cassie," Robert said, his voice gentle. "Or so everyone thinks. I called in some favors, paid off a few people, and had you moved to this facility. It's not a hospital, but it has everything you need. You'll be able to make a full recovery here."

Cassie looked around the room, taking in the small details for the first time. The bed and the machines looked like they belonged in a hospital, but the view out of the window didn't show the cityscape. Mountains and trees lined her view. And now that she'd been clued in, she couldn't hear the hustle and bustle of nurses and doctors tending to patients beyond her four walls.

"Why?" Cassie asked. "Why do all that?"

"I've lost too many people to this cause. I know we haven't known each other for long, but I couldn't throw you back to the wolves like that. This way, Apex won't come searching for you. And they'll stop badgering your friends and family, too. Anastasia is too smart to toss the altered video of Jason in the trash, but she'll lock it away in some drawer somewhere. He was just collateral damage. They really just wanted you."

"My family," Cassie choked out. "Jason. They'll be devastated."

Robert nodded. "But they'll be safe."

And just like that, she understood the gift Robert had given her. There was nothing she wouldn't do to make sure her loved ones were off Apex's radar. Even if it meant destroying any trust they had in her to begin with.

Looking back up into Robert's waiting gaze, she said, "What's our next move?"

Robert's face stretched into the first genuine smile she'd ever seen on his face. "Don't go getting ahead of yourself just yet," he said, retreating to the door. "I'll get the doctor in here and you'll listen to everything she has to say. You're no good to anyone if you don't recover first."

"Fine," Cassie bit out. "But then you've got a lot of explaining to do."

"I suppose I do." He pulled open the door. With one more look, he said, "Hang tight."

Cassie watched him leave before settling into a more comfortable position. For once, the pain took a backseat to the single thought that raged inside of her.

It was time to burn Apex to the fucking ground.

Cassie Quinn returns in *Risen from Ashes*! Pre-order your copy now: My Book

Join the LT Ryan reader family & receive a free copy of the Cassie Quinn story, *Through the Veil*. Click the link below to get started: https://ltryan.com/cassie-quinn-newsletter-signup-1

Return to Ashes

Love Cassie? Hatch? Noble? Maddie? Get your very own L.T. Ryan merchandise today! Click the link below to find coffee mugs, t-shirts, and even signed copies of your favorite thrillers! https://ltryan.ink/EvG_

THE CASSIE QUINN SERIES

Path of Bones

Whisper of Bones

Symphony of Bones

Etched in Shadow

Concealed in Shadow

Betrayed in Shadow

Born from Ashes

Return from Ashes (2024)

Love Cassie? Hatch? Noble? Maddie? Get your very own Cassie Quinn merchandise today! Click the link below to find coffee mugs, t-shirts, and even signed copies of your favorite L.T. Ryan thrillers! https://ltryan.ink/EvG_

ALSO BY L.T. RYAN

Find All of L.T. Ryan's Books on Amazon Today!

The Jack Noble Series

The Recruit (free)

The First Deception (Prequel 1)

Noble Beginnings

A Deadly Distance

Ripple Effect (Bear Logan)

Thin Line

Noble Intentions

When Dead in Greece

Noble Retribution

Noble Betrayal

Never Go Home

Beyond Betrayal (Clarissa Abbot)

Noble Judgment

Never Cry Mercy

Deadline

End Game

Noble Ultimatum

Noble Legend

Noble Revenge

Never Look Back (Coming Soon)

Bear Logan Series

Ripple Effect

Blowback

Take Down

Deep State

Bear & Mandy Logan Series

Close to Home

Under the Surface

The Last Stop

Over the Edge

Between the Lies (Coming Soon)

Rachel Hatch Series

Drift

Downburst

Fever Burn

Smoke Signal

Firewalk

Whitewater

Aftershock

Whirlwind

Tsunami

Fastrope

Sidewinder (Coming Soon)

Mitch Tanner Series

The Depth of Darkness

Into The Darkness

Deliver Us From Darkness

Cassie Quinn Series

Path of Bones

Whisper of Bones

Symphony of Bones

Etched in Shadow

Concealed in Shadow

Betrayed in Shadow

Born from Ashes

Blake Brier Series

Unmasked

Unleashed

Uncharted

Drawpoint

Contrail

Detachment

Clear

Quarry (Coming Soon)

Dalton Savage Series

Savage Grounds

Scorched Earth

Cold Sky

The Frost Killer (Coming Soon)

Maddie Castle Series

The Handler

Tracking Justice

Hunting Grounds

Vanished Trails (Coming Soon)

Affliction Z Series

Affliction Z: Patient Zero

Affliction Z: Abandoned Hope

Affliction Z: Descended in Blood

Affliction Z : Fractured Part 1

Affliction Z: Fractured Part 2 (Fall 2021)

Love Cassie? Hatch? Noble? Maddie? Get your very own L.T. Ryan merchandise today! Click the link below to find coffee mugs, t-shirts, and even signed copies of your favorite thrillers! https://ltryan.ink/EvG_

Receive a free copy of The Recruit. Visit:

https://ltryan.com/jack-noble-newsletter-signup-1

ABOUT THE AUTHOR

L.T. Ryan is a *Wall Street Journal & USA Today* bestselling author. The new age of publishing offered L.T. the opportunity to blend his passions for creating, marketing, and technology to reach audiences with his popular Jack Noble series.

Living in central Virginia with his wife, the youngest of his three daughters, and their three dogs, L.T. enjoys staring out his window at the trees and mountains while he should be writing, as well as reading, hiking, running, and playing with gadgets. See what he's up to at http://ltryan.com.

Social Medial Links:
- Facebook (L.T. Ryan): https://www.facebook.com/LTRyanAuthor
- Facebook (Jack Noble Page): https://www.facebook.com/JackNobleBooks/
- Twitter: https://twitter.com/LTRyanWrites
- Goodreads: http://www.goodreads.com/author/show/6151659.L_T_Ryan

K.M. Rought is a writer and editor hailing from Upstate New York. Through she graduated with a degree in Art History, she fell into a career of freelancing, fulfilling her childhood dream of being a published author.

Now residing in Ohio, K.M. spends her days writing, playing video games, and telling her cat that no, it's not time to eat yet. Her obsessions include foraging for mushrooms, buying neon green kitchenware, and reading every single book by Rick Riordan.

You can find her on Instagram @karenrought.

Made in the USA
Middletown, DE
11 August 2025

12060514R10166